"Brilliantly conceived and executed. . . . Complex, breath-taking. . . ."
— *Globe and Mail*

"Graphic and powerful."
— *Ottawa Citizen*

"Bush has given readers what is not only a heartfelt depiction of pain but also a thought-provoking read for anyone who, like Claire, uses their head."
— *Books in Canada*

"Bush is never false. She possesses in spades the gift of sincerity which brings her strongest characters bounding to life."
— Montreal *Gazette*

"A neurological thriller. . . . Bush is a deeply intelligent and empathetic writer."
— *Edmonton Journal*

"Catherine Bush is a master of geography. She has a knack for highlighting the sensory minutiae of place so vividly that you feel like you're tailgating her characters through the spaces they inhabit."
— *NOW* magazine

BOOKS BY CATHERINE BUSH

Minus Time (1994)
The Rules of Engagement (2000)
Claire's Head (2004)

CATHERINE BUSH

CLAIRE'S

HEAD

EMBLEM EDITIONS
Published by McClelland & Stewart Ltd.

Library and Archives Canada Cataloguing in Publication

Bush, Catherine, 1961-
Claire's head / Catherine Bush.

ISBN 0-7710-1753-7

I. Title.

PS8553.U6963C53 2005   C813'.54   C2005-901267-6

We acknowledge the financial support of the Government of Canada through the Book Publishing Industry Development Program and that of the Government of Ontario through the Ontario Media Development Corporation's Ontario Book Initiative. We further acknowledge the support of the Canada Council for the Arts and the Ontario Arts Council for our publishing program.

The first epigraph is taken from *In the Land of Pain*, by Alphonse Daudet, trans. Julian Barnes. Copyright © 2003 Julian Barnes. Reprinted by permission of Alfred A. Knopf, Random House, Inc. 1745 Broadway, New York 10019.

SERIES EDITOR: ELLEN SELIGMAN

Cover design: Kong
Cover image: R.J. Muna © Graphistock
Series logo design: Brian Bean

Typeset in Centaur
Printed and bound in Canada

This book is printed on acid-free paper that is
100% ancient-forest friendly (40% post-consumer recycled).

EMBLEM EDITIONS
McClelland & Stewart Ltd.
The Canadian Publishers
481 University Avenue
Toronto, Ontario
M5G 2E9
www.mcclelland.com/emblem

1 2 3 4 5   09 08 07 06 05

For H. W.

and my grandmother, Hilda Maud Hawes

"Pain, you must be everything to me. Let me find in you all those foreign lands you will not let me visit."
— Alphonse Daudet,
In the Land of Pain, trans. Julian Barnes

"Now I can do no more ... What will become of me?"
— Lewis Carroll, *Alice in Wonderland*

When the phone rang, Claire was upstairs in her study, drawing the shoreline of Lake Ontario by hand. She liked to test her recall of the intricate patterns of coasts and shores — every inlet and promontory. As she picked up the phone, she noted the time, 3:42 in the afternoon. She was aware of her coordinates: she faced east, the window to her right, south, open just a crack, perhaps four centimetres.

"Is this Claire Barber?" asked an unknown male voice.

"Yes," she said. "Who's this?"

"My name's Brad," he said. "Brad Arnarson. I'm a friend of Rachel's. Your sister. I'm calling from New York. I was wondering when you last heard from her." Claire glanced out the window, mentally spanning the distance from Toronto to New York.

"In March." It was now Saturday, June 3, 2000. Not only did she not know Brad Arnarson, but she had never heard Rachel mention his name, which was not necessarily significant, since

Rachel, four years older and given to courting mystery when she chose, could be quite reticent about her private life. "We spoke the night of March 14." The date had stuck. Then again, precision was Claire's forte. "She was in Montreal on a trip and called me from her hotel the night she arrived."

"I talked to her the night before she left," Brad Arnarson said. "At least that's where she said she was off to."

To have heard nothing from Rachel, her oldest sister, in two and a half months was not all that unusual. Claire assumed she had been busy. A writer specializing in medical issues, Rachel freelanced and travelled a lot, often on assignment. In April, Claire had e-mailed her to see how she was doing and when Rachel didn't respond, Claire had not thought too much about it, since Rachel was not always dependable about staying in contact.

"She told me she was in Montreal to interview someone, a doctor, a migraine specialist, for an article."

"The thing is," Brad Arnarson went on, "I don't think she's been back to New York. I've called and left messages. I've gone up to her door and knocked. I've asked around in the neighbourhood, in shops, the health food store, the dry cleaner's across the street from her building, and no one's seen her. My place isn't that far away. On 12th Street. I've walked along 9th at night and the only light I've seen lit is one I know she keeps on a timer. I have a set of keys. I could let myself into the apartment, but I thought I should talk to someone else first."

"You're a close friend?"

"Yeah, pretty close."

"Did she give you my number?"

"No, first I tried to find your other sister, Allison, but I couldn't."

"She's listed under her husband's name."

"You were the first C. Barber."

Had he been spying on Rachel? Stalking, only Rachel wasn't there to be stalked. Were there reasons to be suspicious of him, for all that his concern seemed genuine?

"I'll call you back. Can you give me your number?" She wrote his home and cellphone numbers on a piece of drawing paper, not yet certain how worried she should be.

The last time she'd spoken to Rachel, Rachel had not sounded well. But then Rachel had been in the grip of a migraine, which Claire had intuited, from the rasp in her voice, before she'd said more than a word. When Rachel's headaches were particularly bad or when, because of them, she was feeling despondent and lonely, she called Claire. How bad, Claire had asked that night. 2.85, Rachel croaked, which was at the high end of their private code, the Barber Pain Scale. It ran from zero to three, broken down, at Claire's suggestion, infinitesimally within that range. Was it the flight, Claire asked, although she was more often the one who suffered migraines while flying. Maybe, Rachel said, maybe flights were beginning to be a trigger for her, too, although they never used to be.

She'd felt the quiver of something before leaving. She'd eaten a sandwich at La Guardia before catching her plane. There'd been a slice of cheese in the sandwich, and dairy *was* a big trigger for her these days. She'd taken the cheese out, but maybe there was some kind of residue. On the flight, feeling a headache coming on, she'd had a sip of coffee, no more than a sip – she'd been trying to be so careful about such things, about too much caffeine, although sometimes, conversely, a swig of coffee early in the migraine cycle would nip the pain in the bud. This time the caffeine only made things worse. As soon as she got to her hotel room, she'd medicated – a Zomig, two Tylenol 3s – but the drugs didn't seem to be working.

"How long ago was that?"

"Couple of hours."

"Give them a chance. Perhaps you just need to sleep it off. Or if you can't sleep, try to relax. Breathe deeply. Think of the sea, something calming."

Claire knew how inane her words sounded, how hard it was to offer comfort. When a migraine came on, the pain swelled, like the sea over a small boat, overwhelming the horizon. It wasn't just in the head, but down one side of the body. All of you felt disturbed, helpless, assaulted.

In the two and a half months since that conversation, it had struck Claire now and again that Rachel hadn't called seeking solace when in pain. Odd, if she'd broken a nasty and persistent bout, that she hadn't let Claire know what had done the trick. Perhaps she'd been feeling so well, so blissfully pain-free, that thoughts of Claire and headaches had fallen by the wayside.

"I have to talk to this neurologist tomorrow," Rachel had said from Montreal. "About some new migraine research. It seemed like a good idea when I set it up."

"Maybe the neurologist will be able to help you."

Phone in hand, Claire padded down the upstairs hall to Stefan's study at the front of the house. He looked up as she entered, away from a computer screen radiant with shifting colours, his chin and neck retracting as he swivelled his chair towards her. "Who was it?"

"A friend of Rachel's. Some guy from New York named Brad. I'm not sure what kind of friend. He hasn't heard from her since just before she left for Montreal to interview some researcher, and I haven't heard from her since the night she arrived there. He doesn't think she's been back to her apartment."

Stefan picked up the marble that he liked to play with while he worked and circled it in his left palm. "Maybe she went back home and took off again."

"It's possible."

"Maybe she was invited to someone's beach house in the Caribbean. Or a yacht. Maybe she's having an adventure and is on a yacht somewhere."

"It's possible, but not very likely."

"Have you talked to Allison?" He set the marble down in a little white china dish.

"No, no, I was just about to call her."

It had been four weeks since Claire had spoken to Allison, her middle sister, which was not unusual given the hectic pace of both their lives, Allison's even more than Claire's. Although Claire had not heard from Rachel, Allison surely had. Rachel was more faithfully in contact with Allison than anyone else, since for the past four and a half years, Allison and her husband,

Lennie Lee, had been raising Rachel's daughter, Star, along with their own two daughters.

When Claire called Allison's house, seven-year-old Amelia answered. Behind her, Belle, the mutt, barked, four-year-old Lara yelled, and six-year-old Star yelped back, while Lennie tried to mollify them. The two cats, Maggie and Georgia, had no doubt skedaddled somewhere. "Hi Claire," Amelia shouted. "My mum's at the zoo."

"Thanks, sweetheart," Claire said. "I'll talk to you later."

Saturdays, Allison, a senior zookeeper, was not usually at work. The woman who answered the phone in the Indo-Malay keepers' quarters went to get her. "Someone called in sick," Allison said, "and one of the rhinos is under the weather, so things are kind of crazy around here. What's up? This'll have to be quick."

"When did you last hear from Rachel?"

"Speak to her? When she was supposed to come here in March and left a message saying she couldn't come after all."

"Do you remember the date?"

"Not the exact date. Mid-March. She called from Montreal."

"Do you remember what she said?"

"Not her exact words but something like, I can't make it right now. Something's come up. She didn't make it seem like she was going to be away for a while."

"How did she sound?"

"I don't know. It was a message. Guilty. Rushed."

"And no calls, no e-mails, nothing for Star since then?"

"She sent Star a postcard from Montreal, that's it."

"You don't think it's weird?"

Allison gave a sigh. "I've left messages. I guess I thought she was busy. Or away. It's odd but I've been busy. You haven't heard from her either?"

"Not since the night she arrived in Montreal. I just got a call from this friend of hers in New York who doesn't think she's been back to her apartment since Montreal, and he's worried."

The last time Claire had seen Rachel, at Christmas, she'd looked tired, perhaps a little paler than usual. She had come to Toronto for ten days to stay at Allison's east-end home and spend time with Star, although she had also brought her computer and had a piece to finish, something on narcolepsy. On Christmas Eve, Claire and Rachel had found themselves briefly alone together in Allison's living room, while Stefan and Lennie trooped down to the basement with the three girls. Allison had sprinted upstairs.

"How's your head?" Claire had asked, because all fall Rachel had been complaining, once in a bleak phone call from Shanghai, that her headaches were worse than they'd been in a while.

"Not great," Rachel said, rubbing her index finger along the ridge of bone beneath her right eye. "I feel like I keep reacting to more triggers. Food triggers. Caffeine, alcohol. Smoke." She shrugged. "Yours?"

"Okay," Claire said carefully. "The drugs work mostly. The hormonal ones are bad but there's not a lot I can do about that."

Allison stuck her head through the doorway, heard what they were talking about, and retreated. Girls' voices rose up the basement stairs.

For dinner, they had pan-fried Chinese dumplings and pizza, which Rachel didn't eat. They grazed off paper plates while lounging around the living room, and attempted to stop the girls from handling every present under the tree. Rachel spread herself out on the carpet beyond the coffee table and cajoled Amelia and Star and Lara into giving her a massage by offering to pay each of them a quarter. Neck and scalp, please. They seemed happy to oblige, in a rather manic and distracted way, fingers probing her as if she were a pudding and ruffling her long, dark hair while they shouted, Give me money. Rachel said, You have to work for it first.

Later, Star, whose given name was Astra, lay curled between Rachel's legs, her head on Rachel's thigh, while Rachel, still on the floor, leaned against the sofa and stroked Star's pale-brown forehead — like any mother and daughter.

Allison wanted to read a story. Lennie suggested a round of Rummy 500, no, Crazy Eights, all right, Go Fish, since this was all Lara, at four, could manage, and even Claire, who hated card games, agreed to play. Only Rachel, who hated them even more, wouldn't. She left the room momentarily. Claire heard the faint pop of a blister pack being opened, a pill no doubt extracted, then a rush of water from the tap. When Rachel returned, she was chewing smoked salmon on a cracker, the last of the hors d'oeuvres, a glass of soda water spiked with lemon in her hand.

Originally, Rachel had booked her return ticket to New York for the second of January, insisting that she feared none of the dire predictions of millennial disaster and wanted to be with her family, her daughter, for the giddy countdown to a new millennium, but on the morning of the thirty-first, she called Claire at home to wish her a Happy New Year and said she was flying back that afternoon. She'd decided she wanted to be in her own place. Had a more enticing offer of celebration turned up? She didn't say. Was she nervous about the warnings of disaster after all? Had something happened at Allison's? Had she lost some internal equilibrium and had all she could manage of that chaotic household?

After she and Allison hung up, Claire tried Rachel's cellphone, which Rachel was forever forgetting to turn on or recharge, or losing, and which she hadn't used the night she'd called from Montreal. Claire sent her an e-mail and left a message at her New York number for good measure. If she had known the hotel where Rachel had stayed in Montreal, she would have tried there, too, as doubtful as it seemed that Rachel was still on the premises.

No messages of any sort on Sunday. Yet if something terrible had happened, surely they would have heard. Heard something, heard somehow.

On Monday morning, as they did most days, Claire and Stefan walked together to work, east along Queen Street, past Bathurst, then Spadina, before turning north up University towards Dundas. On the northwest corner of Dundas and University, they kissed and parted, Stefan continuing up University to the hospital that housed his molecular medicine lab, while Claire set off east, 512 more steps, past Yonge to Victoria, where, in an unassuming office building, the City Map Department resided.

She had worked in the map department for just over seven years, since shortly after her parents' death. She had loved maps ever since childhood and, as a child, had spent hours drawing them, of both real places and imaginary. From the start, mapping had been a way to give the world order, to hold back the riot of sensory signals that sometimes threatened to overwhelm her, and to compensate for the disorder that, more frequently than she liked to admit, was let loose inside her. Making a map, any map, was a chance to bring a little more clarity and form to the world.

These days, mapping no longer meant being able to draw but, in an age of digitized information, to be able to assemble maps from banks of data. To sort and select the details you needed. Map-makers were data organizers. So Claire had adapted. Where once you had to be able to inscribe a line a thousandth of a centimetre thick, now you simply had to be able to recognize the difference between a line of five thousandths and one of seven thousandths of a centimetre. Sometimes the map-makers had competitions. But there was more to the work than data, crowed their boss, Charlie Gorjup, chief map-maker and former surveyor: every single city department depended on their maps. The city itself, he boasted, would not exist without them. They were geographic enablers, in the business of leaving a record both of what happened and what could be.

For her first three years, Claire had worked as a photogrammetrist, up in the eyrie of photogrammetrists, who sat in a row behind a glassed-in window a full storey above the floor where most of the map-makers worked. The map department was housed in what had once been a gymnasium, built puzzlingly at the top of the building rather than at ground level. Charlie called the photogrammetrists his aerialists, a visual pun, since what they did was translate aerial photographs. When Claire had worked in the upper tier of their domain, she *had* been drawing, converting the scanned-in photos of the city into lines. Grid by grid, they'd assembled a new base map of the city: every building, every street, every tree, everything that could be marked in outline. All the other maps they created would draw on this master data, be a subset of the base.

Now the photogrammetrists huddled towards their double-screened computers like strange movie viewers, wearing the same kind of 3-D glasses, staring at twin frames of aerial photographs stereoscopically, and converting the information that revealed height (bridges, lampposts, roofs) into full 3-D computerized display.

After three years, her eyesight growing wonky, Claire asked to be transferred down. Charlie Gorjup, who prided himself on being a flexible man, on letting his mappists work odd hours, on shifting people around within the department if they requested and it was possible, brought her to the gymnasium floor to work on custom maps, between New Names and Utilities.

She was lucky to have landed a job that suited her so well, and to have so sympathetic a boss. The building she worked in didn't make her sick. The two storeys of air in the converted gymnasium weren't stuffy or rancid with carpet or cleaning chemicals. Charlie was accommodating about her occasional missed days or headache-induced late arrival or early departure, without Claire having to acknowledge to him how deeply her life was shaped, or distorted, by the coming and going of her migraines. A combination of drugs kept her headaches relatively under control and managed the pain when it came, although she was conscious, at times, of the fragility of this stability.

All day, as she worked on a map for Parks and Recreation of city wetlands, which meant every watery surface imaginable, for use in mosquito control, Claire's mind kept returning to Rachel. Where was she? Travelling? What had happened to her in Montreal? And if she had run off, why now?

Once, Rachel had vanished without a word for over three months, but that time there had been a reason, an obvious catalyst. Eight years ago, in May, on May 15, their parents had been killed in an accident. (For the first five years afterwards, the three of them had spoken on the anniversary of their parents' deaths; the sixth year, only Claire and Allison had done so, and the last two years, Claire had simply noted the date to herself.)

Rachel had not disappeared right after their parents' death. No, in the immediate aftermath, she had flown to meet Allison and Claire in Frankfurt, at a hotel, not far from the airport, where the accident had taken place. After Frankfurt, she had come to Toronto for the funeral and together they had travelled to the West Coast, to Victoria, where both their parents' families had settled and where their mother's mother and father's father still lived.

Accompanied by their weeping grandparents, they had scattered their parents' ashes within a grove of trees, and then flown back to Toronto to begin the difficult task of sorting through the belongings in their parents' west-end bungalow, the home of their childhood, and putting the house up for sale. In those agonizing days, it was Rachel who had taken charge, ushering them through what needed to be done, solicitous to the way that grief threatened to overwhelm them all. She had overseen the consultations with lawyers – German and Canadian – who were trying to determine if there would be a court case or just an insurance settlement. She kept on when both Allison and Claire were too overcome to do much of anything.

Then, at the beginning of that December, just when she might have been thinking of returning to Toronto to spend that first parentless Christmas with Allison and Claire, as they had assumed she would do, Rachel called to say she was going on a trip. Neither Claire nor Allison spoke to her directly. She did not say, in her messages, where she was going, or for how long.

There had been no word from Rachel at Christmas, which Claire shared with Allison and Lennie in their ground-floor apartment, in the house on Booth Avenue where she lived on the second floor. On Boxing Day, while Allison and Lennie set out for Montreal to visit Lennie's family, Claire, somewhat anxiously, allowed Stefan Simic, her new boyfriend then, to bear her off to his mother's house in Ottawa.

Weeks went by and there was still no word from Rachel. No postcards or letters arrived. Michael Straw, the architect with whom Rachel had lived for six years in her 9th Street apartment, until shortly before their parents' death, had not heard from her. The lack of word was puzzling, and yet Rachel had always been impetuous, a little willful and unpredictable, and somewhat blind to the effect of her behaviour on others.

More weeks passed. Phone messages left at Rachel's New York apartment went unreturned. Once or twice, however, the line rang busy. Late one night, near the end of March, Allison, who was having a harder time than Claire coping with Rachel's absence, managed to land a voice on Rachel's line, not Rachel, but a woman who gave her name as Mary Po, who began by stuttering that she was Rachel's roommate. Where was Rachel, Allison demanded. Had she received any of their messages? When Allison threatened to bring in the police, jittery, squeaky Mary Po relented and said that she was really more a subletter than a roommate, since Rachel wasn't actually there, but the sublet wasn't legal, so Rachel had instructed her not to answer the phone and all she knew was that Rachel was travelling and had said she would give Mary two weeks' notice before her return. She'd thought Rachel had spoken of coming back at the end of February but hadn't heard from her.

Allison hired a private detective. It had been a horrific year, and she couldn't put up with any more craziness. With remarkable efficiency, the detective tracked Rachel down at a beach resort in Thailand. From some palm-thatched lodge, Rachel called Allison (so Allison told Claire), and said, after everything they'd gone through, she'd just needed some time to herself; she was on vacation; they were all adults now; surely they did not have to know at all times where she was. Anyway, why would they assume the worst?

Shortly thereafter, she returned to New York and, perhaps as an act of penance, paid a visit to Toronto, tanned, apparently healthy, vague about whether she'd travelled alone or with anyone and what her itinerary had been, although she mentioned India and the Andaman Islands. She came back, Rachel told Claire, when she ran out of prescription migraine drugs.

"Hey, Claire," shouted Parker in New Names, "Does Falling Street sound like Colleen Street?"

His voice made her jump, even though she was used to him calling out such questions.

She raised her head from her computer to consider it. If she called back yes, the developer who had proposed Falling Street for some new field-engulfing residential tract would have to go back to the drawing board, since no name that could potentially cause any confusion when someone dialled 9-1-1 would be accepted. "Yes."

There was a Rachael Street in Toronto but no Rachel Street. In Montreal, there was a rue Rachel. In March, in Montreal, Rachel had sounded depressed, and desperate, but no more so than she had at other times. As they both did, at times. When it seemed as if a headache or a round of headaches would never end.

If Rachel had indeed gone travelling, this time she did not appear to have left a squeaky-voiced subletter occupying her apartment, at least not according to Brad Arnarson. Which suggested less premeditation. Or what?

Next to Claire, Bianca was complaining about the map of head lice cases that she was constructing for the Public School Board: where infested students lived, where their parents worked, in order to document the infestation's spread.

Logan, at the large-screen computer beyond, told Bianca to pipe down. His forensic map, for the police department, drew on information given by suspects and witnesses in a High Park rape investigation to establish people's walking patterns, to determine *confidence regions* – how close, based on the evidence and statements, witnesses and suspects could have been to the crime at the hour in question.

All mapping, Charlie Gorjup argued, was forensic, a kind of investigation.

Claire stood up.

At five, she reversed her path and set off west towards Stefan, who, like her, worked ten floors in the air. It would have been convenient if, a true aerialist, she could have tightrope-walked ten floors above Dundas Street to meet him.

He was not at his desk when she entered his research team's office, not examining DNA arrays on his computer, colour-coded grids of control cells and those subject to experimental conditions, over which he pored to see which were expressing under different sets of conditions. He worked with a fierce concentration that Claire loved. He, too, was mapping things. His research involved testing the responses of cancer cells at low-oxygen levels, searching for particular molecular pathways to target in cancer treatment.

Nor were there any other researchers around, which might mean they were beavering away in the lab somewhere or had already left for the day. Claire pushed through the door at the back of the office with the poster of the Bridget Fonda movie *Point of No Return* taped to it and made her way along the corridor off which opened the labs themselves — some filled with beakers or a centrifuge or refrigerator units, some sealed behind doors emblazoned with biohazard signs — until, turning left at the end of the hall, she came to a small door with a square window which emitted a glow of red light. And there was Stefan, on the other side of the door, in the tiny room where she often found him, crouched over the fluorescent microscope, the narrow curve of his spine shifting as he moved, dark hair drifting over his checked collar, olive skin rouged. She liked watching him think, unobserved – a heated, familiar rush that never failed her. Was love possible without admiration? How bony and agile his back and neck, his invisible mind ticking. When she knocked and waved through the portal, he turned and waved back, happy to see her, and without needing to move from his stool, opened the door. She had to do no more than slip into the gap between his legs and clasp his hands, room for only the two of them in this rose world.

"Claire, what's wrong?" Stefan touched his fingers to her temples, his glimmer of anxiety transferred to her.

"Thinking about Rachel."

He kissed the side of her neck. "Rachel's perfectly capable of looking after herself."

The next night, Tuesday, Claire called Brad Arnarson back.

"Have you heard anything?" she asked him, although she assumed, even before he responded, that he hadn't. "Have you been in touch with any of her other friends?"

"I don't actually know a lot of Rachel's friends. I've run into a couple of people but no one seems to have seen or heard from her recently."

"Did anything happen right before she left?"

"I don't know. I keep wondering. She was under kind of a lot of stress and she didn't seem very happy."

Claire wished she could visualize him. Blond? Dark? A Scandinavian surname. Rachel had always said she had a thing against blond men, so perhaps not blond then. Claire could not reliably get a grip on Brad Arnarson from his voice. Friend, he'd said, which could be euphemism – coyness or reticence. She was indebted to him for calling her but remained internally at odds about the nature of his concern.

"I'm thinking of coming to New York to check up on the apartment myself," she told him. She had a set of keys that Rachel had given her on an earlier trip to New York and had told her to hang on to, so that she would have them on subsequent visits and in case of an emergency, although the emergency that Claire had contemplated was Rachel losing her keys or having them stolen and needing dependable Claire to courier the extra set to her.

On Wednesday night, Claire called Allison once more, but got only voice mail, which probably meant that Allison and Lennie were putting the girls to bed. At 9:17, Allison phoned Claire. "Nothing," Claire said.

"Nothing here either," said Allison. "In the past year we haven't heard quite as often, every couple of weeks or so. But she visits. I knew we hadn't heard and I've been meaning to do or say something but things get so crazy around here. I suppose I convinced myself she'd be in touch by Star's birthday, which is like three more weeks, but, yeah, I guess I'm worried."

As Claire hung up the phone, the right side of her temple began to pulse. A point in the centre of her scalp. A second one at the base of the bone above and behind her right eye. Another point at the base of her skull, beneath the occipital bone, on the right. (Rachel said there was a point on the sole of her foot that ached whenever she got a migraine.)

Claire had no desire to get on a plane and fly to New York. She was thrown off-balance even having to consider it. She racked her brain for the names of the one or two of Rachel's friends she'd met on previous visits — Sophia, was it Sophia, whom they'd bumped into on Avenue A? Or Eileen, with whom they'd shared a quick dinner in a café on the corner of First Avenue and St. Marks Place? If she couldn't remember their surnames it was likely because Rachel hadn't mentioned them.

From the fridge, Claire pulled a carton of leftover Thai food. She'd eaten an early dinner, right after work, before heading to a yoga class. Now she spooned chicken with basil onto a plate and set the dish spinning in the microwave.

Stefan came home. He'd stayed late at the lab and gone straight to the gym. Wet-haired, he swept in the front door, trailing his slim shadow, drawing the scent of lilacs in with him.

Claire wiped her lips on a napkin. They kissed, Stefan touching his fingers to the back of her neck. She loved him, loved the life they shared. She did not want to be pulled away from this. She could, of course, sit tight for now, do nothing. There would be an explanation for whatever Rachel was up to. And yet something kept gnawing at her. Stefan poured himself a drink, cracking ice cubes into his glass, and sat. Wrapping her feet around the rungs of his chair, Claire fed him a forkful of chicken.

"What's the harm in having this guy look in on Rachel's apartment?"

"I have no idea who he is. He might be a murderer."

"And there's no one else you can think of to ask."

"Not offhand. And even if he goes in, I'm not sure he'll notice the right things. He could wreck things – clues."

Through the screen of the open window came the snuffling of the neighbours' bulldog along the foot of their shared fence. Here, too, the perfume of lilacs penetrated. Five and a quarter metres away, on the far side of the alley that ran between their narrow row of yards and those belonging to the houses on the next street, a security light blinked on.

"We could go down together next weekend," Stefan said. "I can't this weekend. I said I'd go into work. I'm supposed to look over some results with Rob." He didn't want to go, Claire knew. He believed Rachel would turn up. In her own sweet time. She was flighty. She was (she knew he thought this though he wouldn't say it aloud) a woman who had abandoned her child. "Why not give her another week to see if she shows herself? Now she knows everyone's trying to get hold of her." This sounded reasonable.

Claire frowned. She rubbed the occipital point at the back of her neck. When she caught Stefan looking at her, she dropped her hand. "I may go down to New York this weekend."

Claire had migraines long before her parents' death. She'd had migraines since childhood. She'd suffered from them even before Rachel had.

Where did the pain begin? She could not remember anything as decisive as a first headache, rather she had a growing awareness of their being part of her life's landscape. They were not as frequent during her childhood, however. And when they came – when they shook her, when she was capsized into them – the headaches always took her by surprise.

She had no sense, then, of warning signals. Nor was she able to attribute the migraines to any obvious cause, if they were in fact caused by anything outside her body and its complicated neurochemistry, her faulty nervous system with its particular sensitivity to pain. No one had yet used the word "migraine" around her. *Now* she was aware of triggers – things that didn't strictly cause the migraine but made her more vulnerable to its processes – but not then.

Then, the pain simply appeared. It was. She became it. One side of her head was seized, one side of her body. It took her over, like a fit. Even without a headache, she'd feel suddenly at sea and vomit. (Once, she remembered being terrified by a big black dog, then being put to bed with a headache, although no one else in her family recalled anything about the dog. Another time, when she and her sisters were left overnight by their parents with some friends, she must have come down with a migraine, though what she remembered was throwing up all over their baby-blue carpet.)

At home, in the bedroom that she and Allison shared, her mother drew shut the curtains and passed Claire a plastic bag of ice cubes to lay across her forehead. Beside the bed, she set a turquoise plastic tub – the barf bucket. Broad-browed, dark-haired, a dry hand to Claire's head, how matter-of-fact her mother was, as if there were nothing very unusual about Claire's pain. How far away she seemed, her hand, her body retreating.

Sometimes, dreamily, the ice pack having fallen from her eyes, the pillow itself now cold and wet, Claire became aware of someone standing in the doorway – not her mother, whom she longed for. Rachel, Allison? Shorts, a haze of longish hair. The figure did not speak. She could not bring herself to open her eyes fully to see who it was.

Slowly, her body was returned to her. She stopped lying still and began restlessly to toss. Once more, voices and the bang of the back screen door before the latch clicked made an impression upon her. She opened her eyes. Three small steps from her bed to Allison's. An oval of brown braided rug separated the two. The print of a Picasso Harlequin hung on the wall beyond her feet. Blue and orange squares and triangles patterned the curtains. The sun glittered faintly through the coarse weave of the cotton. There were eighteen triangles on the curtains. Claire moved her thumb along the edge of the bedside chest of drawers, alive to the ridge of wood beneath her skin, measuring, counting.

There were other symptoms that were probably related to her migraines which, at the time, she had no way of connecting to them. She was easily motion sick. On the plane the summer they flew to England, for instance. She did not actually throw up in the family car but often felt woozy, especially if she tried to read. Rachel and Allison read. They whispered to each other. They teased her. They complained about not wanting to sit next to her in the car in case she threw up — where's the barf bag? — but they both had to because neither of them was prepared to give up her window seat. So Claire, the youngest, stuck in the middle, her feet straddling the hump on the floor, was forced to contemplate the unreachable landscape, visible through the front windscreen and over her sisters' shoulders. She took some small revenge by insisting that either Rachel or Allison keep her window open, no matter how cold it was, otherwise she *would* throw up on them.

There was a fear that overcame her, linked to a sensation of being slightly out of control, as though her body were not altogether hers or the line between the world out there and her in here was very thin.

At night sometimes, as Claire lay in her bedroom beside solid, comforting Allison, her body began shrinking. She thought of it as the elevator feeling: shrinking was like falling down an elevator shaft, being both the one falling and the one who watched herself fall, whole but diminishing in scale. Other nights she grew. Her limbs swelled. If she concentrated all her attention on her right hand, it kept growing: its proportions remained the same, it simply expanded. She could not move. She had no warning which nights the distortions were going to happen. Whether she would be dropped into a deep well or lifted into the sky. Disappear or balloon to fill the world.

She didn't talk about it. She assumed this happened to everyone (Rachel, Allison), and that because the experience was so common, no one spoke of it.

Nor did it seem unusual to desire to measure things, trying to keep the world's wildness at bay. So much sensation — from the whirr of crickets to the whoosh of cars accelerating between stop signs on Rathburn Road, the sometimes bewildering facial expressions of other people, the pressure of others' gazes and skin, the hard plastic curves of a beloved toy figurine lost when it fell through her fingers into a sewer grate, the assault of the penny arcade machines beside an English beach, the overblown sweetness of honey — and so little means of blocking anything out.

One winter afternoon, aged eight, Claire made her way towards her parents' bedroom where the pale curtains were often left half-closed. In this room, she was alone, unobserved. She was not thinking in any plotted way about what she was doing. Her mother, and Rachel, and Allison were down the hall and around the corner, a right-hand turn into the kitchen. Claire peeled off her socks. The radiator beneath the window was sheathed in an aura of heat. She pressed her right foot against it. Her skin and muscle flinched. She persisted. She counted to ten, pulled her foot back, and examined the pink flush growing on her sole. The stinging swelled and receded. No other sensation existed while she did this. Then she tried the same with her left foot.

She began to slip away to her parents' bedroom regularly, in the later afternoon, when she was least likely to be missed, while her mother was preparing supper and her sisters bickering over homework at the dining room table, her father still away at the school where he taught math. Always at the same radiator, beside the rocking chair over which Sylvia hung her worn shirts and pantyhose, faintly sweet with the odour of her feet and shoes. Beneath the radiator's eight pleats, dust gathered amidst the pale blue stubble of the broadloom. Cold air billowed through an open slit of window. Claire did not close the door. She folded her knees, pressed both feet to the hot metal, and started counting. Each time there came a point when she could no longer hold her feet in place, her arches contracting even as she bit her tongue and urged herself to go longer. She did not cry. The pain was worse, far worse, when she pulled her feet away. It bowled her over. She bit her hand to counteract it. But the pain was hers, no one's but hers. She controlled when it started and when it ended, and this produced a satisfaction so deep it became exhilaration. She began to use her wristwatch to time herself — three minutes and forty-four seconds, forty-five, forty-six. Her feet so piercingly tender afterwards it was hard to walk. One step, two steps, three. Once she held her feet so long that she burned them enough to blister. Did she make a sound that time? Someone in the doorway. Her mother in the doorway, bounding across the room, yanking her by the wrist, What the heck do you think you're doing?

Slowly Claire grew aware that Rachel also got headaches. Or, slowly Rachel also began to get headaches. Until then, Claire had only thought of her sisters as people who did things, who sometimes did things to her or made her feel a certain way. Rachel, in particular, seemed out of reach, twelve, nearly thirteen, loping around in that musky, budding body of hers. The year Claire turned nine, they moved to a somewhat bigger bungalow, blocks from the old but far enough that she had to switch schools. She and Allison still shared a room but it was larger, their beds, pushed to opposite walls, four large paces away from each other. Now and again, when Claire came home from school with a headache and took to her bed, she'd open her eyes later to find another person in the room. Rachel not Allison. Out of the dim haze of those afternoons, Rachel materialized, gazing down at her, Rachel lying in Allison's bed. Long, dark hair, long and angular face, her elongated legs growing even as she lay. Sometimes Rachel pulled Allison's pillow over her head. Eyes closed, Claire listened to the rasp of Rachel's breath, her own breath echoing Rachel's. There was comfort in Rachel's presence. They did not need to speak. Their mother came in and gave them each two 222s, aspirin with codeine, to quell the pain. Strange to see Rachel so quiet and stilled. Rachel who ran and won the hundred-metre dash in junior high school track meets. On the shelf beside the window, Allison's gerbils madly spun the metal wheel in their cage.

Sometimes, ten-year-old Allison appeared, swinging open the door. There she was, through the slits of Claire's eyelids, a Band-Aid on her left shin, another on her right elbow — the one who tripped on her shoelaces, who bumped into things.

"You're in my bed," Allison said to Rachel.

"So?" Rachel removed Allison's pillow from her forehead.

"I have a headache," Allison said.

"You do not," said Rachel. Dark hair was matted like a stain across her brow.

"I do so," said Allison. She sat on the edge of the bed, then swung her legs up, forcing Rachel to shift over. There was barely room for the two of them as Allison rolled onto her side, scrunched up her eyes, clutched her stomach and began to moan.

"Cut it out," Rachel said, rising on one elbow. But Allison kept moaning.

"I mean it," Rachel said. And, "Go bother Claire." When she pinched Allison, Allison shrieked.

First came the rap of their mother's footsteps along the hall, then she veered into the room, her left hand gripping the door frame. "What's going on in here?"

"I have a headache," Allison said.

"Where?" Sylvia asked as she approached. "Do you feel sick?"

"All over the top of my head," Allison said. Her eyes were wide open, the whites glistening in the dusky light, the room shielded by curtains.

Sylvia laid her palm against Allison's forehead, as if checking for fever. "One side or both sides?"

They all waited for Allison's response. "Both," Allison said at last.

Sylvia sighed, leaning over Allison to kiss her, which made Claire's heart leap about indignantly. "You'll be all right."

As soon as their mother left, pulling the door almost all the way closed, Rachel turned to Claire and spoke in a gravelly voice. "She has a migraine."

"Who?" Claire asked.

"Mum."

"A what?"

"It's what you have."

"How do you know she has one?"

"From the way she's rubbing her shoulder and her neck."

Word dovetailed with image: her mother's right hand unconsciously working the muscles of her right shoulder, playing with the tight tendons beside her throat, kneading the place at the back of the head where the neck joined the skull, where, beneath her skull (as in her head, as in Rachel's), on one side the pain was beginning to throb. And it came to Claire that she had seen her mother like this not just minutes ago, leaning over Allison's bed, but on other occasions.

Claire arrived at La Guardia late on the Saturday morning. The world shone with a supple, exquisite brightness that was not normal because she so seldom experienced airports without some level of pain-induced perceptual interference. This time, the hour-long flight, the dry air of high altitudes, the convulsive shifts in pressure, had not given her a headache. She bought a bag of almonds and an apple to tide her over on the food front, then headed down the flight of stairs to the baggage claim, her overnight bag in one hand. She did not take the escalator.

By the baggage carousels stretched banks of pay phones, their silvered surfaces built right into the walls. The first one she tried didn't work but the second one did, its buttons clicking as she pressed Stefan's number at the lab. She left him a message saying she'd arrived, her head was fine, and she'd try him at home that evening. If he needed to reach her, she'd be at Rachel's.

Fishing Brad Arnarson's number out of her datebook, she called him. He picked up after four rings, a little hoarse, as if he'd just woken up, although it was nearly noon. He'd told her to call as soon as she got in and they would make plans to meet. Claire said she was still at the airport. "What time do you want to come by Rachel's?" she asked.

"Say two?"

Outside, the sun shone brilliantly, battering car windshields. The drivers of yellow taxis leaned on their horns. A black man yanked down the baggage doors of a Manhattan-bound airport bus. A beautiful day and such blare all around her. As Claire raced for the bus, she kept her eyes peeled for Rachel, on the off chance that Rachel, wheeling her flight bag behind her, was about to make a sudden, miraculously timed reappearance.

A man in attendant's greens sat smoking on the fourth of the six steps that led up to Rachel's apartment building on East 9th Street. He was watching a teenaged girl coax a shivering, hairless dog down another set of stairs to the basement veterinary clinic. On all sides, heat pressed in. The fetid, cheesy stench of warming garbage rose from a row of metal cans lined against the wall of the building next door. Sweat had already gathered at Claire's underarms, dampening her flowered dress. At home, she might have been sitting in the cool kitchen, reading the paper, or biking with Stefan by the lake. The vet attendant glanced at her as she passed him on her way to the front door.

The door, which was sometimes locked and sometimes not, wasn't. In the vestibule, Claire checked for Rachel's name, there as it had always been, and pressed her buzzer.

After a minute, she let herself through the second door into the front hall. A hole in the ceiling, half-covered with a green garbage bag, had not been there the last time she had visited, on her own, early in the fall. Dog fluff floated down the stairwell. Parrots squawked behind closed doors. Nothing felt askew or in any way sinister, as she mounted the six dizzying flights, 110 steps, that led to Rachel's door.

Claire knocked. And listened, trying to still her racing breath, her flushed face pressed to the crack between door and the metal security plate bolted along the frame's edge. No funky smells from inside. Only the familiar, softly sulphurous scent of gas drifted through the hall. She unlocked the three locks, fumbling over the keys until she got each one to fit in turn, catching her finger on the security plate as she pushed the door open, swearing as her skin smarted. She called out Rachel's name. Sunlight poured through the kitchen windows. Pigeons erupted from the window ledges. The door slammed shut behind her. She locked it from the inside.

Warm air enveloped her, the close stickiness of a place that appeared to have been uninhabited for a while.

Claire dropped her bag.

Fourteen paces to the farthest point in the apartment, through the kitchen, the middle room, the third room that did triple duty as study, bedroom, living room, to the far end where two windows looked over 9th Street. Rachel's champagne-coloured duvet was pulled loosely over her bed, as if before leaving she'd given it one half-hearted tug. Her pillows lay one atop another the way she piled them when she had a headache so that she could lie with her head raised. A small alarm clock – the time was 12:57 – sat on the floor by the bed. Papers lay scattered on her desk, around a gap, twenty-five by thirty centimetres, the size of her laptop computer, black grit coming up when Claire swiped her finger across the space. Rachel's books (anatomy books, medical books, books of all sorts) were lined up on her shelves and in stacks, beneath the shelves, on the floor. The framed photograph of Star and one of their parents, an early snapshot taken in Addis Ababa when Rachel herself was no more than a baby, remained in place on her desk. Yellow Post-it notes clung to the wall above the telephone, while a couple of numbers were scribbled in red ink right on the wall. When Claire picked up the phone, the line pulsed with the quickened dial tone that signalled waiting messages.

Nothing looked, at least superficially, all that different than usual. Dust swirled across the floor. Dust gathered in clumps in the corners of the middle room, skittering over Rachel's Moroccan slippers – but then Rachel hated to vacuum.

Inside the closet, four empty hangers dangled amidst the row of clothes. Spumes of dry-cleaning plastic lay in waves beneath. On the shelf above the clothes' rail gaped a space big enough to hold a small suitcase. In the top drawer of a chest of drawers, Claire counted seven pairs of underwear, four beige, three black. Surely Rachel owned more. On the other hand, she did not appear to have packed for a long trip.

The contents of Rachel's fridge were an opened bottle of Evian water; a shrivelled piece of ginger; a canister of film (which Claire had a feeling she'd seen on a couple of previous visits) rattled in the otherwise empty egg tray; a handful of vegetables rotted in the crisper. A bowl, a plate, a glass, a knife and fork, were stacked in the sink.

Insect corpses lay scattered in the bathtub, three centipedes and the carapace of a cockroach. The water in the toilet bowl had turned an unpleasant rusty colour. In the bathroom garbage basket, long strands of dark hair were coiled among piles of Kleenex.

No note, no sign of a note.

Back in the kitchen, Claire grabbed a handful of nuts from her bag, then opened the door of the cupboard that ran along the wall to the left of the sink. The bottom shelf, just above eye level, served as Rachel's medicine cabinet. Bottles of vitamins and over-the-counter pills, a desperate cornucopia of prescription medications, were jumbled together. Claire lifted the bottles out and set them on the kitchen table.

Among the various abandoned prophylactics – drugs that Rachel had tried to keep headaches at bay – were a half-empty bottle of Sandomigran, and an expired bottle of Elavil, which Claire used at a low dose to ward off her migraines, and another of Epival.

She found an almost-empty bottle of Anaprox, good for calming muscles, which she herself took whenever she had a migraine. It heightened the effectiveness of Zomig, the triptan drug that targeted the specific receptors implicated in the migraine's neurochemical processes. Rachel, too, used Zomig, but there was no sign of any, none that Claire could find, only one partly used cardboard blister pack of Imitrex, an earlier triptan drug, which, they agreed, no longer worked for them as effectively as it used to.

There were other things Claire expected to see and didn't: no Tylenol 3s. And no 292s, prescription codeine with aspirin, so no prescription codeine drugs at all, only a Canadian bottle of over-the-counter 222s. On the other hand, Claire was always cautioning Rachel about codeine overuse, not only because codeine was addictive, but it could actually lower your pain threshold. Which Rachel knew. Rachel had had both Zomig and Tylenol 3s on her in Montreal. Presumably she'd taken all her supplies of those drugs (months' worth, possibly, in the case of Zomig, since Rachel, like Claire, tended to fill her prescriptions in bulk). Odd that she'd left nothing of either at home, particularly the Zomig. This might suggest some premeditation – a determination, even before setting out for Montreal, not to return, at least not soon thereafter. No doubt she had some Anaprox on her, too. While careless about some things, Rachel would never let herself get caught without medication – of this Claire was convinced. Neither of them ever went out the door without a pocket stash of something.

And yet, and yet – the apartment wasn't abandoned. Electricity still juiced through the switches – the overhead light bloomed when Claire flicked it on and the fridge had been humming the whole while. Blue flames leaped to life on the gas stove when she switched on one of the elements. Someone was paying the utility bills. The phone worked. By the looks of such things, Rachel might waltz in the door at any moment. Her landlord had not tried to repossess the place.

Claire scooped up the keys from the kitchen table and headed back downstairs. In the front hall, pieces of mail were practically bursting out of Rachel's mailbox, and when Claire turned the key, the lock stiff with the pressure of the contents, the metal door sprang open, spilling envelopes in all directions.

She picked envelopes off the floor, tugged free those items wedged deep within the box. Folded amidst the real and junk mail was a piece of paper on which someone (the mail carrier?) had scrawled CLEAN OUT YOUR MAILBOX!!!

At the back of the first floor hall, which smelled now of damp dog and garlic, Claire stopped to toss the obvious junk mail in the recycling bin before carrying the rest upstairs. When she re-entered the apartment, the pigeons, who had returned to their perches, leaped up with less ferocity. The heat hit her even more intensely. Before sorting the mail, she set about opening windows, wrestling with the stiff catches, pushing up so hard on the frames that she was frightened of falling out. Now she felt like an intruder, disrupting things, trampling on traces of Rachel. The window ledges were thick with pigeon shit. Cooler air blew in, skivvying the dust. She scarfed down another handful of nuts and gulped the rest of the bottle of Evian water.

There wasn't a lot of personal mail. A couple of handwritten envelopes. A postcard from St. Petersburg from someone named John, who began, *I know you haven't heard from me in years.*

Envelopes from *Elle*, *Vogue*, *Marie Claire* might be cheques, payments for articles. There was a bank statement. Surely under the circumstances, it was permissible to open Rachel's bank statement. At first Claire simply stared. All those zeros. Thirty thousand dollars in Rachel's chequing account. Some of that money might be the remains of the sum they'd each received from the insurance settlement after their parents' death. At the time, Claire had found it funny that Rachel did not do as she and Allison had done: put some of the money into buying a house or apartment. A condo. Allison had no doubt argued in favour of this, but

Rachel had told Claire why bother when she had a cheap, rent-controlled apartment in Manhattan that she liked. This was her March statement. Her rent, $550, disappeared on the first of the month — presumably Rachel had given her landlord a fistful of postdated cheques at the beginning of the year.

Bills were paid by automatic withdrawal. There was an unspecified bank transfer of $1,000 which might be the monthly allowance that Rachel paid Allison towards Star's care. Later in the month there were a couple of automatic withdrawals for several hundred dollars apiece, not even amounts, and accompanied by additional withdrawal fees, which suggested they'd been made outside the country. No further information was offered.

An official letter sent by the post office on April 24 announced that Rachel's mail would be held until further notice, since there was no room in her mailbox; she should contact the Cooper Square station as soon as possible regarding pickup or alternate delivery. There was also what appeared to be a credit card statement — Claire was slicing her finger along the top of the envelope, when, from across the kitchen, the buzzer sounded.

The three buttons beneath the intercom spelled BLT. Like the sandwich, as Rachel had said when she'd shown Claire how to work them. Pressing T, Claire shouted, "Who is it?" She pressed L and listened to a male voice holler back through static. She presumed he'd said Brad. He could have said Bacon. Hitting B, she buzzed him up.

As soon as his footsteps reached the top of the stairs, Claire opened the door. He was blond. A limp mess of uncombed hair.

As breathless and moist as she'd been upon reaching the summit. He looked young, boyish, perhaps younger than he was. At first sight, there was nothing obviously discomforting or menacing about him. His pale skin, despite the flush of his face, gave him an appearance of all-over milkiness, a guileless, quizzical air. His thin plaid shirt hung open, the sleeves rolled above the elbows. A damp white undershirt beneath. A cellphone hooked to the waist of his jeans. A sharp hint of sweat. On first impression, he seemed too mild, too kind, too *unstylish*, to be a boyfriend of Rachel's. He looked like he'd stepped out of a field, or, no, out of a picture of a field.

He was staring at Claire, too, as he approached, perhaps examining the ways in which she did or did not resemble Rachel. Put Allison between them and the connections became clearer. Rachel's face was the sternest, her hair the darkest brown; she also had the best cheekbones, their father's. Allison, the tallest, shared her squared jaw. Claire, the small one, didn't, and her hair was light brown, almost fair, but her mouth and lips were, like Rachel's, their mother's. You saw their resemblance when they smiled.

"Hi." He held out his hand, and Claire shook it. "Have you found anything?" He followed her into the apartment.

"Not really, not yet." All at once she felt like crying but swallowed the urge. She gathered up the medications in handfuls and stuffed them back in the cupboard.

Just as she had done, he walked all the way to the far end of the apartment, glancing about, as if Rachel might pop out from behind the furniture.

"Do you happen to know her phone code?" Claire asked.

"Unh-unh."

"I've used it when I've stayed here but I can't remember it." It drove her crazy that she, who had a good memory for details, couldn't recall it, though it was nothing obvious (like Rachel's date of birth) and she had not visited Rachel all that frequently.

"I've been looking through her mail." They returned to the kitchen. The pigeons had floated back to the window ledges where they were quietly hooting.

Brad Arnarson fingered the postcard on the table, then glanced at the bank statement. Claire hoped she wasn't betraying Rachel by exposing something as private as her finances.

She picked up the credit card statement that she'd been in the process of opening. She really didn't want to be doing this.

On March 16, charges from the Hotel du Parc in Montreal. (Rachel must have stayed until the sixteenth then.) On the seventeenth, a $1,245.68 charge from Air Canada. This was the date the transaction had gone through, which wasn't necessarily the date when the ticket had been purchased, and the statement gave no clue as to where the transaction had taken place, nor where Rachel was flying. It could have been a delayed charge for Rachel's ticket to Montreal or it could have taken her somewhere else entirely.

There were no subsequent charges.

"How long have you known Rachel?" Claire asked, as they pulled out chairs on either side of the table.

"Just about a couple of years."

"And were you — I'm sorry, I don't know a better way of asking — were you a couple?"

"Kind of."

"Does that mean you were and you're not now?"

"I'm not sure. I know that sounds strange. We'd entered some kind of grey zone. It wasn't totally clear."

"It was clearer before?"

"Yeah. For a while, things were pretty intense. But we've both been really busy. We have a lot of commitments. And there were complications. Things haven't been all that easy for her lately."

"Not easy how?"

"With her headaches, for a start. They'd been giving her a hard time and she was having trouble finding anything that helped. So that was depressing her, and obsessing her, kind of, I'd say. And I think she was looking to do more straight journalism, still on medical issues but she was getting kind of fed up with the women's magazines."

"They pay okay, don't they?"

"Yeah, they pay."

"So you think maybe she's on some, I don't know, investigative mission?"

"Could be."

"The last time you saw her —"

"We got together a week before she left — and that was fine, it was great, we had dinner, we had a good time."

"But you spoke to her —"

"The night before she left. She was kind of frantic because she had something to finish before she took off, and she wasn't feeling well. She was kind of on edge. I think she'd been trying to pull back from people generally. So I don't know how personal some of it was. Her mood. We argued. She told me I was too involved. I'd called mostly to make sure she was okay — but there was also something she wanted that I wasn't prepared to do."

Sex, was it an argument about sex?

Was Rachel trying to dump him and he wasn't getting it? If this was indeed the reason for her running off, it did not explain why she hadn't got in touch with Claire, or with Allison and Star.

It was odd that Rachel had never mentioned his name. Did this make the relationship more a delusion on his part than something actual, for all that they had no doubt slept together, spent time (nights?) together in this very apartment? Yet Rachel's accounts of her relationships were not altogether to be trusted. She could be by turns confessional and secretive, and more often secretive — private, she might say. When Michael Straw had moved in, she had said nothing to her family for eight months. Later, she said it was because she'd felt nervous, uncertain about whether the relationship would last. She had been equally oblique when he moved out. There had been other boyfriends whom they'd heard little of, their presence signalled ambiguously in Rachel's conversation by references to "a friend."

Was there something Rachel found embarrassing about Brad Arnarson or was she simply trying to protect herself? If he did not immediately strike Claire as conforming to her sense of Rachel's taste — she would have said Rachel liked her men more assertive, men capable of sweeping her away — well, there were also limits to what she knew of Rachel's taste in men.

Just like that, her head — specifically, the point behind her right eye — began to pulse. Claire leaped to her feet. "I need to get some lunch."

"Want to find something on First Avenue?" Brad rose also.

"Something fast."

"You've got your choice." He listed Cuban, Vietnamese, Filipino, Japanese, Thai, Korean, Indian, Italian, Venezuelan, and Belgian waffles. He did not seem thrown by her sudden shift in tempo but kept pace as they hustled out the door and down the stairs.

"Japanese." Outside, as they bounded towards the corner, Claire pointed north to the Japanese restaurant at the intersection of 11th Street and First Avenue where she had often eaten with Rachel, most recently during her last visit to New York. Last September 13, it would have been, or the fourteenth. Despite being raw, sushi was a good food for both of them — heavy on protein, which helped stabilize their blood sugar and thus warded off migraines, and neutral (just fish and rice). Seaweed (healthy and green) on the side. In September, Rachel had remarked that sushi was the only food she was still eating out with any regularity. It felt safe. Talismanic. Just as there were times when Claire, pitching towards a headache, hung all her hope on a Granny Smith apple, because someone had told her there was something in green apples that counteracted migraines. She wondered if Rachel had told Brad that she also suffered from them. Likely Rachel had mentioned it at some point.

They had barely squeezed into their corner table before Brad waved a waiter over.

"How fast can you bring us some sushi?"

"Sashimi," Claire said.

"Okay, sashimi."

Fast, it seemed, since the lunch rush was over. Once their orders were taken, they turned their attention back to the matter at hand.

"Are you going to call the police?" Brad Arnarson asked.

"Not sure yet." In Claire's mind, puzzlement still prevailed over fear.

"What about a private detective?"

She shook her head vehemently. "Not yet."

That last visit, Claire had flown down on her own to take in a show of antique maps at the Pierpont Morgan Library. In recent years, she and Stefan had usually come down together, twice when Rachel was out of town and they could be on their own in her apartment. Claire, rather than Allison, was the one who had more frequently visited Rachel in New York.

In September, Rachel had seemed in good spirits. She had taken Claire to a boutique on 7th Street run by a friend of hers — Adele, that was the woman's name but Adele what? — and bought her a pair of silver gloves, which Claire had almost never worn.

"Do you know a friend of Rachel's who owns a store on 7th Street?"

"Adele Thomas." Brad was drinking from a cup of miso soup, eyeing her over the rim of the bowl. "Are she and Rachel close?"

"I don't know."

"We can stop by after lunch, if you like."

Their food arrived: teriyaki chicken for Brad, sashimi for Claire, who began to wolf down the glistening strips of raw fish.

In September, they'd sat two tables closer to the sushi bar than where Claire and Brad were seated. Notice anything unusual, Rachel had asked, plucking Claire's arm. No matter how carefully Claire scanned the room and its decor, the cramped tables, the special menus for soft-shell crab and tempura asparagus written in coloured highlighter and taped to the walls, no matter how carefully she revisited her memories of previous visits, nothing seemed to have altered. I'll give you a clue, Rachel said. She nodded towards the three men in white jackets working the sushi bar, little white hats moored like boats on top of their heads. Ah. They weren't Japanese. They were speaking Spanish. I'm amazed you didn't notice, Rachel said. In the last year, it's like this in every sushi restaurant around here.

"When do you go home?" Brad asked. (This day, also, three Hispanic men were chopping fish behind the bar.)

"Sunday evening." The muscles along Claire's right side, at the nape of her neck were seizing up. She was uneasy, that was all, and caught off guard. "I may need to go right back to Rachel's after lunch."

He nodded, without seeming either surprised or perturbed. "I can stop by Adele's."

"It's okay. I can go tomorrow."

Brad shrugged. "Well, let me know if there's anything you want me to do."

"How did you meet Rachel?"

Now he blushed, his cheeks as full of colour as when she'd first encountered him at the top of the stairs outside Rachel's apartment. "We had a professional connection. And then we reconnected nonprofessionally after that."

Ever since meeting him, Claire had been trying to imagine what his professional life consisted of, what lay beyond the plaid shirt and concerned demeanour – actor, computer programmer, banker, grad student? "What do you do?"

His blush had receded. He was signalling the waiter — already — for the bill. "I'm a massage therapist."

Once, Claire had flown to New York to visit Rachel, and arrived with a migraine (not unusual). A bad one (worse luck). Rachel was actually there when Claire, the extra set of keys in her pocket, reached the apartment. As soon as Rachel saw Claire wobbling in the doorway, she beckoned Claire in. C'mere. Gently.

She pulled Claire's bags from her arms and pushed her into a kitchen chair and handed her a glass of water along with a couple of familiar pills. Standing behind the chair, Rachel pressed her fingertips sharply into Claire's shoulders, above the collarbone, then along the vertebrae at the nape of her neck. Oh, babe. Leaning over her, she worked the occipital area, at the top of the nape, on the right side, hard as a wall as a rock. Claire was close to tears, each pulse like a dodgem car slamming away behind her eye, but Rachel seemed to know, without Claire having to say anything, without seeking far, the precise spots on Claire's scalp where the muscles gripped, those strange little muscle joins that the migraine made throb (pain which didn't originate in the muscles but travelled there), the searing place over the right eyebrow. Claire's pain spoke and Rachel heard it. Her fingers, barely stumbling, spoke back. It was the fact that her fingers could identify the pain as much as her attempts to release it that was so comforting.

Once she had returned to Rachel's apartment, Claire medicated herself and stretched out on the bed, on top of Rachel's duvet, head on the raised pillows, eyes covered with the small silk eye pillow that she always carried with her when she travelled. Later, she tossed it aside. Light slid slowly across the walls of Rachel's room. The height of the brass frame of Rachel's bed meant that the view through the east-facing side window, the direction in which the bed faced, offered nothing but sky and rooftops and mostly sky, through which Claire floated. Rachel must have lain here like this, a ghost, an echo. Stefan, too, had sprawled on this bed beside her. How quiet the room was. For moments at a time, Claire would forget, as she drifted, that she was here because Rachel was missing. She could have been almost anywhere. Stefan might walk through the door. The pigeons' voices and the flapping of their wings dropped to a sibilant murmur. From a distant window ledge came the droning of a dove.

It was 9:07 by the alarm clock beside Rachel's bed, and still light, when Claire roused herself and pulled on a T-shirt over her bra and underpants. At eight, Stefan had called and, still murky with drugs, she'd told him she would phone him later, adding that there was no sign of Rachel. Now, her head slowly clearing, she padded from window to window. In a minute, she would call him back. Then she would have to rouse herself further and find some dinner.

On the rooftop on the north side of 9th Street, a woman was watering a garden of yellow climbing roses. In the east, on the roof of the building next door, only five floors up and thus clearly visible from Rachel's sixth-floor apartment, a cocktail party was in progress. Three young men lingered by the south edge of the rooftop, each with a jacket hooked over his shoulder, a martini glass in the other hand. Three young women in diaphanous dresses hovered close to the east side of the roof, the sunset like silk on their bare backs, arms smooth as bones. It was a Saturday night, for others only an ordinary Saturday night. The pigeons had vanished.

Until her parents' deaths, when she was twenty-six, Claire had always taken comfort in statistical odds. She quelled any nervousness about flying by telling herself that she was far more likely to die in a car crash than in the air. Her parents' accident had savaged that comfort, for the odds of both your parents dying at the foot of an upward-bound escalator in an arrival hall at the Frankfurt International Airport, falling and being crushed beneath their luggage and a metal luggage trolley that had come loose from the patented metal grips on the escalator, were so minute as to be infinitesimal. Yet this had happened.

After the first years of grief, Claire had tried to salvage some consolation. Their deaths offered a kind of statistical inoculation. The odds of something equally terrible happening to another family member had to be as infinitesimal. By this reasoning, Rachel would be safe. Yet there were limits to this consolation. After all, the world was ruled by randomness. People were transformed or vanished or died when you least expected it. She could not forget that if a young woman had not, years ago, leaped to her death from a bridge, neither she nor Rachel nor Allison would even exist.

On Sunday evening, Claire flew home almost but not entirely empty-handed. She'd gathered up the pages that Rachel had abandoned on her desk and stuffed them into her flight bag. Most of them seemed to be notes towards an article on insomnia – at Christmas Rachel had been writing about narcolepsy. On another page were scribbled words which Claire deciphered as *trigeminal nerve, migraine generator, brain stem,* and a phone number with a Montreal area code for a Dr. P. L'Aube.

She had spent the day searching through Rachel's belongings. In particular, she'd looked for Rachel's passport, or a datebook, or an address book, none of which she found. There was no sign of a cellphone either, although in the right-hand bottom drawer of Rachel's desk, Claire found three sets of cords and adapters – the remains of lost cellphones? The upper drawers of the desk, and notably the shallow middle drawer, were strewn with business cards, as if Rachel had simply emptied her pockets into them. Claire sorted through the cards and pulled out the ones marked with the names of editors at magazines: she would try calling these from work the next morning. Also Rachel's bank and phone company.

At lunchtime, she'd knocked on the door of Rachel's neighbours, two men, a couple, whom she had met briefly in the past, but they weren't in. She slipped a note under their door. Nor when she stopped by Adele Thomas, the boutique, was Adele there, only a young underling with very short hair who said that Adele would be in France for the next two weeks but gave Claire Adele's home number.

Back in Rachel's apartment, Claire tried the phone numbers written in red ink on the wall, which proved to be a car service, a Japanese restaurant, and a pharmacy on Second Avenue. She even called information and got the listing for Michael Straw, who now lived in Brooklyn with a woman Claire believed to be his wife. She was acutely aware that for him Rachel was history, as he surely was for her. When Michael came on the line (of course he remembered Claire, he said), he commiserated but was clearly relieved that Rachel's peregrinations didn't concern him any longer.

Home to downtown Toronto. How strangely quiet and empty, after New York, the evening streets seemed – York Street as Claire walked north from Front, where the airport bus had dropped her off, towards her streetcar stop on King. How few other pedestrians there were, all of them lost in scale beneath the glass-clad office towers. Her perception of space was entirely different here: the bank towers barely seemed to crowd each other, and between the green gleaming walls spread wide slices of azure sky.

Too much space, Rachel had complained. Everything so spread out. She claimed it was one of the reasons she'd left Toronto for New York.

On the other hand, Claire loved the way the streets stretching east and west became ribbons of two- or three-storey hundred-year-old buildings rather than corridors of five- and six-storey tenements. It pleased her to live in a city full of houses and vistas that opened through trees to the sky.

She loved living close to the lake, too, that inland sea, loved the sense of expansiveness the lake offered. The air felt different in its proximity even when you couldn't see the water. There were breezes, yes, but also the invisible promise of a wide horizon nearby.

Not that she and Stefan had consciously searched for a house close to the lake. Claire was aware of a certain constriction in herself when she moved inland, and perhaps she suffered from an unacknowledged desire to find a city within this city as unlike her childhood suburban home as possible (Stefan had spent his childhood in Hamilton, not Toronto). Growing up, she certainly had not thought of herself as living by a lake; the lake, then, had seemed far away.

They had looked for months before buying a house, before daring to make an offer; then were nearly outbid. So many of the houses they saw were hopelessly, heart-sinkingly ugly – old houses modernized with lurid broadloom and vile veneer cabinetry, panelled doors replaced by hollow wood, rooms stuffed with dolls or sports plaques, quaint but unnecessary second-floor kitchens, closed doors behind which lurked vicious dogs or aquaria filled with snakes, old washing machines with hand-turned mangles in the neat basements of deceased old women, other basements fat with vats of homemade wine. They kept to the west end, traipsing the kilometres west from Bathurst to Roncesvalles, from College south to King. Neither of them had ever lived with anyone before, which made Claire nervous. Surely that was a bad sign, that neither of them had managed to live with anyone before, though she was only twenty-six and Stefan twenty-seven when they'd met. She had already almost convinced herself that she would never meet anyone with whom she would be able to live and who would want to live with her.

The house they bought needed work, a brick-fronted Victorian semidetached on Adelaide Street not further abused by anyone else's terrible taste. It had seemed solid enough, which was important to Stefan, the angles of its walls and floors not too, too wonky, and Claire, who loved its antique trim and the height of its ceilings, allowed herself to be pulled along by Stefan's conviction that this was the place for them.

They had the money from the insurance settlement to help with their renovation. Under the circumstances, there was something reassuring about Stefan's own obsessiveness and tenacity. He was a good person to be renovating a house with, as careful and methodical as Claire was. Together they tore out old mouldy carpets and stripped the hideous speckled wallpaper, deliberating, sometimes for hours, over choices of light fixtures and faucets. They were both fastidious about cleaning up as they went and about measuring everything accurately. There was pleasure in such exactitude, Claire thought, passion in order, until the day when she struggled to get two corner joins of the new bathroom baseboard to line up properly and collapsed in tears at a three-millimetre gap, a gap that, as Stefan reassured her, would be filled in with silicone and hidden behind the toilet. Stefan proved as inconsolable when, trying to move the porcelain pedestal of the sink, he dropped and chipped it, and lay on the hall floor for over two hours, despite all Claire's efforts to drag him to his feet. But such moments were few, and they were pulled onward.

Flight bag in hand, Claire hurried up the three steps onto the front porch. She could, by now, count her way through these rooms in her sleep. Nine steps from the front door to the entrance of the kitchen, where the clock on the stove read 8:26. Stefan had left a note on the counter: Out playing basketball, back any minute, love, love, love, S. Up the twenty-one narrow stairs to the second floor, where she paused at the top before taking four more steps down the hallway to the entrance of their bedroom.

Once explorers had mapped the country by counting steps. Sir William Logan had counted his steps until the soles of his shoes fell off in tatters and his feet grew ragged. For three months, he had walked through clouds of mosquitoes, mapping the coastline of the Gaspé cove by cove, from dawn until the sun fell at night. Claire had fallen in love with exploration stories like these. Of course, there was no more room in the world for this sort of mapping.

All the time that she and Stefan were renovating the house, Claire was working on the base map of the city. Home cosmography, Charlie crowed. That's our legacy. Claire and the other photogrammetrists moved through the city grid by grid, aerial photograph by aerial photograph; the photographs were updated each year around the third week of April, after the snow had gone but while the trees remained leaf-free, before a cover of foliage enshrouded the city from view. They worked it out so that each of them got to transfer their own immediate neighbourhood from photograph to grid and as luck would have it they lived far enough apart that there were no conflicts.

Claire got: part of Lakeshore Boulevard, the old Molson Brewery, Fort York on its hump of land squeezed between the elevated Gardiner Expressway and the railway tracks. King Street, Queen Street, Dundas Street as her northern boundary, Bathurst Street to the east, Dufferin Street to the west. To the south, the shoreline. Once upon a time, just out of her cartography program, she'd specialized as a mapper of coastlines, entranced by their finicky, fractal details.

She stylus-drew the footprint of her house, and the house attached to it, the property lines, the ailanthus tree in the backyard, the alley. She did not inscribe what everyone on the block called the Ugly Garage, across the alley from their yard, its patched-up walls of Insulbrick listing so much that they swayed in one direction, then another depending which way the wind blew. One door was painted dung brown, the other a foul green. Plants that tried to grow up its sides, even deadly nightshade, withered and died, leaving desiccated skeletons. Strange smells seeped beneath its doors: car oil, vinegar, sulphur. The tarpaper roof was littered with empty pigeon coops and pigeon shit. Now, on the city map, the Ugly Garage didn't exist; it had been erased, this being what they and all their neighbours wished for. A small act of cartographic defiance. Someone else might catch and correct it. It didn't matter. When Claire had worked for a map publisher, before coming to city maps, they routinely left at least one small inaccuracy on every map as a way of tracing the map as theirs. These mistakes marked their claim to uniqueness. If another company's maps appeared with the same inaccuracy, they'd know their maps had been copied.

The last aerial photographs that Claire had worked on were those taken on April 22, 1998. She asked everyone she knew where they had been and what they were doing that day between the hours of eleven and two to see if by chance she could find them as she blew up the shots to work on. A fool's game, really. Pedestrians were dots; at most, blobs with shadows. Cars appeared clearly, identifiable more by colour than make. Even Rachel happened to be in town that day, visiting Star, and was out there somewhere, perhaps in Allison's white Subaru, Star strapped beside her, in one of all the white cars snapped and stalled forever in the southbound lanes of the Don Valley Parkway.

In the dark, hours after Claire had returned from New York, she and Stefan quietly untangled their bodies. He stroked the skin between her shoulder blades, then laid his right hand on her left hip, which she registered as a different signal, the desire for the continuation of another dialogue.

"If we had a baby we wouldn't be lying here, like this," she said, covers half off, his damp sports clothes abandoned at the foot of the bed beside her flight bag.

"We might be."

"If we had a baby, and if I ended up in pain all the time because I couldn't take the drugs I need, would you support me and look after the baby and not resent me, most of all not resent me?"

"Claire, why think the worst? It's not going to happen like that."

"You don't know. You don't know what's going to happen."

Stefan had always wanted a child. He said he believed something would be lost between them if they did not have a child, an idea which bewildered Claire. Things would be different if they did not have a child but would something inevitably be lost? And if one thing was lost wouldn't another be found? One night, two months ago, he'd said that life without a child would be like living in a prison. Or being a monk. A monk? A prison?

Perhaps in their earlier days, because they were younger and had not been together as long, the subject had not come up as frequently. Or perhaps Claire had failed to notice, had not heard the depth of Stefan's longing because she herself had not been thinking much about having a child. She found it impossible to decide in the abstract: How could you think about whether to have a child without first knowing how strong your relationship was? They had spoken of marriage (sometimes Claire liked the idea of being married, although other things were more important: love, a home, being pain-free). Stefan had never been that set on marriage, at least, he said, until they resolved the matter of whether or not they were going to have children.

And now: his long, careful fingers rubbing the smooth skin above her hipbone, as if on a quest. The two of them weren't old, he argued, but were getting older. There was still time but not a lot of time.

"I'm frightened," she said.

"What are you frightened of?"

"If I'm trying to get pregnant or when I'm pregnant or breast-feeding, I can't use the migraine drugs because it's too risky. You've never seen me try to function without good drugs. I was already using Imitrex when I met you, okay, from just after I met you. You haven't seen what it was like when I was younger and there were times, days in a row, when I really couldn't function. This me you love and want to have a baby with, this is me on drugs."

"How do you even know what you'd be like now without the drugs?"

"I don't know but I can imagine." She was thinking of Rachel, of course, and what had happened to Rachel when she got pregnant, which Stefan would guess, although he said nothing to indicate this. What if she attempted to become a mother, and like Rachel, failed? "If I didn't get migraines —"

"Maybe there's some other way to bring things under control."

"I keep trying. You know that. I try everything. I'm open to just about any suggestion."

"Have you ever thought that maybe you think about your headaches too much and possibly that makes them worse?"

And how was it possible not to think of them, not consider their possibility, not be aware of each subtle fluctuation of sensation within her head, her body? It was like an awareness of the weather, the internal weather of her nervous system. He was asking her to be less conscious of the world, of herself.

"Other people with migraines have children." Was it a sign of his desperation, that he was tacitly roping in Rachel, of all people, on his side of the argument? "Your mother —"

"My mother didn't get migraines as frequently as Rachel and I do."

"Why is that?"

"I don't know. Stef, I'm not saying no, I'm just saying not yet."

The next night, after work, Claire drove out to Allison's. Though she'd called to let Allison know she was coming, when she rang the doorbell on Glebeholme Boulevard only the dog barked in response. Perhaps Allison was putting the girls to bed or had locked herself for a brief respite in the bathroom, so Claire followed a dweedle of music around to the side of the house and rapped her knuckles against the window of the small basement room where Lennie was practising. He waved at her with his violin bow. Banker by day, he played in an amateur orchestra on weekends and grabbed half an hour some weeknights to rehearse. He'd grown up in Montreal, west of rue du Parc in a seven-room apartment with his four siblings, parents, and paternal grandparents, who had emigrated from Guangdong province and ran a supermarket in Chinatown. He and Allison had met at university in Guelph and been together ever since.

Bow in hand, slippers on his feet, he let Claire in the front door, fending off shaggy Belle, who kept hurling herself towards them. He kissed Claire's cheeks, asked for news of Rachel, and when Claire shook her head, pointed with his bow and told her Allison would be down in a moment. He offered her a drink but Claire said no thanks, and when she insisted she'd be fine waiting on her own, Lennie nodded and slipped back downstairs, leaving her with the churning dishwasher and head-butting dog and a faint meander of Mozart's *A Little Night Music*.

The stairs from the second floor creaked as Allison made her way down them. "Three in bed," she said, "and the middle one said, I'm not sleeping. At least she's drowsy now." She crossed her fingers, with an air of blithe exhaustion. The one in the middle, Claire knew, was Star.

On the fridge were photographs of the three girls, all black-haired, though Star's hair was thicker and didn't lie as flat. Fifteen months younger than Amelia and already as tall. How uncanny (they had all remarked on it) that in some ways Star looked more like Allison than she did Rachel, more like Allison than either of Allison's own daughters – the same almond-shaped eyes and crease in her left cheek when she laughed. Her two-plus-one girls Allison sometimes called them.

One of the cats, Georgia, a marbled brown, slipped in through a tear in the screen of the kitchen window, bounced from counter to floor and vamoosed in the direction of the living room. Allison's hair, clipped at the back of her neck, sprayed upwards in a cockscomb. She plucked a corked bottle from the counter and raised one eyebrow. Jealously, Claire shook her head. "Kiwi?" Allison tossed one through the air and Claire caught it as Allison tucked the bottle under her arm and carried a clean but smudged glass towards the table. A movement at the top of the stairs, behind Allison, out of Allison's sight, caught Claire's eye – a small figure in a sleeveless purple nightgown gazed down at them. "So –" Allison began as Claire laid her hand on Allison's wrist and without looking up, Allison nodded and said, "Let's take Belle for a spin around the block."

She poured some wine, not into the glass but a child's plastic cup, then dashed downstairs to let Lennie know where they were off to, while Claire turned, intending to wave to Star, but Star had vanished.

The grass outside was damp against their sandalled feet, Claire's mouth full of the kiwi's sour-sweet flesh. The dog lolloped across a stretch of lawn. "So," Allison said again.

"There was no sign that she's been back. I'd say it looks like she left on a regular trip – she took her computer, most of her medications. There's nothing obvious to suggest she was planning on being away for a long time."

Allison exhaled. "It's weird, okay, it is. And the guy?"

"Well, they've been involved."

"There's a surprise."

"He's a massage therapist."

"Oh great, she gets involved with her massage therapist."

"I think it happened afterwards. Anyway, it didn't sound like things were going all that well. They had an argument before she left."

"Is there someone else?"

"He didn't say."

"Well." Allison slugged back a mouthful of wine. "I suppose it's possible she's fallen madly in love and run off. It's not impossible. Except there's Star. Why no word, why would she do that to Star?"

"What have you said to Star?"

"She's travelling. It's an important trip. She can't get to a computer or the telephone. This can only go on for so long, though. Either I think she's sent messages and they've all, all one of them, whatever, got lost, or something's happened –" Allison whistled for the dog. "I can't –"

"I know someone in the police department," Claire said, listening to the soft clink of the dog's tags and the shush of their sandals against the sidewalk. "We deal with the police department all the time. We make maps for them. I'll see what he has to say."

"That would be good."

"And I have the number of a doctor in Montreal, the guy, I think it's the guy she went to interview. I've been trying to get hold of him."

Claire called Matt Patel, her contact in the police department. He wanted to talk about the High Park rape investigation. When she asked his advice about Rachel, he passed her along to a detective named William Bird, who took down the little information she could give him. Montreal. March 14. Hotel du Parc. She hated making Rachel's absence official. It felt disloyal. Its admission of seriousness sent things into a different zone. Detective Bird reassured her that most missing people turned up. Or simply did not want to be found. People left tracks all over: credit card transactions, cash machine withdrawals, border crossings, car rentals, airline flights. As Claire knew. To begin with, he asked, did she or anyone else have any theories about what had happened to her sister? She was having trouble with her migraines, Claire said. She sensed that this was not what Detective Bird was after. She also sensed that he was busy. Rachel was one among a crowd of missing people out there.

Claire tried calling the various editors in New York, whose

business cards she'd brought home with her. None had heard from Rachel in the last few months. She tried again to reach the neurologist, Dr. Pierre L'Aube of the Montreal Neurological Institute, whose phone line, whenever she attempted to call, rang busy in an irritatingly old-fashioned way. After a few more busy signals, she finally reached Dr. L'Aube's receptionist. A lot of journalists call, the receptionist said. Not called, Claire reiterated, came in person. In March. And hasn't been seen since. Could she check with the doctor? Consult his appointment book? Could she please ask the doctor to call Claire? This was Thursday morning; she heard nothing back all day. Friday the doctor's office was closed. Over the weekend, Claire went in to work. On Monday, she tried the doctor again. More busy signals. Trying to reach the doctor by phone was getting her nowhere.

Exasperated, she called Stefan at the lab. "What am I supposed to do?"

"You could do nothing. You could wait. Keep calling."

"What am I obliged to do, under the circumstances?"

"Or you could go to Montreal."

"Maybe I should go to Montreal."

She walked through the warren of desks and down the hall to Charlie Gorjup's windowed office. He beckoned her in. The window looked west, out over the intersection of Yonge and Dundas, the southeast corner penned in by billboards, awaiting redevelopment; on the southwest corner loomed the white bulk of the Eaton Centre. She asked him if she could take a day off. Headache? Not today, Charlie, I'm hoping to take the day after tomorrow. What's up? She might have explained that she had something else to map, and in some fashion Charlie would have understood this. Without meeting his gaze, overcome all at once by a self-consciousness that bordered on shame, she told him that her sister seemed to be missing. Charlie knew her parents were dead and how they'd died. Neither of them made the obvious joke about what extraordinary bad luck it was for another family member to have vanished. Go, Charlie said, waving his hand. Take the time you need. Hey, Claire, most missing people show up.

She called Stefan back and told him what she was planning. She'd take the train. She booked herself a room overnight in the Hotel du Parc. The next day, Tuesday, after work, she caught a cab to Union Station and boarded the five o'clock express.

Some years earlier, shortly after she moved to New York, Rachel had sent Claire a copy of the McGill Pain Questionnaire, the first codified attempt to give patients a tool to describe their pain. Professor Ronald Melzack of McGill University in Montreal had formulated the famous questionnaire, using words gathered from pain sufferers themselves. (Is it flickering, quivering, pulsing?) Possibly Rachel had gone to Montreal to track down Ronald Melzack, although surely she didn't need new ways to measure her pain, only to be released from it. Perhaps writing an article had been a ploy to get herself seen by someone at the renowned Neurological Institute, where doctors would understand something of the migraineur's dilemma, the invisibility of the pain, how few obvious traces it left, how difficult it was to diagnose or describe.

Claire tossed her bag into the overhead rack and settled herself into a seat by the south-facing window. She'd bought herself a notebook, blank as yet, and slipped a photograph of Rachel inside the cover, Rachel laughing — her long face, the sheen of her dark hair. She carried other versions of Rachel with her, too, visions impossible to capture. Rachel's quick, clean stride. Her tumultuous hand gestures. The fixity of her gaze. The way she would rub her index finger back and forth over the darkened skin beneath her eye. By this signal, Claire would know her anywhere.

Six and a half years earlier, right at the end of the year, Claire had received an ecstatic phone call from Rachel. "I've got some news. Eight weeks along, due in mid-July. I know it's still early but I wanted to tell you."

"Congratulations," Claire said, although what she felt upon hearing word of Rachel's pregnancy was a bewildering array of emotions, happiness being only a part of it. Not that the news was entirely a surprise: for the last half a year, since shortly after her return from her mysterious Asian sojourn, Rachel had been speaking openly about her attempts to conceive. (Was her desire sparked in any way by her discovery, upon her return, that Allison was already pregnant and had been so, quietly, privately, sharing the news with none but Lennie, a mere four months after their parents had been killed? Was Rachel's sudden longing provoked in turn by their terrible death?)

The complication, on Rachel's end, was that there was currently no man in her life to be the father of a child. She did not seem to view this as an insurmountable impediment. She required a man, yes, but seemed less convinced about the need for a relationship.

Allison thought she was crazy. Claire did not know what to think. During her six years of living with Michael Straw, Rachel had not spoken of wanting a child – at least not to Claire, nor to Allison from the sound of it. And there were times, during those years, when Claire truly thought that Rachel had settled down and found a man capable of holding her sustained attention. Claire had liked Michael, missed him when he was gone from Rachel's life. Tall, thick-browed, half-Irish, he had an almost abrupt courtliness on first meeting, yet was willing to sing Irish ballads for the family after dinner, in a lilting baritone, during a visit that he and Rachel made to Toronto. He wore white shirts, always, Rachel said, an ironed one to work, yesterday's crumpled one when he stumbled out of bed in the morning. They had seemed happy together. Rachel had seemed happy. She was never bored, she said, which was her idea of fulfillment. Later, she would complain that Michael brooded more and more in private. Towards the end, there were apparently affairs. On both sides. Claire was under no illusion that Rachel was easy to live with. Perhaps Michael wasn't easy to live with either.

Then, after her return from Asia, Rachel began to speak about her longing for a child, for the joy, the new states of awareness and intimacy that a child would bring. She welcomed the potential transformation of her life. She knew now that she did not want to live without this experience.

"Can I ask about the father?" For a moment Claire was terrified that Rachel did not know for certain who the father was.

There had been a handful of hopeful but ultimately unsuccessful encounters over the last few months, from what she'd gathered.

"He's an engineer. It's him, there's absolutely no question. He was born in Bombay, works at MIT. He sat down next to me on an Amtrak train. We were on our way to Boston. It all happened very fast. He's incredibly good-looking and has an extraordinary mind, extraordinarily sharp. Claire, we just made a connection. The whole thing was extraordinary. I had an immediate sense."

"Did you tell him what you wanted?"

"Yes, eventually, and he was incredibly generous, it was an act of extraordinary connection and generosity."

"You spent time together in Boston?"

"No, Claire, no, it all happened on the train."

In Kingston, Claire woke up. The Japanese couple sitting across the aisle from her had gone, replaced by a tanned young man in a denim shirt whose sleeves were not rolled but ripped above the elbows. A copper bracelet encircled his right wrist. He had the look of a student, whether or not he was one. He was leafing through Peterson's *Field Guide to Mexican Birds*.

She wondered, not for the first time, about the nature of Rachel's train encounter — was it the first, the only one on public transport? (How exactly did you go about seducing a stranger on a train, on a plane, or allow yourself to be seduced?) Presumably, Rachel's desire had been palpable, her avidity, her curiosity, her restless desire to be desired, her confidence that she would be, augmented by her longing for a baby. Claire had no idea how you got from here – sitting beside a man on a train – to there – having sex with him. What did you say? Had Rachel asked about sexually transmitted diseases? Surely, for the sake of her child-to-be, she'd made certain that the engineer didn't get migraines.

Claire's gaze travelled along the chestnut arm of the young man across the aisle. He looked up as if her regard were a touch, but his glance did not appear to be an invitation. What could she say to the reader of *Mexican Birds* (strange choice for a trip through Ontario), or he to her? What had the Bombay-born engineer seen in Rachel? (Her longing? Her beauty? Her grief?) Had he and Rachel made their way to the train compartment's tiny bathroom singly, or together, heedlessly, bodies already helplessly brushing, figuring they'd never see anyone around them (including each other) again?

Claire's room in the Hotel du Parc was seven floors off the ground and faced south. It was four paces wide and eight paces long. It contained a king-sized bed, a desk, and a bureau that held a monstrous television above a locked mini-bar. She walked straight to the window and switched off the air conditioner, stopping the chemical flow of coolant into the room. She tugged open the small panel of window that vented to a real, murky city breeze as Rachel, even in winter, had no doubt done. Travel by train was not as bad as air travel, but any sealed environment posed hazards. Hotel rooms weren't the worst but had their perils: recycled air and powerful cleaners and chemically suspiring carpets.

Claire had told Rachel about a man she knew who'd been a vet, until the smells of the disinfectants used in the clinic where he worked began to give him migraines. It took him a while to figure out the connection, and it depressed him when he did, because he loved animals and loved working with them, but the recurrent pain was making it difficult for him to function. So he became a travelling salesman for veterinary products, hoping to keep his hand in the business somehow. As he criss-crossed the country, the headaches came back, as strong as ever. He realized he was reacting not only to veterinary products but to the cleaners and aerosol sprays used in hotel rooms. He hit upon a temporary strategy. He'd go for product conferences and, walking into his hotel room, fling open the windows. He refused to stay in rooms where the windows didn't open. He'd instruct the housekeeping staff not to clean or enter his room while he was staying in it, although they often disobeyed him and he'd return to the telltale traces of air freshener. Eventually, he gave up on animal care altogether, went to architecture school, and became a city planner.

With her head out the window, Claire listened to the city of Montreal, its streets swollen with tourists out for a stroll or a late supper on a muggy summer night. She could order from room service or go out to join them. If Stefan had been with her, they would have gone out. She felt the imagined clasp of his hand in hers. They had been to Montreal together five years before, staying with a friend of Stefan's who lived on a flat and treeless block of Hôtel de Ville. They had walked hand in hand, Claire in a brand-new yellow rayon dress, along Mont Royal to the park and up the mountain. Now she was in no mood to surrender to the city: Montreal felt like a tunnel she had to manoeuvre through. She lay down on the bed and breathed deeply. Then she rose, swiped on some lipstick, ran her hands through her hair, and made her way downstairs.

An older couple in identical pantsuits was checking in. Once they were done, Claire approached the young woman who had welcomed her a little while before. "Puis-je vous aider?" The hotel clerk made her uniform look almost voluptuous, a white shirt, tight over her breasts, above a narrow maroon skirt.

"I'm trying to find out some information about a hotel guest. Not one who's staying here now. She was here in March. Rachel Barber. She's my sister. I think she checked in on the fourteenth and checked out on the sixteenth, but I'd like to confirm those dates. She hasn't been heard from since."

"I'm not allowed to give out that kind of information," the clerk said in accentless English. "I'm really sorry. Maybe if you speak to the manager but she's not here right now. Can you try in the morning?"

Managers were never here right now.

"Just the dates?"

"I'm sorry," the girl repeated, her eyes scrunched as if it were easier not to look at Claire full on. "Have you gone to the police?"

"Yes, but I'm trying to find out what I can by myself."

The hooks of the girl's plucked eyebrows shrugged.

"I'll go down on my knees," Claire said. She couldn't believe she'd said that. She pulled out the photograph of Rachel.

"I'll take that," the girl said. She stared at the photo, then at Claire. "I can see if anyone remembers her."

"I'll have to make you a copy."

"There's a Xerox shop over on Parc. Look, I'm not saying anyone will remember — unless she's three foot high and limps."

Hair dark enough to seem black in certain lights. Red-tinted at the ends. Shoulder-length when last seen though it could be any length now. A long brown braid at one time. Of middle height, though sometimes she looked taller than she was. Slim. Those runner's legs. Those cheekbones.

How hard it is to fix the details of what is not in front of you — the room at your back, those who are gone. To remember anything is to select some details and leave out others. How difficult to recall eye colour, for instance: it's as shifty an item of memory as any, even the eyes of those we are closest to, perhaps because they come to us bearing traces of so much more than colour (unless we can deduce them to be brown). Claire struggled to remember her parents' eyes, both, like Rachel's, in the blue-grey spectrum, but where, more precisely? Were her father's closer to the blue of certain clouds, her mother's the green-grey of a lake? And what of Rachel's? The purest grey, Claire thought, but she was guessing. And Stefan's?

Back upstairs in her room, she called him.

"You're out of breath," she said when he picked up the phone. It was already dark in Montreal, but in Toronto, farther west in the same time zone, the sky, she knew, would still be the jade of twilight.

"Just got in."

"From work?" She angled herself so that, despite the 545 kilometres between them, she was facing in his direction.

"I stayed at the lab working on some arrays, and then we went to a movie. Rob and Maria and I, a horror movie. Claire, you would have hated it." If he sounded sheepish and perhaps a little guilty, it was because he loved going to movies (loved horror films, none more than those involving killer bugs and mutant viruses). Claire found it difficult to sit through any movie (the flickering image, the visual overstimulation), a state of affairs which even she found pathetic, though there didn't seem to be much she could do about it. Scary movies, in which her whole body succumbed to a seizure of tension, were the worst. Occasionally, she and Stefan went to see films anyway, although Stefan never tried to convince her to accompany him, any more than he encouraged her to do anything — drink alcohol, hang out in smoky bars — that might cause her to react. She did not mind him dashing out to a movie as soon as she left town. "And how was your trip?" he asked.

"Unmomentous and almost on time. I miss you."

"I miss you, too. How are you feeling?"

"Fine, I'm feeling fine. I don't think the hotel's going to give me any more information, though."

"They probably won't unless you bring in the police. Presumably that Detective Bird will contact them."

"I'm really not sure what Detective Bird is planning to do."

"Well, we'll bug him."

"I suppose I'm counting on the neurologist."

Long ago, Rachel had talked about becoming a doctor, even a neurologist – towards the end of high school and during her first two years at university. She had taken a range of science courses and done well but backed away from the idea of medical school in the end because, she said, her migraines were too disruptive. She did not think she had the stamina for it.

Claire, who had never thought she would hold down a full-time job, understood this. Map-making had appealed as something she might be able to do on her own, on her own time – she had never expected to stay at City Maps as long as she had.

Later, she and Rachel had joked that since neither had become a neurologist, one of them ought to have married one, preferably a migraine specialist who was on top of the most cutting-edge research and who would, in addition, understand their neurochemically volatile condition. Rachel had even given the imaginary neurologist a name, Tom Lukacs. Now, she said, all she had to do was meet him. Claire had come close, with Stefan Simic, star medical researcher, whose father's family hailed from Dubrovnik, who dreamed of creating customized treatments for individual cancer patients by targeting the particular molecular pathways of individual tumours. The pin-in-the-right-place approach, he called it. How could Claire possibly begrudge him his fixation on lethal cancers, or argue with his priorities, when her neurological quirk resulted only in pain, which made you suffer, but couldn't kill you.

The moment Claire hung up the phone, the red message light began to flash. There was one message waiting. The young woman spoke in a breathless volley. "Rachel Barber checked in on March 14 and checked out March 16. She stayed in room 514. Please delete this message immediately, and don't tell anyone how you got the information."

Claire sank to her knees and offered up a prayer of thanks to the hook-eyebrowed girl at reception. Not just the dates, but the room number. Numinous detail. Only given this much information, greedy, she wanted more: what about Rachel's itemized hotel bill, which, if she'd charged long-distance calls to her room (conceivable, knowing Rachel), would have listed not only the ones to Claire and Allison but any others.

She would call Stefan to tell him, but first she left the room and hurried to the elevator, riding it two floors down to the fifth floor. She counted nineteen steps along an identical hall to room 514, on the other side from her own, facing north. You'd see the mountain through the window. The illuminated cross on top. You might, possibly, between buildings, pick out the rooftops of the Royal Victoria Hospital and the Neurological Institute, on avenue des Pins, nestled halfway up the mountain. In the bay just beyond the room, ice roiled and crackled in a machine. Claire laid her hand on the door. She pressed her ear to its mute, painted wood.

One night at dinner, the year Claire turned fourteen, Rachel (who would have been eighteen and on the verge of heading to university) asked Hugh, their father, Why didn't you stick it out at medical school? We could certainly have used a doctor in this family. They were, as Claire remembered it, all five of them at the kitchen table, not in the dining room, which probably meant a Friday night. Perhaps Rachel was teasing him, being mouthy rather than accusatory. Without saying a word, Hugh screeched back the legs of his chair and left the room.

"Jeez," Rachel said.

"Nothing you can joke about," Sylvia said. That was all she said.

"Clearly," said Rachel.

"Rachel."

"Forget it," Rachel said and stormed out.

What they knew, what Claire understood then, was that as a young man, not long after Rachel's birth, their father had dropped out of medical school. He had not flunked out, he had simply decided not to go back for his final year. There was no indication that Rachel's birth had in any way provoked his decision. He had simply decided that medicine was not for him. His first love was, had always been, mathematics. He would teach. Claire was not certain why, if his love was pure mathematics, he didn't go to graduate school and consider a research career instead of hightailing it to Addis Ababa, with Sylvia and six-month-old Rachel in tow, to teach in an international school.

He needed money. A job. Still.

They understood, if not then, then a little later, that by abandoning medicine he had become a disappointment to his family, to his parents who had wanted him to become a doctor, who had uprooted themselves from London's East End and come to Canada in order to give their children, Hugh and Al, but especially Hugh, the oldest, the brightest, the scholarship student, the opportunities they did not think he would have in

England. He was sixteen when they emigrated. All the rest of his large family – his uncles, aunts, all his cousins, his grandparents – remained behind.

He was a gifted teacher, from all reports, whether or not he had sensed this talent in advance. His math whizzes, whom he coached for national and international competitions, loved him, as did the students who only came to love math through the flare of his teaching, his conviction that mathematical skill was not innate but could be taught. He won teaching prizes, ran a math club for hours after school. At home, they saw glimpses of his galvanizing light, never more so than when they asked him for help with mathematical problems. Then he came to jumpy life, gesticulating, leaping up from his chair, urging them onward, although it was clear to all of them that they were not, and never would be, in the league of his best students. Some of these came in quiet, nerdy clusters to the funeral. He and Sylvia had flown to Frankfurt for a conference on math pedagogy – they were to rent a car, afterwards, and travel south towards Strasbourg – when they were killed.

In late spring of the year Claire turned fifteen, their grand-mother was diagnosed with esophageal cancer. As soon as the school year ended, Hugh returned to Victoria to help out his father and brother, who lived only a ferry ride away in Vancouver, with her care. The cancer was terminal but his mother was not immediately dying. Gruelling though her treatment was – radia-tion, chemotherapy – she appeared to be responding to it.

When he came home to Toronto, late in the summer, Hugh

announced that they should all think of moving to Victoria, or perhaps he alone should do so, if only temporarily, although after that one night, to Claire's relief, the idea was never mentioned again. Occasionally morose before, he was more so now, even sulky. Sometimes, out of the depths of his fatigue, he would stare at Claire as if he barely saw her, or as if there were something about her that baffled him. And how, even when she had a headache, could she dare make a bid for his attention and sympathy? Her headaches went away. They came back but they did go away. He nagged Sylvia to set up an appointment for Claire with a neurologist, who prescribed her pills (a beta blocker called Propanolol), but these did nothing to help.

Rachel was no longer living at home by then but in a shared house on Huron Street, downtown near the university. She came home occasionally for dinner and would regale Claire with stories: of how once, in the thick of a migraine, she'd lurched out of a subway car and thrown up over the edge of the subway platform. Once, when no medication worked, she'd ended up in the emergency room at Toronto Western, brought by a frantic boyfriend convinced she'd had a stroke. When she went into the hospital for a knee operation to repair cartilage torn at the end of her high-school track career, she got shot up on Demerol, which, she claimed, deadened all pain from the knee but didn't touch the headache keening through her as she was wheeled into the operating room. Claire did not know if her parents heard these stories. Rachel swore that none of the pain was affecting her studies – she was fine, she was doing fine.

And they coped, they did. Most days when she came home from high school, Claire would down a couple of 222s, before collapsing on the sofa for an hour. She was not a malingerer. She didn't believe her life would go on like this, although so far it had.

The summer after Grade Twelve, she found work in an antiquarian bookshop on Bathurst Street, south of Dupont, whose owner, elegant Irene Tate — tall and boyish, her silvering hair held back in a ponytail — also got migraines, as Claire discovered a week after starting the job. Once, Irene said, she'd had a headache that had lasted ten years — no joke, it waxed and waned but never entirely disappeared until in the end it gradually faded away. These were the years when she was raising her two sons, which might have had something to do with it. Irene, too, carried pills on her at all times, always something in her purse or wadded into a Kleenex in her pocket, as she showed Claire. On some afternoons, she left Claire on her own under the shop's rickety ceiling fan while she retreated to her upstairs apartment. What Claire felt in Irene's presence was not only horror at the thought of the ten-year headache but also relief and comfort: there were others outside her family, others with migraines even worse than hers.

Time ran along two parallel tracks: pain time and ordinary time. You slid from one to the other, one as familiar as the other. Pain time did not progress: you fell into it as into a ditch, you followed it like a fractal shoreline that, at any scale, repeats and repeats itself.

Was it the Christmas after Grade Twelve that Claire and Rachel and Sylvia all came down with migraines at once? No, it was later. Looking back, it was impossible to remember the pain. It was retrievable only through context. Propped against the counter, Sylvia basted the goose, brown bruises beneath her eyes, nearly oblivious to the fat spitting at her from the roasting pan. Rachel busied herself silently setting crystal and silverware on the dining room table, swearing under her breath. Claire tried to slice root vegetables without cutting her fingers off. Meanwhile, Allison, taller and skinnier than any of them and the only one without a headache, would look at them balefully now and again as she carved open chestnut shells for a chestnut purée, ripping at the skins with such vigour and without cease that the tips of her fingers bled.

For dinner, Hugh opened a bottle of fine Alsatian wine, lamenting that there was hardly any point in doing so, although in the end he and Allison largely polished off the bottle between them, in addition to making inroads into a bottle of port, so that by Boxing Day, as far as heads were concerned, they were all much in the same shape.

The night before, they had put on the tissue paper party hats that came in paper crackers, and at the end of dinner, Allison convinced them all to sing a round of *We Wish You a Merry Christmas* and so followed a tuneless, monotonal dirge over the flaming pudding. As the brandy burned, wild and blue, and they fell silent, Hugh rose to his feet and, without preamble, blue tissue-paper crown still balanced precariously on his head, began to recite Lewis Carroll's "The Walrus and the Carpenter."

Claire had had no idea that he knew all the words to "The Walrus and the Carpenter" (for all that he kept books of Charles Dodgson's mathematical puzzles piled at his bedside for nighttime reading). Where and when had he learned the words? She'd certainly never heard him recite the poem before. In fact, she had no memory of him reciting any poetry to them during her childhood, even though he admitted to a love for the rollicking rhymes and raucous northern adventures of Robert Service's Yukon sagas.

Now here her father stood, just under six feet tall, heavier than in the photographs from his youth, leaning over the table, his fingertips resting lightly, as if for balance, upon its surface. His smile was suffused, it seemed, with sadness (but then it was a sad story he told, of all those self-sacrificing oysters) as he offered them this love song, this distraction, this gift of himself.

At eight-thirty in the morning, Claire climbed avenue des Pins, past the grey stone weight of university buildings, through heat, weaving among the summer students and nurses, until she reached rue de l'Université, which rose steeply from Sherbrooke below and dead-ended, on the other side of Pine Avenue, partway up the mountain. She turned right onto the little dead-end stretch of University and stepped into shadow, pinned in on the left by the tall stone walls of the Royal Victoria Hospital, and by the Neurological Institute on her right. Ambulances were parked some four metres ahead, near where an elevated passageway linked the two buildings. Inside the Neurological Institute, she found Dr. L'Aube's room number on the wall directory. First floor. To the left. Fourteen steps later, she entered his reception area. She'd hoped she might reach him before his appointments began — at nine, she'd assumed, but no, he'd started at eight-thirty.

"I spoke to you by phone," Claire told the receptionist, tipping back her sunglasses. "About Rachel Barber. The journalist who's been missing since she was here in March. The doctor didn't call me back. So I came from Toronto. I'll only take a few minutes of his time. I'm free any time until four today." She was booked on the five o'clock express train back.

The receptionist, bottle-black-haired, bare-armed, solid in her swivel chair, looked vaguely disgruntled.

"He has appointments, but have a seat in the waiting room, I will see," she said.

"Five minutes," Claire said. "I just need to know for certain if she spoke to him and if so, what they talked about."

In the doorway of the waiting room, she sniffed the air, testing the stuffiness, the currents of circulation. Waiting rooms often gave her headaches. Being confined in one was like submitting to a plot to reproduce your symptoms in order to confirm, before you saw the doctor, that you really had them. This room was better than most: bigger, high-ceilinged, with tall and no doubt leaky windows. The chairs arranged around the perimeter made it feel a little like a dance hall. The magazines were only a few months out of date, not archaeological. And there was a telephone, whose real dial tone droned when Claire lifted the receiver: they were not, glory be, sealed off from the outside world.

Two women sat side by side in chairs pushed against the wall opposite the windows, one older than the other, the older one wearing a wide-brimmed straw hat. Neither spoke. Claire sat in a chair facing the door, at a right angle to the women. There were four chairs, in total, against the opposite wall, four beneath the windows, one on the other side of the telephone table. The walls were easily twelve feet high. The voice of the receptionist came to her, intoning now in English, now in French.

A middle-aged man in a white coat, eyebrows thick as shrubbery, appeared in the doorway, tilting from the waist as he spoke. "Elaine Stephanopolos." Both women stood.

"Excuse me," Claire said, rising also.

"Not yet," the doctor said. "I will be with you shortly."

A woman in red sandals towed two small children into the room.

Claire spoke to the receptionist again. "I have mentioned you," the woman said. "He says he thinks he remembers the name."

"I have a photograph."

If Rachel had been here, what would she have done? In March, had her migraine of the night before resolved itself by the time she arrived at the Neurological Institute?

Dr. L'Aube had led the two women past the receptionist back into the main hallway, which branched in two directions. The reception area lay in the corner where the corridor turned. Claire left the waiting room. To her right, the hall, lined with closed doors, led back to the main entrance. The left-hand corridor, also lined with closed doors, terminated in a large room filled with spanking white medical equipment. Vessels for bodies, lacking only those bodies.

She set off back towards the entrance, past notices tacked to bulletin boards advertising neurological conferences, a bipolar clinic, an epilepsy study that needed volunteers. When she retraced her steps and re-entered the main vestibule, she realized, with a start, that she'd stepped into a brain.

On first impression the room looked merely like a near-spherical womb of honeyed wood. Peering closer, she saw that the dark lines of dendrites wriggled towards neural cells across the panelled ceiling, and the amber walls were speckled with dots that rose in greater and greater concentration to a line marking the edge of brain tissue like the crest of a wave. The wooden radiator casings were stacked cervical vertebrae. The effect of the whole was deliriously quaint: a moment of mid-twentieth-century neurological knowledge preserved architecturally, in wood. Claire read the plaque that said the room had been built to the specifications of Dr. Wilder Penfield, the Institute's founder, the pioneering Montreal neurosurgeon who had done some of the earliest brain mapping.

Anyone standing in the middle of the room became part of the brain, a live neural connection.

Yet this brought Claire no closer to Rachel. She left the vestibule and was halfway down the hallway's left-hand branch, keeping her eyes peeled for Dr. L'Aube's office, when a man in a white lab coat, younger than Dr. L'Aube, burst out of a doorway, directly opposite the closed door with Dr. L'Aube's nameplate upon it.

"Excuse me," Claire said.

He stopped, waylaid in midstride, parts of him (hands, one leg) still in motion, flinging themselves away from his body. His name tag read Dr. Michael Tagliacci. "What can I do for you today?" Words spilling into one another.

"Are you a colleague of Dr. L'Aube's?"

"I am." A tenor voice, light as a cello.

"Are you a migraine specialist?"

"That, too."

"I'm looking for someone. My sister. I don't think she's here now. She's missing. She's a journalist. I think she talked to Dr. L'Aube back in March, the day before she vanished. Maybe you'll recognize her. Her name's Rachel Barber." She handed him a colour Xerox of the photograph, Rachel in the kitchen of her apartment in New York.

He took it. His whole trajectory shifted. "Let's sit down for a minute." He checked his watch, reopened the door to his office and ushered Claire in, beckoning her towards an armchair in front of his desk, simultaneously lifting a stack of books from the chair with his other hand. A room four metres by three. Electric guitar propped in the corner by the door. Walls jammed with books, shelves crammed with teetering piles. Desk surface, 155 centimetres wide, half-buried under paper and a desktop computer. At the front of the desk: a plastic model of a brain. A room arranged for work, not meeting patients.

Dr. Tagliacci dropped the colour Xerox onto his desk, tugged back his sleeve, and glanced at his wristwatch once more, wedging the phone receiver between his neck and shoulder. "Hey, Mike here. Give me ten." He set down the phone but remained standing, gathering strands of black hair into neat strips running back from his forehead. "Canadian, from New York?"

Claire nodded.

"It was a magazine piece of some sort, wasn't it? Name again?"

"Rachel Barber."

"I spoke to her."

"Here? In this room?"

He nodded.

"Do you know if she also spoke to Dr. L'Aube?"

"L'Aube's the clinician. He tends to get pretty jammed up. He sees the patients, I'm primarily a researcher. Of course he researches, too. He heads up the team but we work closely together. Presumably he passed her on to me."

He sat. He handed her a business card and she, inscribing her home phone and e-mail on the back, gave one of hers to him.

"She's missing," he said.

"She hasn't been directly in contact with anyone since she left here."

"Shit, eh? You're not accusing us of abducting your sister." His grin vanished. "Sorry. That was in terrible taste. You've gone to the police?"

Claire nodded. "Can you possibly tell me what you talked about when she was here?" She pulled out her notebook and uncapped her pen, taking him in a little more now: good-looking in a way that might have appealed to Rachel; cleft chin; a manner that seemed both smooth and congenitally nervous.

"So she left here —?"

"She checked out of the Hotel du Parc the next day. March 16. She was supposed to go to Toronto afterwards but she cancelled her plans. She said she was coming to Montreal to interview a neurologist for an article on migraines. She left Dr. L'Aube's name on a piece of paper on the desk in her apartment."

"No other leads?"

"Nothing yet."

"So we're it — well, we talked about migraines."

"Can you please be more specific?"

He pulled in his chair, straightening himself, the mauve cuffs of his shirt extruding beyond the arms of his lab coat. Stubble spread across his cheeks, around his jaw, under that firm chin. "We talked about developments in serotonin-based research."

"Okay, but more."

"You know migraine results from a deficiency in regulating serotonin? Used to be thought of as a vascular problem, but it's actually a neurological problem."

Claire nodded.

"During a migraine, blood flow increases in the brain stem and other cortical areas. Medications such as sumitriptan or other triptan drugs can lessen migraine symptoms but don't seem to affect blood flow in the brain stem. Two areas of the brain stem, the dorsal raphe nucleus and the nucleus raphe magnus — tell me if you want me to slow down or explain anything — contain large amounts of the neurotransmitter serotonin. This is what our research here is concentrating on. We're trying to measure, using PET scans and fMRI's, the serotonin levels in various areas of the brain throughout a migraine. There are also sex-based differences in serotonin distribution. Men have more in the left frontal lobe, women's is more evenly distributed. Women don't retain brain serotonin levels as well as men without eating foods containing tryptophan, which the body converts to serotonin. Serotonin levels drop precipitously during a migraine attack, as much as 60 per cent. We're trying to fix where the serotonin activity occurs, what triggers the drop, all getting back to the fundamentals of what exactly initiates migraine."

"Give me a sec," Claire said, scribbling. "Did she say who the piece was for?"

"Probably. I don't remember. L'Aube might. It's true we never heard back from her but that's not unusual with journalists."

"Was there anything particular in what you said that seemed to catch her attention, that she might have wanted to follow up on?"

"We talked a little about drugs, too. The failure of current triptan drugs to cross the blood-brain barrier and thus affect what's going on in the brain stem. That's the goal, ultimately."

"To cross the blood-brain barrier."

He nodded.

"How close are you to that?"

"Well, first we have to understand the mechanism."

"Did you give her any other leads? People to contact?"

"There's the guy at Sunnybrook in Toronto. Some good people in the UK."

He gave her names and she wrote them down. "Did she happen to mention that she gets migraines?"

"She mentioned it. Not auras but pretty frequent, severe, kind of drug resistant by the sound of it."

"Would you happen to know if she had a migraine when she came to see you?"

"At one point she said so but she wasn't obviously incapacitated."

"Did she seem in any way upset or on edge?"

"No, but she wanted something I wasn't prepared to give her. We do these studies, examining serotonin levels in patient volunteers during the course of a migraine. You have to have not taken any drugs in the last twenty-four hours and we put you through a PET scan. She said she hadn't taken anything and was willing. But she wouldn't be in town for any kind of follow-up, and that's part of the study. And there's a preliminary interview. We're not set up for walk-ins. Though she was very persuasive."

"So, what happened?"

"I told her, under the existing protocols, I couldn't use her in the study. That was pretty much it."

"When was this?"

"Around three, four in the afternoon. Hang on, I'll check the date." He picked up the phone and dialled. "Pierre, a quick one. Got a woman here whose sister's disappeared. Journalist, here in March. Yeah, I talked to her. You spoke to her by phone. Okay. It's in your book?" He looked at Claire. "March 15. Three p.m." Hung up the phone. "You get them, too, don't you?"

Which took her aback. "Yeah. Do you?"

"No, go on, hate me. You seem to know the language. There's a physiological predisposition that runs in families, as I'm sure you know. Mother? Grandmother?" Claire nodded. "Yours as bad as your sister's?"

"Not quite as bad."

"The usual tyramine-based triggers – chocolate, red wine, et cetera, et cetera?"

"Other ones, too."

"The drugs work for you?"

"Mostly."

He rose to his feet. "I hope some of this helps. I hope you find her. If you have any more questions, let me know."

Dr. Tagliacci swept Claire out of his office, the pressure of his hand still on her palm as he sprinted ahead of her, white coat flapping, down the hall. She wasn't sure what to make of him. After bumping into Pierre L'Aube in the reception area, who confirmed that he had spoken briefly to Rachel but not seen her, she exited the Neurological Institute at ten past eleven. She had just under six hours until her train left. She had already checked out of her hotel room. She'd found something, proof that Rachel had been here, and, for the third day in a row, had been suffering from a migraine, but where this led she did not yet know.

From the east, a bus clambered up the hill of Pine Avenue while a breeze tossed up by the river to the south climbed the slope of University, the hot bus wind and sultry river breeze intersecting at the point on the slope where Claire stood. Rachel, too, must have stood on or near this spot, in March, in the snow and near-dark, spurned, it would appear, by Dr. Tagliacci, without a PET scan, her stubborn head still aching. (She'd been prepared to lie to get her brain scanned, if she'd claimed that she'd been medication-free for twenty-four hours.)

Presumably, in this state, she had returned to the hotel. In the morning, if not wholly well, she'd nevertheless felt well enough to check out. When had she called Allison to say she wasn't coming to Toronto, in the morning or the previous night? At what point had she decided to leave Montreal, to vanish from the island?

*T*he doors to the Indo-Malay pavilion were locked, but lights were still on and human figures visible among the trees. Claire rapped on the glass and one of the figures, a young man in green T-shirt and khakis, approached and tried to shoo her away. The zoo was already closed to visitors for the night. She had parked over by the administration building, as she did on her occasional visits, and walked into the zoo from there. I'm here to see Allison Barber, Claire shouted, pointing in the direction of the keepers' quarters. She was uncertain whether the young man could hear her, but he unlocked the main doors and let her enter the pavilion's tropical interior.

"I'm Claire, Allison's sister," she said.

"I think Allison's in with the orangs." Not the actual orang-utan enclosure, it would seem, visible near the centre of the pavilion as they made their way along a path near the periphery, and where a woman, not Allison, was hosing the cement floor. Far above their heads, birds hooted as they settled for the night in the thirty-foot rafters or among the high canopies of the trees. Leaves brushed against Claire's arms.

The young man opened the door to the keepers' quarters and led Claire fourteen steps along a corridor to another door, which he unlocked. Then he called into the large, turquoise-walled interior, "Allison. Allison, your sister's here."

"My sister?" Allison appeared, also in a green T-shirt, carrying a handful of keys. Sweat made the planes of her face shine. At the sight of Claire, she looked worried.

"No big news," Claire said. "I got back from Montreal last night. I drove out because I thought it might be easier to talk to you here."

Allison nodded. Three days a week, she worked an early shift, rising before dawn and arriving home just as the three girls were let out of school. Two days a week she worked late and came home in time to tuck them into bed. "Only I can't be too late. Let me check that everyone's locked in."

They walked together along the row of barred enclosures, the orangutans' night quarters, which rose to skylights overhead, the turquoise walls and evening light that fell from above making the enclosures bright enough. In high school, Allison had spoken of wanting to be a veterinarian but, after getting a degree in animal husbandry, she had come to the zoo to work full-time. She loved the exotics, she said, having a continent's worth of creatures under her care, and she didn't want that care to be exclusively medical, even if some days all they seemed to do was clean — clean up shit.

"Which one's Dido?"

The orangutans were divided by age and rank (an old, sour male slumped in a cage by himself at the far end). Most sat quietly munching leafy twigs. Allison pointed to a young female in a pen with two others, lolling on her back in a patch of straw. There was no sign that her upbringing had been in any way unusual, that she had, in fact, been raised by a team of keepers, including Allison, who now, at least in front of Claire, paid no special attention to her. A young male pressed himself to the bars and spat at Allison as she passed.

"A normal bit of attention-getting," Allison said, wiping off her forearm.

When she switched off the lights, the room softened to blue. (Once Claire had asked Allison if she thought the orangutans, or any of the great apes, got migraines. Allison said she didn't know. It would be hard to tell. One of the mountain gorillas over in the Africa pavilion suffered epileptic fits. Sometimes one of the female orangutans rubbed her head as if she had a headache. Since migraines were recorded across time and in most human populations, it was not impossible that apes suffered them, too.)

They passed back through the keepers' kitchen. Through the animal kitchen, where a young woman was snapping plastic lids over the buckets of monkey chow, and out, again, into the pavilion. Claire followed Allison around to the back entrance of the orangutan exhibit, which Allison unlocked. The woman who had been cleaning the floors had left.

Inside, the door locked again behind them, Allison seated herself on a rectangular riser of cement, on top of a tidied pallet of straw. "You don't mind?" A tire hung above them from a rope attached to a roof beam. A film of sweat was spreading over Claire's skin.

"It's fine." The Plexiglas enclosure, vaulting to the heights of the glass roof above, was echoey but private: only in daytime would people peer in. "She talked to a doctor, but not the one I thought she'd spoken to. One strange thing is she wanted him to give her a brain scan — he was doing some kind of study but told her he couldn't use her."

"That's weird if she was there as a journalist."

"I guess."

"Did she think something was wrong?"

"I don't know."

Allison wiped her hands on her khakis. "I wish I could remember what her last message said. Now of course I wish I'd saved it but why would I? I know I listened to it in the morning, which would have been March 16, right? But I don't know when she sent it. I was pissed off. She'd said she was coming and then she wasn't, and however sorry she sounded, I was the one who was going to have to tell Star. I keep thinking maybe she said something about trying to visit a couple of weeks later, not that it matters now, but I could be making that up."

"I've talked to her phone company and bank but they say they can't give me any information because of privacy regulations."

"Won't Detective Bird get that sort of thing?" Allison was grazing a piece of straw back and forth against her left wrist. "What I keep wondering is if all this has something to do with Star. Everything seemed fine at Christmas. Didn't it? I know she left early, but I don't remember anything upsetting happening.

Star wants to know if Rachel's coming for her birthday. But what if she feels it's too difficult, even like this, that somehow it's better if she's not around, if she's not around at all." Allison looked at Claire. "Did she say anything to you about this?"

"No, she didn't."

This was what Claire knew: nearly four and a half years ago, one Saturday afternoon in January, Rachel had arrived without warning on Allison's doorstep, along with eighteen-month-old Star strapped in her stroller.

According to Rachel, as soon as Allison opened the door, she had bolted into the house, leaving Star on the doorstep with Allison, and raced to the downstairs bathroom where she vomited into the toilet.

In Allison's version, ashen-faced Rachel had stood there, and said, I've made a mistake. I need your help.

According to both, Rachel had spent most of the afternoon in bed in what was then Allison and Lennie's guest room, while Allison entertained Star along with two-year-old Amelia, and it wasn't until that evening, after the girls had been put to bed, that Allison and Lennie and Rachel sat down in the living room to talk.

I've made a mistake. Apparently these were the words that Rachel kept repeating. And, I can't go on like this.

You're exhausted, Allison told her. Which was totally understandable. And possibly depressed, which happened to some women. But, as Allison pointed out, Rachel was not exactly without means. She had money from their insurance settlement.

Even if she had qualms about it, she could put Star full-time in daycare, at least for a while, or hire a nanny, or stop working for a spell — give herself a break until she got some of her energy back. Why didn't she consider leaving New York, which wasn't the cheapest or easiest place to raise a baby, particularly in a six-storey walk-up? Why not come back to Toronto for a bit, where she had family to help?

The thing was, as Allison reiterated to Claire, she had made all these suggestions before, earlier in Star's babyhood, although, until now, Rachel had claimed she didn't need help. She would figure things out on her own. She couldn't stop working, she argued, because she was a freelancer and if she stopped altogether she would lose her contacts, and she did not want to leave New York. For the first eight months of Star's life, she had swapped apartments with a friend, who lived in the West Village on the ground floor of a building near the corner of Grove and Bedford streets, but Max's apartment, for all its accessibility, was also small and dark, made claustrophobically smaller by being stuffed with antique furniture that Max had recently inherited from a deceased aunt. After eight months, Rachel decided that she couldn't bear it any longer, fled its mausoleum-like interior and brought Star back to the airy heights of her own apartment.

They could take Star for a couple of weeks: this was Allison's initial suggestion. No, Rachel said, no, actually I was thinking more like a couple of months. She said she was at the end of her tether. She didn't think it was good for Star to go on like this either.

And so, Allison said to Claire, what were she and Lennie sup-posed to do when no amount of encouragement seemed to shift

Rachel? Even though her first response was one of disbelief. You couldn't have a child and then change your mind about it.

When Allison asked if Rachel was planning to go away somewhere, Rachel said no, or anyway not for very long. All she really wanted was to crawl into bed for a month and sleep.

It wasn't that Star was an especially difficult child. She wasn't colicky. She didn't always sleep through the night but a lot of babies didn't. She wasn't as easy as Amelia, but then everyone agreed that Amelia had been an almost unnaturally easy baby.

A span of two months was longer than a holiday. It was long enough for Star, who had cried herself to sleep every night for the first week when Allison told her that her mother was going away *for a little while*, to settle and adapt to their household. Perhaps the whole thing would not have been possible if Star had been less self-reliant and Amelia less happy-go-lucky. Perhaps it would just have been harder. Perhaps it had been unwise – unwise? – to reassure Rachel so vigorously that Star was fine because after two months she asked Allison if Star could stay a little longer, she had an assignment that would take her for a week or so to Georgia, not the state but the country, to Tbilisi, and then, a few weeks later, she called and said, if Star was so at home, perhaps, if they could manage it, she could stay on a month more. She was nervous about disrupting her. She was terrified of things going back to the way they'd been. If Allison and Lennie couldn't – she began to talk a little wildly about putting Star up for adoption.

Lennie was the one who said it would be a terrible thing for Star to be raised by someone who clearly didn't want to do it, but if they were going to take her in, they would have to work

out a formal arrangement. Neither he nor Allison was prepared to condemn Rachel's behaviour outright, at least in front
of Claire, perhaps because they were trying to protect Star, or
wanted to give Rachel's motives the benefit of the doubt. (If she
was so unhappy, perhaps she *was* doing the right thing, and it
was true that afterwards she did seem calmer and for a while her
migraines eased.) They would make the best of the situation, a
situation which was about to become a little more complicated,
since Allison, who swore she'd never set out to recreate their own
lost family, had just become pregnant with Lara.

And yet, Allison said, there was no sign that Rachel had ever
mistreated Star, even if it was impossible to know what had gone
on when the two of them were on their own in Rachel's apartment. Allison had seen more of Rachel and Star together than
Claire had, and spoken to Rachel about Star more frequently. At
first, Allison said, she'd been nervous about Rachel's lack of pre-
paredness for motherhood, despite her rampant eagerness, and it
was true that she was given to uttering aloud some of the things
that other mothers only thought: there were days when she
wanted to chuck the baby out the window. Of course she had
never meant this literally.

There were times when she had seemed almost relaxed,
happy as a mother. Hadn't she? The day they'd all met out at the
zoo, for instance. This was Allison's doing. Rachel, who'd been
in town with nine-month-old Star, had made plans to drive out
to the zoo with Allison, and Allison had convinced Claire to join
them. This was during the period when Allison was fostering

Dido, also nine months old, one of a team caring for Dido around the clock after her orangutan mother, Sunny, refused to accept her. They took turns in eight-hour shifts, holding her, always holding her – in a sling against the breast or on the back or scooped against the hip – to simulate as much as possible the experience of a baby orangutan who does not leave her mother's body during her first two years of life. It was exhausting work, Allison said, especially with Amelia waiting for her at home at the end of the day, but thrilling, too, given Dido's need for love and her fight for survival. Allison had gotten it into her head that she wanted Star to meet Dido because they were the same age. She wanted to see them interact, compare them developmentally. Rachel was game. And Allison wanted Claire there, she wanted them all to be together.

Claire drove out to meet them on a Saturday morning. They walked, Rachel pushing Star's stroller, from the administrative parking lot back through the admin building to a room off a corridor that ran along the rear of the building. A plain room with a sink and metal counter, cupboards above, pillows on the floor, some rubber toys, a couple of stuffed animals (a monkey, a lion), which they pressed Dido to when they needed a stretch break or to make a bathroom run. Another woman handed off Dido to Allison, who hugged Dido to her hip, Dido's long arms draping over Allison's shoulder. Rachel unbuckled Star from her stroller.

Had Rachel seemed happy that day? Allison had seemed happy, happy to have brought them all together, to reaffirm that they were still a family. And Rachel, too, had seemed glad to be with them, affectionate with Star. It was perhaps only to Claire that her garrulousness appeared a little forced, as if she were covering up something, but then Claire was particularly attuned to the ways people hid certain internal states from others. And surely her surprise at the sight of Rachel being so maternal – lifting Star from her stroller, burying her face in Star's neck and kissing her – revealed more about her than it did about Rachel.

Allison held Dido and Rachel Star close enough to each other that Dido, small-eyed, protuberant-mouthed, haloed in orange fur, extended an arm and wandered her long fingers through Star's fine brown hair. Take a picture, Allison instructed Claire – the youngest, childless sister. Wriggling in Rachel's grasp, Star reached out and, before they could stop her, slipped her fingers between Dido's lips. Dido didn't bite.

"Baby don't do that," Rachel said, raising her eyebrows at Allison as she wiped Star's hand matter-of-factly on her shirt, then slid Star's fingers into her mouth and sucked them clean. "You crazy monkey."

Allison offered Dido to Claire, who took her hesitantly, clasping Dido to her chest, feeling Dido's fingers track across her back and wind themselves into her hair. The curious, restless pressure of those fingers was so intimate as to be almost alarming and sent a surge through Claire not unlike that she'd felt when holding Amelia or Star. Rachel wouldn't hold Dido. Which seemed surprising, even at the time. She said she had her hands full. She said she didn't feel like being fondled by a baby orangutan although she let Dido examine her hand and play with her hair. Claire thought that Rachel had been fighting the effects of a migraine that day. But perhaps she had been thinking even then about what she would do nine months on. Was some idea being planted in her head as she watched animated Allison hold Dido and Star together, or did the thought not occur to Rachel until later?

Surely Rachel must have foreseen that getting pregnant and giving birth to a child would involve pain of one sort or another. When she called Claire during those couple of years it was more often to talk about her migraines than the baby. She'd stopped using most drugs when she began planning to conceive but, just back from Asia, she did not seem to be terribly troubled by headaches. During her pregnancy, her migraines grew worse, no doubt in part due to the hormonal shifts going on within her. Sometimes she didn't make it out of bed for days, she said, but she had a friend, friends, checking in on her. She cut back on work. She rallied herself by repeating that she was only going to be in this state for a matter of months.

(There were also those stairs, hefting her pregnant self up those six flights to her apartment. It was as if, whatever longing had possessed her, Rachel had never stopped to consider in practical terms what being pregnant and having a baby in a six-storey walk-up would be like.)

After Star's birth, things did not get better. Sleep deprivation gave Rachel migraines, and of course there was more hormonal turbulence. She gave up breast-feeding after two months so that she could go back to Imitrex and Tylenol 3s. She was swallowing Imitrex like crazy, she said, when no one even knew the long-term risks of the drug, but she didn't feel like she had a choice when she really couldn't function without it.

What had she hoped for? Optimistically, dangerously, had she gambled that getting pregnant and having a child might make her migraines vanish? This happened to some women — some free at least for the duration of pregnancy, some forever. It might happen to Claire but the possibility didn't seem worth counting on or even worth thinking too much about, especially given what had happened to Rachel, who now claimed she'd take the pain of childbirth over suffering through a really bad cycle of migraines — *not* that this meant that she ever wanted another child.

In the orangutan enclosure, seated on their concrete box, Allison frowned at Claire.

"So what are we supposed to do?"

"I don't know," Claire said. A flicker of fear passed between them. "But I feel like I need to do something."

"Even if she needs help," Allison said, "she may not ask for it."

They had been schooled in self-reliance, it was true. This was part of their legacy: stories of coping, of determinedly going it alone, had been handed down to them by their parents.

There was, for a start, the story of Rachel's birth.

Two days before Rachel was born, their father, still a medical student, had fallen ill, so ill that he took a taxi to emergency at the Toronto Western Hospital where he was admitted and diagnosed with hepatitis. He was flat out on his own hospital bed when Sylvia went into labour across town at the Toronto General. He was still there a week later when Sylvia brought Rachel home. For three weeks Sylvia could not even visit her husband because he was too contagious; then she would leave her baby with friends while she made the trip to his bedside. For the first six weeks of Rachel's life, Hugh did not see her except in the photographs that Sylvia brought to show him. He would joke in later years that the terror of his first child's birth had made him sick, which, it would turn out, was perhaps not such a joke, after all.

Meanwhile, Sylvia and Rachel were making out on their own in the Clinton Street apartment. An only child, Sylvia had almost no experience of babies. She swore she'd never even changed a diaper. But she coped. She did not move in with any of her friends. Her mother did not come out from Victoria to help her. Perhaps she had not asked for help. (Or turned it down when it was offered?) Surely it could not have been easy, those six weeks, alone in the apartment with her first child, navigating the slippery winter streets, unprepared for the isolation, anxious about both her husband and her baby, prone to migraines. Surely those weeks must have been bewildering and exhausting. Perhaps there were days when *she* wanted to chuck the baby out the window.

And then, mere months after that, her husband announced that he would not be returning to medical school, that he was abandoning his plans to become a doctor. A four-month-old child, her plans for the future tossed up in the air, her husband jobless and in debt, what was her state of mind then? Hugh found a job, in Ethiopia, of all places. So they picked themselves up and moved across the world to a compound in Addis Ababa, and yet they did not seem to have been undone by these upheavals. Bird-crazy Sylvia bought herself a parrot, which she named Theodotius, and Hugh a second-hand Jeep and a motorbike, on which he made solo expeditions into the countryside, and Rachel was put in the care of an Ethiopian nanny named Desta, whom she adored and who spoke to her only in Amharic. Two years later, she would return to Toronto speaking more Amharic than English, and one word more than any other, the Amharic word for yes, pronounced *ow*.

Claire arrived back in New York on the Friday night. She had arranged to take another day off work and return home on Monday. As she eased open the door to Rachel's apartment, she breathed in the faint odour of gas, the lock clicking into place as she bolted the door behind her. She stopped to catch her breath. There was a strange relief in returning to the familiarity of this place. She set down her bags by Rachel's closet in the middle room, her overnight bag and her laptop computer, and struggled with the windows to let loose some of the appalling heat.

"A day and a half was not enough," she'd said to Stefan as they sat in the kitchen, late in the evening of the day she'd visited Allison at the zoo.

"Why not let Detective Bird do his work?"

"All he's doing is making some phone calls."

"Give him a chance. And we can always hire a private detective. That worked last time."

Lennie had set up a missing person Web page for Rachel and listed her name with various on-line missing-person sites. They had sent out an e-mail bulletin to everyone they could think of, asking for news, any word, sightings, but nothing useful had come back yet.

Claire tapped the rim of her glass. "There's got to be something down there that'll help. I know I could wait a little longer but next weekend's the long weekend and then everyone's going to start going on vacation. And Allison can't do very much." Also, although she hesitated to speak of it to Stefan, she felt that she owed this to Allison: because of all that Allison did do, for a start.

"Maybe she doesn't want to be found," Stefan said. "You've considered that, haven't you?"

"If we knew that — but we don't know. Maybe it's not just an adventure." She reached across the table and squeezed his fingers. "And then the two of us can spend next weekend, the long weekend together, do something, or just hang out."

"We could take out the bikes. We haven't done that in a while. Go out for dinner." He ran his fingernail in delicate whorls across her palm, waiting for the very lightness of his touch to make her shudder, as it always did.

Standing by Rachel's sink, Claire let the water run up through the pipes before pouring herself a glass. She swallowed a small round cream pill and an ovoid yellow one. Zomig. Anaprox.

An uncomfortable band of sensation was pressing against her forehead; it had not yet congealed into a pulsing on one side of her head but inevitably would.

She called Brad Arnarson at home and left him a message saying that she was back in town and asking him to call her at Rachel's. From her bag, she pulled out some of the food supplies that she'd brought, a package of rice cakes, a small jar of cashew butter, and spread some of the nut butter onto a rice cake. She deliberated over whether to get out a plate and didn't, just used her fingers to scoop up fallen crumbs from the floor. She kept being unnerved by the thought that even now Rachel would see their worry as an overreaction and insist that they keep their noses out of whatever she was up to. It was her own business. If only one could assume that.

Across the hall, the neighbours' door banged. A whisper of voices, the faintest of footsteps echoed through the wall. So they were there this time. It was late. In the morning, whether Rachel would approve or not, Claire intended to go and talk to them.

A flicker of breeze reached her. Rachel used to have one of those window-mounted air conditioners. Claire had no idea where she stored it. She stumbled to the front window to check on the rooftop rose garden on the north side of 9th Street. The umbrella was furled for the night. Two weeks on and different roses were blooming, a scattering of white ones, pale smears in the dark, on the bush next to the one that had been in profusion during her last visit, as if a dial had turned, one degree to the west.

On the roof next to the garden, two couples were sharing a late-night barbecue. The women lounged on white ribbed lawn chairs near the edge of the flat surface, their ankles resting on the cornice, wrists dipped over the rooftop, flicking the ash from their cigarettes into the air over 9th Street.

How quiet it was in this apartment, how quiet it always was, unusual for New York or any big city – and how much of the life in this city took place in the air. Perhaps these were things that Rachel also loved, reasons she'd refused to move anyplace else: however much she liked to travel, she also liked to return here.

She had first moved in as a graduate student back in the mid-1980s when the East Village was a raunchier but already desirable place to be. In those days, she slept on a futon and her guest bed was a couch draped in pink fun fur, magazines strewn about it. Then Michael Straw moved in. His drafting table occupied the space between the two front windows. He remodelled the place: built Rachel a proper desk, bookshelves, the closet, kitchen cupboards. They slept in a loft bed in the middle room.

When Michael Straw moved out, he took his drafting table, his whiskey, and since he was the one who cooked, every piece of kitchen equipment bought during his tenure (all the items that Rachel had bought for him, plus those that they had purchased together). Rachel made him dismantle the loft bed, and thereafter slept on the mattress alone, a homemade Murphy bed that she lowered to the floor at night and during the day tipped up against the wall. She got rid of the sofa. Briefly, the apartment was Rachel's and Star's, until their sojourn in the West Village. After their return, Star slept in a crib at Rachel's side, then on the mattress beside her, her stroller wrapped with three feet of thick chain and locked in the stairwell below.

Three years ago, Rachel had bought her current bed, brass frame, new thick mattress and box spring, and set it up in the front room. Her first real bed, she insisted. Claire, who had witnessed the apartment's transitions on visits over the years, thought the bed's prominence a paean to sleep or sex rather than invalidism. A new beginning. Although perhaps she was not taking account of how a history of pain lurked here, as throughout the apartment.

With her silk eye pillow over her lids, Claire stretched out on Rachel's bed. She had never felt as desperate to escape – to escape Toronto, to begin with. The cartography program that she had wanted to attend was in the city, so there had been no need to move away for college. She had travelled – more so when she was younger – and this had satisfied much of her urge to explore. She had a friend, Maura Addison, who had moved to New York to redraw borders on maps for the UN, and another, Louisa Herskovitz, who went north to Yellowknife to slug it out with the male surveyors, but at the point when Claire had felt most restless and in need of a different home (even then she had not been able to decide where she would go), she had met Stefan.

Yet putting things this way failed to acknowledge the part that pain had played in these choices, how it gave rise to a deeper ambivalence within her. Sometimes, when her migraines were bad, she wanted nothing but to be housebound, her desire, then, only for stillness, for the recognizable smell of her own sheets, the known dark corners and memorized ceiling of her own bedroom. Longing was reduced to a dream of return, the return of the familiar. On the other hand, there were times when a bad headache, or a succession of bad headaches, made the familiar seem toxic. The same sheets, ceiling, the creak of the fourth stair became merely a conduit for pain, and she longed to be anywhere not associated with pain. It was like the way Allison's old arthritic cat used to wander from room to room, moving from chair to closet to floor, as if somehow a different place would by itself offer the necessary balm. Likely Rachel felt something similar. Perhaps this state of mind had simply overwhelmed her. The question was, escape to where?

In the morning, after eating a quick breakfast, Claire knocked on the door across the hall. The neighbours invited her inside, reintroducing themselves as Jim and Alex, and offered her a mug of tea. They had lived in the building even longer than Rachel had.

Their kitchen was cooled by air conditioning and dim – spatially the mirror image of Rachel's but nothing like the bright pallor of her walls, or her kitchen's warm stuffiness. Theirs had the air of an elegant cave, a burgundy-tinted salon. In a dark silk dressing gown, Jim slumped over a squat teapot while Alex, a soft-bellied older man in tank top and shorts, lounged in the doorway to the room beyond.

Jim's brow creased. He said they'd received the note that Claire had left two weeks ago but didn't have anything to report. It was true, they hadn't heard much noise recently from across the hall; the last few years, it was sometimes hard to tell when Rachel was there and when she was away. They both seemed sheepish, a bit furtive, as if they ought to have noticed something else and hadn't. All March, they'd been away in Mexico. They'd been upstate the last time Claire had come to town. Jim rested his hand on Claire's back as he handed her a mug. Had she talked to Otto, the guy at the other end of the hall, who was admittedly a creep (not dangerous, just weird) – and what about the girls downstairs?

They'd last seen Rachel – Jim shot a bashful glance at Alex, who rubbed his knuckles back and forth across his upper lip – in February? February. Sheepish again. A Friday night? They'd run into her on the landing. She said she was off to a meeting. She did not say what kind of meeting. Nothing more, nothing out of the ordinary to report.

"Did you notice the mail piling up in her box?"

"Yes," laconic Alex said. "Assumed she was out of town."

"Do you have any idea why there's no mail now?" Claire was convinced the post office was still returning it, although when she'd called, the woman she'd spoken to seemed to have no idea where Rachel's mail had gone.

"Could be she's having it forwarded to another address."

In the lower left-hand drawer of Rachel's desk: seven files of notes and clippings of articles. All old. Some half-used note-pads. At the very back, a single photograph of Michael Straw, and a file of Star's drawings, some of which still bore crease marks from having been folded in the mail. Big-headed figures, a fat sun shining over three blue creatures that might be dogs. To Mum, Love Star. To Rachel, love Star. Another file folder, right at the back, marked M & D, which Claire took out and opened on her lap.

Inside there were only two objects. A card with a picture of Monet's water lilies on the front contained a message in Sylvia's hand: To our beloved Rachel on her thirtieth birthday. Hope you're living life to the fullest and may you continue to do so for years to come! Love, Mum and Dad. The other object was more mysterious. It appeared, at first, to be nothing more than a pad of blank white paper. When Claire examined it more closely, she realized that indentations of her father's handwriting were scored into its pages. He must have penned a note on a sheet that had been torn off, the pressure of the pen leaving these grooves beneath. Their father had never, almost never, written them things. Birthday cards, postcards were always in their mother's hand, signed from the two of them. Claire had one postcard that her father had sent her, from San Antonio, Texas, where he'd gone alone to a math convention when she was twelve. She could not make out all the ghostly words on the pad. Sylvia — that was clear. Blue suitcase. Zipper. Hugh. How familiar the cursives of his "g," the final jut of his second "h." Had the indented letters faded over the years? Had Rachel been able to make out all the words? His presence was summoned up anyway, the heft of his body, the timbre of his voice. Rachel must have taken the pad from the house when the three of them had cleared it out, keeping this find to herself. Perhaps she considered it such an odd item to hold onto that she feared they might tease her, or perhaps she thought that neither Claire nor Allison would care about something of so little apparent consequence. And yet Claire found it hard to put the pad back. She could think of no justification, at this stage, for removing it. If she simply, carefully ripped out an underlying page, on which the grooves of their father's writing were a little less deep, Rachel would never know, and yet such an act felt like stealing, violating the integrity of the object. She slid the pad back into the folder, the folder into the drawer.

In another folder were years' worth of medical insurance statements and receipts for prescription drug purchases. Rachel tended to do as Claire herself did: stock up every four or five months. Her last purchases, on February 15, 2000: forty-eight Zomig (several hundred dollars' worth), two hundred Anaprox, one hundred Tylenol 3s. Thirty Ativan. Before that: thirty-six Zomig on November 12, 1999. Claire took note of the prescribing doctor's name. How long would forty-eight Zomig last Rachel? There was also a chance that Rachel had phoned in for more renewals from wherever she was.

Though the pill count was high, it was not, to Claire's eye, out of line. Rachel had always relied on drugs, even more than she had. Rachel was the one who'd tried hard-core painkillers, who'd suffered through an addiction to Fiorinal. For women's magazines, she wrote about all kinds of treatments, from the mainstream to the kooky, and passed on any migraine-related tips that came her way, but for herself scoffed at anything that seemed too alternative. Claire was the one who'd tried an osteopath, a cranial sacral therapist, two naturopaths, three acupuncturists, a biofeedback specialist, none, so far, to any long-lasting effect. Friends with migraines had found cures – magnesium had done the trick for Irene Tate – but nothing so far had really worked either for her or Rachel.

From the bottom right-hand drawer, Claire pulled out an answering machine, a relic from the days before voice mail. The phone line still beeped with messages that she could not retrieve. Before leaving Toronto, she'd called Rachel's New York number and discovered the voice-mail box to be full. Perhaps, by connecting the answering machine to the phone and wall jack and setting it to pick up after two rings, she'd be able to intercept the line, before the voice-mail function kicked in, and retrieve any new messages.

She set up her laptop on Rachel's desk and began to feed into it the computer disks jumbled in the desk's top right-hand drawer. Four were empty, the rest contained files full of articles in various versions, all old, and some out-of-date software. None of the magazine editors whom she had contacted had commissioned the migraine article that Rachel was ostensibly working on at the time of her disappearance. Claire had tried to locate the article on-line, without success. Of course this did not mean that Rachel hadn't written it, although perhaps she had abandoned the attempt, or the article itself was a ruse, a way to get herself seen by the neurologists in Montreal, and experts elsewhere.

Claire searched for signs, however minute, that Rachel had returned in her absence, that she might be hiding out close by or trying consciously to elude them. She'd checked the depressions in the bed upon entering the night before, the fridge, the contents of the bathroom garbage, the position of the tube of toothpaste beside the kitchen sink and the indentations in it, Rachel's assemblage of pills in the kitchen cupboard, the pattern of dust on her desktop.

And now: the number of pairs of underwear in the chest of drawers in her closet, the items of clothing on hangers, the arrangement of empty hangers. And then, since nothing seemed to have altered, Claire began to slip her hands into the pockets of Rachel's trousers and jackets, as one might search through the belongings of the dead, fingers closing around Kleenexes, lint-covered pills, old MetroCards, more business cards, but there were no obvious clues as to where Rachel had gone or why, no longed-for secret message. Cardboard filing boxes were stored on a top shelf. On the closet floor, within a slim, clear plastic shopping bag was folded a slinky silver top, tag still attached. The impression of Rachel's feet hollowed out her worn shoes.

Claire had to stop and collect herself. She was back in Etobicoke, in the old bungalow, with Rachel and Allison, only they weren't in the room with her. She was in her parents' long double closet, in the dark, the sliding door pulled shut, surrounded by their clothes. What she wanted to bear away with her was not the clothes but the scents that clung to them, the particular commingling of her father's nut-like musk and her mother's perfume of citrus and rose, an essence impossible to capture. Even if she managed to bottle it, it would fade.

She sat on the floor of Rachel's apartment with her head in her hands. She was here because of them, too, because surely her parents would have wanted her to do something to help Rachel, especially since they could no longer do anything themselves.

At 11:52, Brad Arnarson called, his voice staccatoed by the crackle of a cellphone. "Hey, what's up?" His call caught Claire batting away dry-cleaning plastic as she dragged a fan from the back of Rachel's closet.

"Looking through Rachel's stuff. Why?" His offhand tone and question threw her. What did he think she'd be doing? "Where are you?"

"– on 11th Str – outside Danal – on line for brunch – long are you around?" His line kept breaking up.

She yelled. "Till Monday afternoon."

"I've got a pretty insane schedule all weekend." She sensed a falling off of his concern, a glimpse of the life he lived beyond Rachel. Perhaps he felt he'd done what he needed to do by alerting her to Rachel's absence. The work of finding Rachel was hers.

"Did a Detective Bird call you?" she asked.

"Yeah, and I told him pretty much what I told you."

"Do you have a moment now?" He mumbled something. "What exactly did Rachel say about how bad her migraines were before she left?"

"What — Claire, sorry — just a sec."

She shouted her question again.

"Bad," he said. The connection got suddenly better. Perhaps he'd changed location. There were still street sounds around him. "But I don't really have a point of comparison. She said she kept reacting to more triggers and she was worried about reaching some point of total toxicity. I stopped by at a meeting of this pain support group she went to a few times — kind of an AA thing. They get together once a month in a basement on St. Marks Place."

"Rachel went to this?"

"She said it was totally not like her, but — Anyway, I asked around and no one there has seen her since January."

"At Christmas she mentioned this Chinese doctor."

"Oh, the herb doctor. Some friend of hers recommended this doctor in Chinatown who got her boiling up herbs every day for like weeks. The whole apartment stank. Then she had to drink the, what, the tea, the broth?"

"Did it help?"

"Honestly? Maybe. Not really in the end, I guess."

"Do you have the doctor's name?"

"Fin? Fung? Someone on East Broadway." The line went shrill with sirens, a man, a woman calling his name. "Claire, I've gotta go."

She set down the phone. A pain support group? An herbalist? She retrieved the fan from the closet and stationed it far enough from the desk so as not to ruffle the papers on the surface. Gathering the business cards, minus those she'd taken home on her last visit, she began to sort them, dealing them out like playing cards. Medical professionals, assorted media, beauty treatments, other — the curious detritus of Rachel's life. Other included IT workers, bankers, an economist, a hypnotist, a professor of astronomy. The air filled with the thwacking of pigeon wings. A breeze from the fan played across Claire's sweaty back. She stood in front of the fan, arms raised, as if showering in air. Down below, a dog barked. She went to the sink and gulped down a glass of water. Back at the desk, she came upon a card for a Dr. Win Toong on East Broadway.

It was a Saturday. She decided to try the number anyway. The woman who answered the phone said the doctor was finish for today. I'm just wondering if I could speak to the doctor? Finish, you want an appointment? Well, Claire said, I guess, if there's anything available Monday, say, Monday morning. Monday, twelve noon.

She was scheduled to fly out at 3:50. She ought to be able to make it down to East Broadway and back in time to catch her flight.

At one, wearing a hat and sunglasses, Claire went out for lunch. The curbs glowed white-hot. Pedestrians kept to the shady side of the street. In Veselka's, on the corner of 9th and Second Avenue, she ate a tuna-salad sandwich and listened to a waitress taking a man's order as a bus blew squealing in along 9th Street. "Something to drink with that?" the waitress asked.

"Mustard," the man replied.

Instead of returning to Rachel's apartment, Claire kept walking, south along Second Avenue, past a young woman who suddenly turned to her male companion and asked, What is a falafel? Further south, a man coasted by on a scooter, chanting, Wherefore wherefore where — It was an afternoon of such auditory oddities. At Houston, a man was squatting on the sidewalk, a wool hat upended in front of him, shouting what sounded like gibberish, which then clarified into *shellfish shellfish* as she approached, and then, uttered with ever increasing speed, *please help please help*, as she drew even nearer. She tossed a handful of coins into his hat.

All of this seemed familiar. She and Rachel had walked together down Second Avenue, sometimes cutting across 4th Street or 3rd, sometimes continuing south to Houston, before heading west. Through Rachel, she had a history on these streets, a history that brought Rachel close and reached back years, ever since Rachel had moved to New York, at twenty-four, to attend the Columbia School of Journalism. (Later, she would manage to finagle herself a series of work visas through positions on various magazines, which became in practice, if not on paper, steadily more freelance over the years. She found a good lawyer and got a green card.)

Two Decembers in a row, as soon as her fall semester of college classes ended, Claire had taken the twelve-hour train journey south to visit Rachel. During the hours when Rachel was busy, she had walked the streets and avenues on her own, back and forth, up and down, counting blocks, committing them to memory, storing the streets inside her.

On her first trip, she discovered that tree-sellers had taken over stretches of lower First Avenue, below 7th Street, erecting wooden scaffolds and leaning Christmas trees, cut spruce and Scotch pine, against them. She walked through these temporary bowers, inhaling pitch and spice. The tree-sellers, she realized, by observing the licence plates on the trailers parked beside the trees, were Canadian. Presumably they camped out on First Avenue during these weeks before Christmas. (Where did they shower? What did they eat?) They sat on folding metal chairs behind the trailers, those with Quebec licence plates speaking nasal French to each other, the Nova Scotians with noticeable accents. It was an odd place in which to discover a sense of complicity and fellowship with her countryfolk, and she felt a sudden nostalgia for the land she'd so recently left.

The following year, Claire wanted only to vacate her life in Toronto, empty her heartbreak into these other streets. Four months had passed since Kevin Giddings, her first boyfriend, had left her, the loss of him papering over all the questions she'd had about their relationship, once the initial euphoria of having a boyfriend, an actual boyfriend, had worn off. They'd met at Sheridan, where Claire studied cartography and Kevin, landscape gardening. He'd abandoned her for an interior design student. It wasn't that she was coming to Rachel for comfort, she didn't particularly want to confide in Rachel about her love life. Rather she wanted to be enveloped by the magnanimous, energetic pleasure that Rachel would take in steering her, the younger and less sophisticated one, towards gallery shows and shops and cheap restaurants that she might not otherwise have heard of. As on her last trip, they would have dinner together, and wander through tiny boutiques trying on odd-shaped dresses and expensive shoes. Only as soon as Claire arrived on Rachel's doorstep, it was clear that Rachel was in the grip of a migraine.

Before Claire had even set down her bags, Rachel beckoned her over. "Feel this," she muttered, indicating the back of her neck, and when Claire, after removing her gloves, squeezed her fingers over the skin, the muscles beneath were hard as stone. Rachel exhaled softly. There were times when Claire's own neck felt like that. She rubbed Rachel's neck a little longer.

"Bad?" It was a stupid question.

"I thought it would be over by now," Rachel said. Her voice had dropped a note, a side effect of heavy codeine use. "It's into its third day."

Folding her coat over a chair, Claire filled the kettle and put it on the stove. She took the heel of bread and rind of cheese that Rachel offered her, which seemed to be all the food there was in the apartment.

"Look," Rachel said. Pulling back the sleeve of her shirt, she flexed her bicep. The muscle was well-defined without bulging grotesquely. "I was reading an article the other day about junkies, and how toned their muscles can be, from tension, not from strength, and I thought, that's me. Do you know how depressing that is?"

"But you were always athletic," Claire protested.

"Was," Rachel said. "Emphasis on was."

"Are you taking care of yourself?" Claire asked. "Maybe you're working too hard or taking too many pills."

"Honey, I have to work."

Rachel's futon was pulled out across the floor of the middle room. Claire had to leave her bags in the kitchen since there was no way to get from the kitchen to the front room without stepping on the mattress. Rachel wouldn't go out for dinner. "If you want to go out, you'll have to go by yourself."

So, although Claire had envisioned setting out with Rachel for a late meal in SoHo or Chinatown, she squelched her disappointment and trudged around the corner by herself to the Café Mogador on St. Marks Place.

When she climbed back up the six flights, a bag of groceries in her arms, and knocked on Rachel's door, Rachel opened it, in the midst of pulling on her leather jacket.

"What's up?" Claire asked in surprise.

"I have to run an errand."

"Do you want me to run it for you?" Because, as Claire had understood it, an hour and a half ago Rachel wasn't feeling well enough to go anywhere, and her pallor and the swerve at the edge of her movements did not seem to have subsided in the meantime.

"No," Rachel said. It seemed a given that Claire would accompany her.

They descended the six flights without speaking.

Outside, they turned in the direction of First Avenue and crossed at the lights, heading east, where, on the far side of First

Avenue, a handful of dark men jittered in the shadows, crying, *sin sin sinsemilla*. Without a word to Claire, Rachel stepped into the deeper shadows with one of the men, leaving her in the middle of the sidewalk. A moment later, Rachel returned, pocketing something.

"Are we going back?" Claire asked.

"No," Rachel said, "we're going to the park." It was mild for December, cool enough for gloves but not cold enough to see your breath.

"Rachel, no," Claire said, "I just got in. I'm starting to feel exhausted. Let's go back."

"I thought you wanted to go out," Rachel said. There was something mean in her voice. She hadn't yet given Claire a set of keys, which, on some level, she seemed aware of.

Claire thought, I can go back. Or anywhere else. Abandon Rachel, only this wasn't really Rachel, she told herself, this was Rachel's migraine speaking.

They crossed Avenue A and entered Tompkins Square Park. Claire had no idea why Rachel felt she had to go to the middle of the park in the middle of December to smoke a joint, at night. This was a place that at the best of times, as Claire understood it, was not somewhere the two of them should be hanging out after dark. She had no interest in smoking a joint. She did enough drugs as it was and dreamed of fewer altered states, not more.

The park smelled of smoke and shit and urine. There were rustlings in the bushes. Footsteps exploded in Claire's ears. Her limbs felt loose and watery, her heart a sieve. They seated themselves on a bench, directly under an old wrought-iron lamp,

Rachel's concession to Claire. Rachel pulled out her packet. Dark hair fell over her eyes. She swore: she'd forgotten to bring any cigarette papers.

So they had to make their way back out to Avenue A, to the bodega on the corner of 11th, where Rachel discovered she didn't have any more money on her and Claire had to cough up the necessary cash while Rachel hovered beside her.

"Does this work for you?" Claire asked on their way back to the park. She'd heard it said that marijuana helped some people's migraines.

"Don't know yet." There was a note of desperation in Rachel's voice.

Back on the same bench, Rachel rolled a fat little cigarette and offered it to Claire.

"No, thanks," Claire said. She hated being made to feel prim, fearful and prim. She was aware of the twinges of something now, right side, faint pressure and pulse. "I went to a neurologist a couple of weeks ago and he wants me to keep a record of when I get them, how bad they are on a scale of one to three."

"Three," Rachel said, "that's pathetic." She leaned forward. "I met a woman in the laundromat who got migraines and said the only thing that cured them was sex. Whenever she felt a migraine coming on, she went out and had sex. Didn't matter who with, just sex." The skin beneath Rachel's eyes was so pale it looked swollen. "Guess what I asked her?" Rachel tamped the cigarette, still unlit, against her thigh.

"I don't know."

"You do. Did it have to be good sex?"

"And did it?"

"The better the orgasm, the better the effect." Rachel was silent for a moment; then she said, "I would do it."

"Do what?"

"If someone was in terrible pain and having sex could help them, I would do it. Would you?"

Claire said nothing.

"How are things with your guy?"

"I don't have a guy," Claire said. She wished she'd never mentioned Kevin Giddings to Rachel. "When I was in Victoria in the summer, he met someone else." Tears welled in her eyes. "Whatever. Doesn't matter. When I have a headache I don't usually feel like having sex and when I had a headache Kevin didn't seem all that interested in having sex with me."

Rachel rested her left hand gently on top of Claire's right. "It's all right." Then she began to rub at the skin under her right eye. "I know a guy whose migraines are cured by arm wrestling." She could be irritating, but she was also generous, and brave, and if brave, then by extension, surely Claire must also be, for pain made twins of them. There was no other being so neurochemically, so metabolically close.

On another visit, Rachel told Claire a story about a man from London, England, who suffered frequent and debilitating migraines until he came to New York on a business trip and had no headaches at all. So he arranged all his affairs to return, with the same result. And the next time, and the next. Finally, he decided to make a real trial of it, took a leave of absence from his job and spent an entire month in New York. He still didn't suffer a single migraine. He flew back to London and told his wife they had to move to New York. In that city, he was pain-free. He was meant to be there. She refused to accompany him. Instead she asked for a divorce. His widowed mother died of an aneurysm. Still, he did not change his mind about leaving London. He and his wife sold their flat, he abandoned his well-paying job and accepted a transfer to an inferior but potentially less stressful position with the American branch of his London firm. After weeks of searching he managed to sublet a studio apartment in the West Village for several thousand dollars a month. A week later, still pain-free, ecstatically roaming the nearby streets, he stumbled upon a cheese shop. In London, he had eaten a lot of cheese. It had been his habit, on a Friday afternoon, to stop at Neal's Yard Dairy after work, buy a half-pound of Caerphilly, and eat it on the way home to his wife. In New York, he had scarcely eaten any cheese. Instead he'd discovered the joys of takeout sushi. At Murray's Cheese Shop on Cornelia Street, he bought a half-pound of Wensleydale, a fine English cheese, the sight and smell of which made him suddenly wistful. Musing as he walked, he unwrapped the cheese, devoured it all, and two hours later was felled by a migraine.

Now the question is, Rachel said, was it a physical reaction to the cheese or some delayed reaction to the stress of all he'd lost or a reaction to the release from stress, which of course is a common moment for illness to appear, or some combination of all of the above.

Dr. Win Toong was younger than Claire had expected. Dr. Toong was also a woman.

When Claire had counted her way along East Broadway and turned in at the most sanitized and medicinal-looking herb shop she'd passed, she spotted a figure at the far end. Behind the woman, white shelves rose to the tall white ceiling, shelves that were partitioned to look like boxes, holding jars and plastic sacks of roots and vegetable matter. The glass cabinetry of the counter was similarly subdivided, filled with ground powders (what was in those powders?) on white porcelain plates, more roots. The woman approached, smelling of salt and anise, a distillation of the shop's pungency. She wore a short-sleeved cotton shirt and a navy skirt that fell to just below her knees. Though Claire had been to acupuncturists before, she had never been to a doctor who worked out of a Chinatown herb shop.

"I have an appointment," Claire said. She realized she'd forgotten to ask how much her appointment was going to cost.

"This way, please." The woman led her behind a curtain hung across a doorway, through another doorway, and into a room, white-walled and drably carpeted, where she motioned Claire to the chair in front of the desk and took the seat behind it. The six-foot desktop was wood veneer. On the eight-foot-high wall behind the doctor hung a series of diplomas. To her right, on Claire's left, a map of the body was divided by meridians, the arms of the figure held out in supplication. "How can I help you?" Dr. Win Toong asked.

"I get migraines," Claire said. This wasn't what she had meant to say, but she'd woken to a low pulsing. On the left side, not the more usual right. By now her left nasal passages were blocked, neck muscles tensing, the place behind her eye commencing its dull throb.

"How often do you get them?"

"Two to four times a week." Which was a lie: could be two, three, four, five, six, more than she would ever admit to.

"When did they begin?"

"When I was a child. Six or seven."

"Stick out your tongue." The doctor's voice was curt, brusque but not unkind. "Stretch your arm." If Rachel had come here, perhaps she had done so because it seemed so far from any treatment she'd sought before: the powders, the roots, the herbs. Perhaps this step was a measure of her desperation. Perhaps someone she knew had been returned to health after coming here, and for all her cynicism, she'd been drawn by the possibility of what lay behind these doors and in these drawers, or perhaps she'd been seeking treatments like this far longer than Claire knew.

"Have you had acupuncture before?" the doctor asked.

Claire nodded.

"Has it helped?"

"Not really. I thought you used herbs."

"Yes, but acupuncture stimulates the body. Have you ever tried moxa?"

Claire shook her head.

The doctor led her into another room in which there was an examining table. Metal cabinets lined the wall above a small metal sink. On the counter, packages of needles were laid out on a silver tray. "Take off your shoes and socks." The doctor ripped open a packet of needles.

"I came here," Claire said, "because I believe my sister saw you. Rachel Barber. She's taller than me, with darker hair, a little older. It would have been earlier in the year. In January or last December, maybe."

The doctor stopped in the midst of extracting a needle from the packet. "How is she now?"

"I don't know. We don't know where she is. She seems to have disappeared. I was wondering if you could help. If you could tell me when you saw her. How she was. Do you remember her?"

"I will see." The doctor pointed to the table. "Lie down." Claire unfolded herself along the vinyl-covered surface. Perhaps the doctor wouldn't tell her anything about another patient, even if that patient was Claire's sister.

Dr. Toong began to touch Claire's body – the inside of her arm near the elbow, a point along the rim of her ear, another between her first and big toes. The doctor's fingers were cool and rough. "Does it hurt here? Here?" Some of the points were exquisitely sore, points which Dr. Toong located swiftly and without fuss. In each sore point, she stuck a needle, which did not startle Claire or hurt exactly. The doctor laid a palm across her forehead. "Relax. Whatever happens, you must learn to relax. I will look for your sister." She dipped her fingertips in a black paste and smeared it against the ends of some of the needles. Then she flicked a lighter to life, an ordinary cigarette lighter, and held it to the paste-smeared needles, until they began to smoke. Without another word, she left and closed the door behind her.

In the dark, the moxa glowed. Tendrils of smoke drifted towards the ceiling. Claire's body resembled a series of small, perspiring volcanoes. Heat travelled down the spines of the needles. She had never seen her body give off smoke before.

Time passed. One or two of the needles – the ones between Claire's toes – became uncomfortable. Places travelled up from inside her, as if carried upward on the smoke. The mosque at First Avenue and 11th Street. The parking lot on the southwest corner of College and Bathurst in Toronto. The corner of First Avenue and 6th Street. The Petit Pont in Paris. The Bloor Street Viaduct. Places appeared but there were no people in them.

She kept having the feeling that she was missing something. Fragments of e-mails that Rachel had sent and that she'd been poring over, back in Rachel's apartment, drifted through her head. *Terribly and suddenly after a glass of milk, a single glass of milk, 2.6 on the BPS.* That was from October. (Why was it that Rachel had made the most use of the Barber Pain Scale, while she, who measured everything else, had been reluctant to do so?) *Off to Shanghai next week to find out about arsenic as a cancer-fighting drug. No milk in the meantime.*

If pain is a call for attention, what exactly is ours calling attention to (and why why why are our headaches so persistent)?

Claire tried to puzzle out what time it was but had stupidly taken off her watch and left it on the examining room's counter, and although by now her eyes had adjusted to the dark, there was no clock. She began, restlessly, to measure the room, using the needle in the crook of her right elbow as her ruler: the walls, twelve needles high. At first there were sounds from outside, the doctor's voice in the shop, two other voices speaking what might be Cantonese or some other dialect, then the doctor's and one of those voices moved to the office, but now nothing, for a long time nothing.

An hour, Claire's internal clock said, an hour and a half. It couldn't be, though, could it? She'd never been left so long in a doctor's office before. Usually the problem was how quickly you were booted out. Was the doctor trying to find some record of Rachel's visits? Had the doctor forgotten her? She had to go back to 9th Street to pick up her bags. It had seemed a reasonable plan beforehand, in lieu of lugging her computer and overnight case downtown. It was hard to relax. If her head felt better, it might be because she was distracted. Perhaps the doctor was at lunch. Could you set someone on fire and then lose track of them? Could she begin pulling needles out by herself? Could she get up, needles still in place, and wander off in search of the doctor? What *was* she missing? At last, without a sound, on slippered feet, the doctor reappeared, through a second door, to Claire's right. Two hours or none at all. "How are you feeling?"

"I have a plane to catch," Claire said weakly. If patience was what counted then she, like Rachel, had surely failed.

"Why didn't you say?" Dr. Win Toong plucked out needles as if they were bits of string. "We can call you a car." When Claire sat up, she said, "Your sister Rachel came three times. Last time February. Three times is not enough."

"Did she think the treatments were working? Did you think they were?"

"Sometimes the herbs take longer. Two months. Six months."

"How did she seem to you?"

"Her system is stressed. It take time to work."

"Do you have any idea why she didn't come back?"

The doctor shrugged.

On the counter in the shop were two large paper bags, each stuffed to the brim with small clear plastic bags filled with vegetable matter. Roots? Twigs? Burdock? A second older woman, with liver-spotted hands, had joined the doctor behind the counter. The visit cost seventy-five dollars. Six weeks' worth of herbs would be three hundred dollars. Dr. Win Toong did not take credit cards. After that Claire was to come back. She began to blush. "I can't do this. I'm sorry. I really can't." Worse than Rachel. She couldn't possibly carry these bags home across the border. Any customs official would take one look and flag her. Paying for her appointment used up just about all the cash she had. Pink-cheeked, Claire dashed into the street. There were no taxis in sight, only a black sedan car pulled up at the curb, the young Asian driver signalling to her.

This time, there were messages — three! — waiting on the answering machine when Claire burst into the apartment, intent simply on grabbing her luggage and bolting out again. Breathless, she pressed the playback button.

Elise Bray from *American Beauty* asked what had happened to the piece Rachel had been assigned, due April 16, on genital warts.

A hang-up.

Hi, Rachel, Amy Levin here, calling for Ariel. I left you a message last week too. Anyway, reminding you that Ariel wants you to know there are still a few openings for appointments in Amsterdam next week if that suits you and he won't be back in New York until September. You missed him here last month but since you did see him in Amsterdam in March, maybe you're still in Europe or are heading back. Anyway, can you get back to me either way when you get this message? We don't have another number for you so I really hope you pick this up. Ariel sends greetings and says he really, really hopes to see you and wants to know how you're doing.

Claire dropped her bags and scribbled down both numbers. She called the second number immediately.

"Hello?" Amy Levin said.

"This is Claire Barber, Rachel Barber's sister."

"That was quick."

"I've been staying at her place. I got your message. Rachel isn't here. Do you mind my asking, who's Ariel?"

"He's a healer."

"And Rachel definitely saw him in March? In Amsterdam? Can you tell me the date?"

"Um." Pages rustled. Claire's muscles gripped. "March 21."

"And she definitely saw him."

"Yeah, well, it's marked here as paid and he mentioned it. Why?"

"That's the last time we know of anyone seeing her."

"Oh my God. What happened?"

"We don't know."

"Do you want to talk to Ariel? I do the bookkeeping and the scheduling, especially for the New York clients. Oh my God, I'm so sorry. I can give you his number in Tel Aviv. He's flying tomorrow to Geneva. You may have a hard time getting hold of him. I can give you the number in Geneva too. But he doesn't usually answer the phone. I'll tell him to call you as soon as I speak to him."

"What kind of healer is he?"

"He does this totally amazing energetic work. He's Israeli. People come to him from all over the world."

From Montreal Rachel had gone to Amsterdam. She had jettisoned her plans to visit her daughter in order to see this man, this healer.

"What's his number?" Claire asked.

*T*he weather turned. Beneath the summer duvet, Claire folded her body against Stefan's. Outside the partly open window, just beyond the head of the bed, rain teemed into the eavestroughs and chortled through the downspouts, the sound so close as to be almost in the room. A fine mist drifted through the screen, the curtains left open, too. Only if the rain grew worse and began to billow in would she rouse herself to shut the window, but she liked the feeling of permeability, of being close to Stefan in the midst of the tumult, for all that she sometimes felt besieged by her body's porousness to the outer world.

Stefan wasn't yet asleep. Sometimes it still surprised Claire to find herself here with him, to find herself loved. When she'd met Stefan, he had seemed worldly to her, having had three girl-friends, Gwen and Uma and Jenny, relationships that had occupied most of his twenties and lasted for years, unlike her two involvements (the second more of a heartbreak than the first), which had each endured only for a matter of months.

At twenty-two, in the office where she was working for the summer, she had met an architecture student seven years older than she was. Tom Speck had a girlfriend, but a month after meeting Claire, he said he was leaving his girlfriend for her. For two and a half months she lived in a state of rapture, half-delirious in his presence, hardly daring to believe her luck, until the night Tom took her out to a restaurant and told her he'd made a mistake and was going back to the girlfriend he'd recently left. After that, Claire dated no one for years, until a mutual friend introduced her to Stefan, saying they'd either drive each other crazy or be perfect for each other.

She held in her mind an image of him from early in their relationship. Stefan had invited her to a dinner dance, a black-tie affair sponsored by a scientific research council. Until this point their encounters had been more low-key, hesitant and wary on her part. Their movies, dinners, café rendezvous had already involved Claire in explanations, as offhand as she could make them, about why she couldn't watch a lot of films and barely touched alcohol. (At least, if necessary, she could still sneak home alone at the end of the evening to medicate.) This invitation seemed more serious in its intent.

There was Stefan, slim, olive-skinned, neat in a borrowed tuxedo, his dark hair newly trimmed. At the end of the meal, as the tables were being cleared, he told her emphatically that he did not dance. Ever. He hated dancing. As the music began, they sat a little awkwardly over the dregs of their coffee, watching other couples, most older than they were, take to the floor. When Claire asked him if he'd change his mind for just one dance, he shook his head. Then, at the end of the next song, he relented. As they rose together, he did not take his eyes from her, as if that would help overcome his self-consciousness. He was not as awkward a dancer as she'd feared. Bashful but not graceless. He was doing this for her, to please her. The gesture moved her fundamentally towards him, towards love.

Five weeks after they met, her parents died.

Every night she'd spent away from him, and there had not been many, she would turn herself ritualistically to face whatever direction he was in relation to her and bid him goodnight: north-northwest in their own bed from Rachel's apartment in New York. Away from him, she drifted to sleep imagining his body beside hers, turned from her as he turned just before sleep, an act that she intuited not as withdrawal but as vulnerable exposure, as trust. He offered her a view of himself – the curve of his shoulders, the scape of his back – that he could not see. She had never minded his absorption in his work, his late hours and weekends at the lab, the fact that she could walk up behind him as he sat hunched over his computer at home, unaware of her until she laid a hand on his shoulder. His powers of concentration, his capacity for self-immersion had always seemed like good things, and attracted her, perhaps because she found in them some mirror of herself.

The night she got word of her parents' accident, Claire had called Stefan, weeping, from Allison's apartment, downstairs from her own, Allison seated on one side of her, Lennie on the other. When Stefan asked if she wanted him to come over, she said no. Perhaps it was the pressure of his longing to comfort her and the uselessness of that comfort that she hadn't been able to bear, although she would beg his forgiveness before flying off to Frankfurt the next day.

There had been no vulnerability like that she'd felt after her parents died. Danger lurked everywhere. She could not step off a curb without thinking of falling. The horror and randomness of their deaths terrified her. She quailed in the face of it. How fragile her body was. She shook climbing into a car, panicked if she had to drive for more than half an hour at a stretch. Avoided elevators and escalators, had nervous attacks in the echoing, cement-walled stairwells of buildings in which she climbed stairs to avoid the elevators or escalators. Every journey, no matter how tiny, held the possibility of death within it. Within one possibility lay others, lay innumerable deaths, all the way to the molecular level. Standing on a subway platform she was certain of tumbling onto the tracks. Or being pushed. A cyst at the base of one finger meant cancer. Her reactions were hysterical. Knowing this didn't help. Claire's only reassurance was that Kyra McCloud, a friend whose father had died of leukemia two years before her parents' death, had gone through almost the same thing.

It saddened Claire that Stefan would never know her as a woman with parents. In those first five weeks, she had not yet been ready to introduce him to them. Instead she found herself reduced to photographs, to anecdote. (Here's my mother with her parrot in Ethiopia, my father outside Addis on his motorbike.) Stefan would never see her in her parents' presence, have her revealed in some new, idiosyncratic light by how she behaved around them. She had met Stefan's mother, Helene, and stepfather, Richard, on several visits to Ottawa. They welcomed her with the slightly exaggerated warmth of people who felt a little sorry for her (both parents, so young, such a tragedy). Stefan did not talk much about his father, Tomas, an importer of what Claire was never quite certain, who lived part-time in Florida. She'd met him once, over an awkward restaurant dinner.

She played Stefan the last recording that she possessed of her parents' voices, captured on what had been the tape from her answering machine. A couple of weeks before they flew to Germany, Hugh and Sylvia had each phoned and left messages on the same night, as if unaware that the other had done so. A power generator had blown in the east end of the city. Whole neighbourhoods were in darkness. From the west, Hugh called to see if Claire was all right – she lived on her own (if in the same house as Allison and Lennie), and she was his youngest daughter. He had a habit of making such calls. After massive thunderstorms or on nights of sheet ice. Later, Sylvia, on the fainter bedroom phone, invited Claire to dinner, perhaps without leaving the bedroom where she liked to curl up and read on the bed, perhaps without speaking to Hugh, without knowing there'd been a blackout at all. Claire did not get home until late: there'd been no power outage in the restaurant where she'd eaten dinner with friends, or at the house, though she would discover that a friend of hers gave birth that night, a planned home birth not planned for candlelight. After the accident, she took the tape out of the answering machine. It was just luck that she hadn't erased their voices, so unbearably ordinary, having no idea what they were hurtling towards. She listened to the tape once with Stefan, then never again.

During the first months after her parents died, the only thing Claire really wanted to read, it seemed, were maps. She piled them at her bedside, bought atlases the way other people bought CDs, pored over maps of anywhere in the world except Germany. The maps made the world seem reachable, less over-whelming. Stefan brought her road maps, atlases, a glow-in-the-dark globe. She spread the maps out across her bed. She whispered place names to herself, trying to edge towards sleep, a hard place to get to. Oaxaca, Madagascar, Isola di Capri. Sometimes she broke down. She didn't know if she wanted to go away or stay in one spot. She needed the awareness of other places and the rooting of home. On any map, so much is missing. This drew her attention and broke her heart. She clutched an old school ruler of her mother's or slept with it under her pillow. Place names and measurements ricocheted through her head during sex. Small and lean, leaner than she'd be at any other time, Claire tucked herself against Stefan's body. She raged. Some nights Stefan asked if he should stay away. Some nights she said yes. Bewildered, she didn't know what she wanted. (But he was *there*, he came back, he didn't abandon her. He approached her gently. He suggested things they might do together.) Longing felt like something that entered her from outside, a betrayal of grief. Even on those nights when she was alone, she began to shepherd herself towards sleep by imagining Stefan beside her.

Strangely, her migraines seemed unaffected by her parents' death. They did not grow suddenly worse or more frequent, although some days she suffered the uncomfortable illusion of having a pill stuck permanently in her throat, even when she'd swallowed nothing. Rachel agreed that her migraines hadn't worsened either.

Nor did their headaches suddenly ease. Sadly. (In Housing, one floor below the map department, Claire met a woman who didn't have a migraine for two years after her husband died.)

"I spoke to that guy, the healer, earlier this evening," Claire said. The rain had stopped, but water still raced through the drainpipes beneath the window, and the air was full of ozone and the odour of wet bark. "He called me back."

Stefan rolled on his near side to face her. "Where was he calling from? I thought you said he was in Israel or Geneva."

"He was in Geneva. Maybe he likes to make international calls in the middle of the night." The healer, Ariel, had a strong Israeli accent. Over the phone, Claire had not known what to make of him. "He invited me to come to Amsterdam."

"Why? Can't he tell you whatever he knows over the phone?"

"He said he doesn't know where Rachel is. He hasn't heard from her since March. He also said he thought he could help me."

"Help you how?"

It was the healer's insistence, his conviction that he could help that had made the strongest impression, the implication not necessarily being that he would be able to help her find Rachel but that he could help in her own search for health. He had said he would ask his angels for guidance when it came to looking for Rachel. His angels. "With my headaches, I think. But maybe he knows more than he's letting on. I can't tell. I'm thinking maybe I should go. Maybe she's still in Europe."

Detective Bird had finally called them back. He'd confirmed that Rachel had flown from Montreal via Toronto to Amsterdam, on KLM, on March 16. She had cancelled her return date of March 23. The return portion of the ticket had not, or not yet, been used. Of course this did not necessarily mean she was still in Europe. Since Rachel lived in the US, if they wanted to access other records with some efficiency, they might want to hire an American private investigator.

Claire could not imagine Detective Bird having much patience with the peculiarities of a man such as Ariel.

"I'm finding things out, aren't I? I found out why she flew to Amsterdam. Or one reason, anyway. I keep trying to decide how I'll feel if I don't go, if I don't and Rachel doesn't turn up. She went to him three times, and maybe she'd have gone more – we don't know. He's unconventional, clearly, but maybe he does something that works. He says people travel from all over to see him."

"You said he heals with energy." Stefan sounded, not dismissive, but a little dubious.

"He says he talks to angels, too."

"Claire."

"You want me to find something that will help with the headaches, don't you?"

"Yes, okay, yes."

"I don't know how to judge any of this without seeing him."

"Can you take more time off work?"

"Charlie knows what I'm doing. I'll make up the hours."

"When would you go?"

"He's going to be in Amsterdam next week, so I guess some time next week, presumably staying over the Saturday night afterwards so the ticket's cheaper. Anyway, it's not really my money. Think of it as some of the insurance money. I can afford it because of what happened to my parents, and they would want me to do this. Don't you think?" With a finger, she traced Stefan's cheekbone and the familiar line of his long nose. She wanted him to acknowledge the strength of what she was doing, the initiative. "Can I live with myself if I don't go is what I keep wondering. I'm trying to take care of things."

Three years into their relationship, Claire and Stefan had taken a week-long trip to the Caribbean island of St. Kitts. Most of their money and energy was being spent renovating their house, but they were tired of renovation and tired of that long, long stretch of late winter that refuses to concede even the possibility of early spring, and so decided on the spur of the moment to do something neither of them had done before: book a last-minute package vacation south.

Claire did not mind flying, only its physiological effects on her. Those who simply feared flight could drug themselves into a torpor and wake up stunned at their destination. She was awed by those who extracted themselves from airplane seats upon arrival feeling little more than cramped and woozy or sleep deprived. Once or twice she had experienced this, like a miracle, but long flights, transatlantic, anything over an hour, were neurochemically taxing. Flight attendants were as alien to her as those who drank alcohol on planes: she could no more conceive of doing their job than being a seven-foot-tall basketball star or a contortionist. She didn't know how Rachel flew as much as she did, although according to Rachel, drugs still worked for her even when in the air, or had until recently.

In St. Kitts, as she had done upon other occasions, Claire answered the immigration official's questions while silvery with nausea. She was in the midst of the most profound physical dislocation. Other people must experience a version of this but not so intensely or so painfully. Being in any airport was hard even when, like this one, it was open to the air and had no escalators.

Everything outside her was reduced to surface. Suitcase. Floor. Thatched roof. She didn't experience auras but there were other forms of sensory distortion. Bright objects were spiked, sunlight an anathema. Odours heaved towards her: smoke, the miasma of car exhaust. She could identify things but was incapable of providing any context for them or making their relationships clear. Heat. Sky. Stefan's back. The burning point behind her right eye. Walk to the van. Part of her remained mute.

They drove. Sugarcane. Town. Road. Ocean. White hotel.

A chamber-boy led them up a flight of white cement stairs. The stairs were covered but open to the air, windows mere squares in the plaster. Outside: a pile of refuse, palm trees, hydro line, houses with corrugated metal roofs, mountain. On the phone they'd had to choose: room over the pool or room with a view. They'd hesitated. A view sounded good, but Stefan had picked pool, on the theory that the question was rigged and something was missing, namely the ocean. And there it lay, beyond the pool, over the edge of a cliff. Vindicated, he coaxed Claire out to the balcony where they stripped off their shoes and sat for a moment in plastic chairs, their bare feet up on the railing and stared (Claire in hat and sunglasses, eyes slits, perched on the edge of her chair, stomach heaving) out into the blue Atlantic. Three points beat a tattoo along the top of her head. Back inside, Stefan unbuttoned his shirt. How effortlessly the journey peeled from him. Narrow-chested but lithe, he seemed ready to leap from one place to another, the hunch of his shoulders already unfurling. How easily his olive skin, unlike her paler flesh, would tan.

Claire removed her toilet bag from her suitcase. From her carry-on bag, she took the remains of a bottle of water and a small red tin of Tiger Balm. She'd grown accustomed to the orange unguent's burning smell. It had the lustre of the familiar, something to cling to when the rest of the sensory world was at sea. Perhaps it helped ease the muscles of her neck and temples. Or not. The hope that it did counted. She rubbed some into her skin, then tottered to the bathroom, moistened a face cloth and carried the face cloth back, a bleary five paces, to the nearest of the two double beds, where she collapsed. She hadn't thrown up yet and hoped she wouldn't. She unzipped her cotton trousers, stepped out of them, and embarked upon the only act of intimacy she felt capable of. "Stef, can you inject me?"

The first time that she had been injected with Imitrex, the first time that she had ever tried the drug, it was Rachel who had done the injecting. Out of the haze of a Frankfurt hotel room, just off the plane from New York, Rachel had appeared, in a white spring coat, leaning over Claire. Try this, Rachel said quietly, pulling a pale-blue appendage that looked like an oversized ballpoint pen out of her handbag. Allison was also in the room, in a chair by the window, all three of them pale and numb and red-eyed. Claire and Allison had arrived from Toronto earlier that morning. Give me your thigh, Rachel said calmly as she pulled back the sheets and exposed Claire in her underwear. She held the injector to Claire's skin and pressed a small red button at the end of the pen. There was no needle to be seen. Claire simply felt the prick as the point of the invisible needle pierced her. That first time the drug had worked like a dream, releasing her, the erasure of the headache a perverse miracle in those cataclysmic hours after her parents were killed. In half an hour, Claire was able to stumble to her feet.

Since then the drug had never worked quite as effectively. Sometimes she took it as a pill. The injections worked more swiftly but were more expensive. She also hated injecting herself. Because there was no element of surprise, her muscles tensed in anticipation, which left a bruise. Even when Stefan asked *ready?*, she could not predict exactly when he would press the button.

He said he didn't mind giving her injections. He injected plenty of mice on the job. This thought was not altogether comforting, but at least Stefan had no anxiety about needles. Instrument in hand, he approached Claire. Sometimes they tried to make a game of it, although Claire was not often up to this. Once Stefan put down the injector, forehead wrinkling, and said he hated causing her pain, even in a minor way, though he would do whatever he could to make her feel better. Then he jabbed her.

Ah. Claire pulled a sheet over herself and covered her eyes with the face cloth. Here they were on a Caribbean island and she had to fall apart, discover some new neural alignment, before her body would let her enter the new place. The visible world retreated. The drug tightened the breath in her chest. It made her fingertips tingle. In the dark space she'd created, she concentrated on her body's bounded edges and the drug speeding through her, each chemical shift a slight shift in sensation. It was not like being carried towards orgasm in any way except there was an edge, a line you crossed that lifted you towards release and sometimes you travelled there straightaway, you flew, you crossed over, and sometimes you travelled towards but failed to cross the line, you approached then stalled, you knew the state you longed for but you could not long too much. Neither could you give in to despair. You did not know in advance how the journey would go. Wait, patient. Hopeful. Claire lay with arms outstretched, palms raised.

The ecstasy came afterwards, once the pain had passed.

"Why don't you go downstairs and get some lunch? Or go to the pool." Her disembodied voice. "Can you order me a tuna-salad sandwich?" In a couple of hours, she would feel better. She would. For the moment, as much as Claire wanted Stefan with her, she wanted him gone, his presence as forceful as a smell, though her repellence only masked her guilt and deeper exasperation at herself.

The door clicked. Once gone, she wanted him back, desperately. Through the open window, from below, chinaware clanged. Someone smashed into the pool, displacing air and water for miles. A saline ocean breeze flooded Claire, stinging her nostrils, plunging her into a sinkhole of sadness. In her mind, she tried to follow Stefan's path but gave up.

Some time later, the door opened. She removed the face cloth from her eyes as Stefan appeared in blurry outline beside the bed. He asked how she was feeling. Better, she murmured. He sat gently on the edge of the bed but made no attempt to kiss her. Sometimes she did not want to be touched. Sometimes she asked him to lie in the dark beside her, touching but not stroking her palm, this being all the contact she could manage, even the lightest touch communicating all that was active and persistent about him.

Even without touch she could feel his desire to get moving, be doing something. Make plans. Which she was decidedly impeding. At the best of times these were attributes she loved about him. He was trying to submerge, to overcome his frustration. She sensed this. He knew all this was not her fault. He knew she wanted to be on her feet as much as he wanted her to be. On the whole, he was sympathetic and patient with her, for all that he was not a headache sufferer himself, other than occasional muscular twitches that a couple of ibuprofen sent away. He had broken bones, which she hadn't, and infrequently suffered from rashes on his hands and neck that made him horribly self-conscious. He would have preferred her migraines to have a clearly identifiable cause (and solution), but, thankfully, did not seem to think her a hypochondriac. In their early days, Claire had hoped that her happiness in his presence might itself work as a cure, although she had not held it against Stefan when this hadn't happened.

Downstairs, he said, there was an outdoor dining area facing the ocean. You could see the ocean at the horizon beyond the pool and through some palm trees. Blackbirds kept leaping from table to table, stealing crumbs of bread and sugar and sticking their beaks into the pots of jam and ketchup. Someone would bring her sandwich in a minute.

Soon, soon she would try to sit up.

Afterwards came the giddiness, the conviction that everything was going to be all right, everything *was*. Still fragile, still in some chemical flux, at least Claire was standing, showering with Stefan, running her hands, the miniature bar of hotel soap, over his back. They kissed. Towelled dry and changed before her, Stefan seated himself at the white wicker desk and booked a rental car by phone so that they could circumnavigate the island in the morning (Claire's desire), then drive to the beach.

It was still light, if approaching dusk, when they set out for dinner, taking a right turn immediately upon passing through the hotel gate and following the road that switchbacked slowly towards the harbour and Basseterre, the capital, the town they'd barely passed through and which Claire had barely glimpsed, on their way from the airport. On their left, another single-storey hotel was sandwiched between the pastel enclosing walls of private dwellings and hedges of bougainvillea. On their right, through scrubby trees, appeared the cliff that toppled down to the sea.

Stefan had dressed for dinner in a white shirt that he had pressed himself back in Toronto, a shirt on which a line of red stitching ran around the collar and down the front. It might have been something his mother had given him. Like Claire, he wore sandals, his long toes protruding beyond the brown leather straps. She slipped her hand in his.

"Talk to me," she said. He seemed, now, a little distracted.

"I was thinking about when I met you."

"And then my parents died. Our timing was terrible."

"About right when I met you. Not the very first time, the second time, at that party. I was thinking about the way you walked into the room. You'd gone to the kitchen to get drinks and you were coming back. There was something about the way you looked. You seemed so self-possessed. Like you knew how to look after yourself. It was very important to me. Or when we went to that movie and you left your gloves and the guy didn't want to let you back inside because the next showing had started but you insisted."

This was going somewhere, although Claire wasn't yet certain where. "Okay."

"Even when your parents died, you didn't totally fall apart. Half the time I didn't know what to do but you rallied. I admired you so much."

"You could have run away. You didn't."

"But sometimes I worry because even though it doesn't seem like you need looking after, actually you do."

"Everybody does sometimes."

"What about your headaches, Claire? Sometimes you are truly incapacitated."

"I ask you to inject me, and sometimes I ask you to bring me things like crackers or a glass of water but I don't ask you to look after me."

He was frowning at the horizon. "No, I know, I know, but I worry about you. I worry — I worry that I *want* to look after you."

She was puzzled. "And that's wrong?"

"I worry about what the desire means. I told myself, after being with Jenny, that I wanted, I needed to be with someone who didn't need looking after. I was frightened I was falling into a pattern, of looking after people. And when I met you, you didn't seem like that."

Jenny, whom Stefan had been involved with before Claire, was a fellow researcher, who worked in a genetics lab in a hospital just down the street from his. She suffered from depression and sometimes would take to her bed for weeks, refusing her medication, at which point, Stefan, who had never actually lived with her, virtually moved into her apartment in order to take care of her.

Behind Jenny, Claire knew, there was another haunting, probably the greater one, although Stefan did not mention it. During his adolescence, his mother had been so miserable as her marriage to his father broke down that she had spent afternoons for weeks at a time zonked out on tranquilizers on the living-room couch. Stefan, not his older brother or younger sister, had been the one trying to rouse her, to look after her.

What if Stefan *were* unconsciously attracted to her migraines, to her as a woman with migraines? "It's a neurological condition," Claire said. "I deal with it as best I can. I try not to let it stop me."

"And you don't, but in the beginning I had no idea how often you got them."

"You don't have to worry about me, really you don't."

"I'm not saying any of this because I'm unhappy. Claire? I just needed to talk things out a little."

"And you feel better?"

"Yes."

He gripped her hand. They kept walking.

Though Stefan seemed released from whatever had been troubling him, it was Claire's turn to feel preoccupied. Unsettled. Unmoored. They descended into the town and, taking off their sandals, strolled a little way along the sandy shore of the harbour where, a day later, they would watch women scrape the scales from fish with bottle caps nailed to a piece of board, and men press transistor radios to their ears, desperate for the latest on the West Indian cricket team in a Test match, and a girl whose hair formed black burrs all over her head would follow Claire and tug at her skirt and beg to be taken home with them. As the beautiful equatorial dusk dropped into dark, they passed small wooden fishing boats, overturned for the night, and Claire couldn't help noticing the one painted pink with a red stripe beneath the gunwales named *Patience*.

Everything she'd counted on felt suddenly fragile. Stefan. Stefan's support. The life they had, the life they were in the process of creating. Who she was. The nature of her vulnerability. The version of herself that Stefan saw and was drawn to. She had never thought of the migraines as a sign of weakness only as something that had to be borne. But perhaps he did see her as weak, incapacitated, a kind of invalid. Now she was the one feeling frightened.

How much of another's pain can anyone bear? Everyone has limits. But they had come this far, had already been through so much. Surely they would be all right.

They headed back to a seafood restaurant on the near side of the harbour, right on the water, which a woman at the hotel had suggested to them. Cheered now, Stefan ordered a beer and then a Ting, while Claire stuck to bottled water. Beneath the table, Stefan squeezed her thigh. She wanted fish. How could you be by the ocean and not eat fish? But her snapper proved a bad choice, full of tiny perilous bones, and halfway through the meal Claire realized her headache was rising again on the other side. Pain travelled, it traversed the hemispheres. It slipped free of whatever bonds in which you tried to enclose it, its veil cast aside. The migraine moved from one side to the other. This was normal, yet she was on the edge of capsizing into despair, convinced she was doing something terribly wrong only she had no idea what. She was failing Stefan. She downed a 292, despite the fact that codeine was barely useful any more. She couldn't take any more Imitrex until she got back to the hotel. She ordered a tea. Stefan took one look at her and, aware of her distraction and pallor, quietly asked if she wanted to go back.

Claire shook her head. Are you sure? She nodded. So Stefan ordered dessert, a slice of key-lime pie. Claire said she would try a bit. She held on to the sides of her chair, knuckles tightening. The moon was rising round and white through a window beyond Stefan's right shoulder. To remain sitting upright was a feat of strength – couldn't he see that?

*I*n less than twenty-four hours Claire was to leave for Amsterdam. At 3:07 a.m., she had woken cleanly and completely, Stefan shifting restlessly beside her. She was travelling back to Europe for the first time in eight years. She and Stefan had been to St. Kitts and San Francisco and London, but London was not (quite) Europe. They had spoken of going to Brazil together and to Dubrovnik, where Stefan's father's family had come from, now that things had settled down in the regions of the former Yugoslavia, but so far had done no more than speak of these trips. Amsterdam wasn't Frankfurt. There was no reason to think that Rachel had gone from Amsterdam to Frankfurt, was there?

There were times when Claire became obsessed with the minutiae of decisions that had led to her parents' death. Which of them had booked the flight to Frankfurt, and why that flight and not another? It wasn't that she wanted to blame either of them (there were other people, companies, who had legally been declared responsible for the accident), only to understand the sequence of events at every point along the way, as if knowledge of each moment would help to make sense of the calamitous whole. Had her mother or her father picked out that luggage cart? Why that escalator? Why were they riding an upward bound escalator anyway, leaving the arrivals level, rising towards departures? Were there better cafés on the departure level? Were they lost?

At 3:17, Claire slipped from bed and made her way along the hall. In her study, she switched on the light and crouched in front of the bottom shelf where she stored the family photo albums.

Allison had asked for the albums. When they cleared out their parents' house, the three of them had decided that Claire would take possession of them, since she was the most organized and therefore the albums would be safest with her. These days it was possible, even without the negatives (which, in any case, Claire had) to make copies of the photographs and grew easier, as the technology developed, with every passing year, but Allison didn't want copies, she wanted the originals, photographs held in place by little black triangular tabs and labelled in their mother's neat hand. It was true that by the time of the later albums, Sylvia had dispensed with much of the labelling but the earlier albums were all carefully annotated, some photos simply identified with the place and the date, others more suggestively or cryptically marked. The labels, less reproducible than the images, were part of what Allison wanted.

She'd asked to keep the albums — keep them for a while, anyway — at her house. She wanted, she said, to show the albums, the history of their family, to the girls, now that they were old enough to take some interest in them, rather than trying to rip the photos off the pages. Since their actual grandparents weren't there for them to meet, this was the closest they could come to them. Allison didn't come out and say that Claire should think about passing the albums on (at least for a while) because Claire did not have a child, although, to Claire's way of thinking, this was the implication. Allison seemed to be assuming that Claire and Stefan were not going to have a child, perhaps because it seemed likely that if they had been planning to, they would have done something about it, or tried, by now. Claire had not confided in Allison about the current nature of their dilemma or negotiations. She did not think that Allison could help her. Stefan's desire for a child was normal, it was entirely understandable; the problem, if there was a problem, lay with her.

Soon she would hand the albums over. (Wasn't there a certain logic to the contrary argument, that she should retain the albums precisely because, lacking a child, she had no genetic proof of her parents' presence?) She dipped into them occasionally but not often. There were a few gaps on the pages where Rachel and Allison had already taken photographs that they particularly desired. Mostly, the albums just sat on the bottom shelf, lined up chronologically, dusted every now and again. When she and Allison were teenagers, they had sometimes descended to the basement of the Rockingham Drive bungalow to giggle over the pictures of their childhoods, the winged haircuts, bad sunglasses, mile-wide pants. And to puzzle over the earlier photos, from before they were born, photos that gestured towards stories, stories they partly knew but now would never fully know and whose details they now had to reconstruct for themselves.

Claire pulled out an album marked 1964.

Near death in Samburu-Land. Sylvia stood stiffly beside a dusty, aging Jeep, one back wheel missing, replaced by a jack. She must have been twenty-seven. After the year teaching in Addis, Hugh and Sylvia (who was already pregnant with Allison) and Rachel set off south through Ethiopia and Kenya towards Tanzania. In Kenya, somewhere in Samburu country, they got a flat tire (hardly their first) on a stretch of desert road. Perhaps a thorn had tumbled across the tarmac. Watched by a gaggle of goat-herding children, Hugh was trying to boost the vehicle when the unoiled jack seized up. Rachel, only a toddler, was buckled into the back seat (these being the days before and a place out of the reach of mandatory child car seats). Kneeling beside her, Hugh was in the midst of extracting a shovel from the storage space behind the seat, when Sylvia, standing outside, kicked the jack so hard that it released, jouncing the Jeep and Hugh and sending the shovel end veering towards his head — two inches closer and it might have broken his neck.

(Wasn't every life full of potential abandonments and near-escapes from accidental death?)

Bogged down by Lake Bog. Sylvia, pale and squinting beneath a sun hat, was holding hands with Rachel, beside the Jeep, axle deep in mud. Beyond them stretched a bleak lake, Lake Bog-something, whose shore was speckled with white dots. The dots were flamingos. Sylvia had been driving, desperate to get as close as she could to the shore and the birds, when the Jeep went down in what was perhaps a rainy-season riverbed. Frantic, Hugh was convinced it would take days to get them out. He'd heard tales — people stuck for weeks. They were in the middle of a wildlife preserve on a Kenyan national holiday and no one was about. Perhaps Sylvia offered to go in search of help, since she was the one who'd got them stuck in the first place, but Hugh refused and told her to stay put. He left Sylvia and Rachel in the Jeep and trekked four kilometres out to the park entrance and beyond, until he stumbled upon a farmer ploughing his fields, whom he convinced and paid to drive his tractor back into the park. Four hours later, perched beside the driver on top of the tractor, Hugh returned to find the Jeep, mud-mired, sun-soaked, and empty. He panicked. He banged open the Jeep's doors, screaming their names, until, rising over a lip of land, down near the shore, a tiny figure in a hat appeared, waving, calling out, Hulloo, hulloo, an even tinier figure attached to it — as the flamingos rose up en masse, leaving nothing but a sea of guano, and fled to the far bank.

There were no photographs from either their mother's or their father's childhoods during the Second World War, only ones taken before the war and after. Hugh had spent the war years in London, apart from some months when he was sent to stay with cousins in Surrey, until, in his presence, a dog fight tore down the main street of Oxted — a German fighter plane, a Messerschmidt, twisted on its side, two English pilots in pursuit, wing tips inches, or so it seemed, above his head as he fell to his stomach in the middle of the sidewalk. After that, his parents demanded his return. Sylvia lived through the war at home in Norwich. Her house was not bombed, although the school at the end of her street was. She claimed not to remember the bombs, not to remember the war at all.

After the war, Sylvia's father, Granddad Hill, who had worked for the airforce in civil defense, went back to his job in the city hall library, a job he hated and from which he could not get promoted because the man he worked for was mean and possibly crazy. Frustration made him unhappy. Unhappiness made him angry. Her mother, who suffered from what she called sick headaches, would close the curtains and take to her bed. Eight when the war ended, Sylvia was nine when her parents sent her to stay with her father's aunts, Lucy and Nell, in the countryside near Newmarket. It was her duty to go, they told her. In times of hardship, everyone must put up with things.

The years after the war were as hard as the war in their way. There was little food (endless meals of bread and dripping) and little coal, and what coal there was was lousy and barely stayed alight. They were always cold. There was not much more food at the aunts' (no more sugar, no more meat) and the house, being made of stone, was even colder than Sylvia's parents' house had been. Her first winter in the country, the terrible winter of '47, it did nothing but snow. She and the great-aunts all suffered chilblains but at least the aunts were cheerful about them. Sometime around then, Sylvia's own headaches began. She was allowed to keep Slim, the aunts' wire-haired fox terrier, on her bed when she felt ill, although the company she really craved was that of their parrot, Dottie, who spoke in a Norfolk accent as broad as that of any local farmer. In addition to the dog and parrot, they kept a goat and chickens and harvested apples from their half-wild orchard. The aunts insisted Sylvia keep bird lists. They rewarded her with an apple for each new bird she spotted. They made apple sauce, apple pie, apple bread, apple charlotte, apple snow, apple wine. Every few months, they sent Sylvia home to her parents for a visit, laden with goat cheese, eggs, a bag of apples. She must have assumed that her life, at least her childhood, would go on like this, in the company of the great-aunts, visiting her parents, that she had been partially, if not wholly, given up by the latter, which was not, perhaps, such a terrible thing. When she was eleven, however, her parents sold their house in Norwich, stole her back, and took her away with them across the ocean to the farthest fringe of Western Canada to begin a new life (another new life), where there were green mountains but where she knew none, or almost none, of the birds.

High Park, Toronto, April, 1960. At twenty-three, her spring coat open, her dark dress flowing over her knees, Sylvia sits on a picnic table, her toes pressed against the picnic bench, her heels raised, her low pumps slipping away from her feet. Her posture is a little stiff, as if she is about to take flight but is restraining herself. Her expression is quizzical or self-protective, nearly a squint. She is not obviously beautiful, not glamorous, her dark hair puffed and a little mussed. She seems about to raise her hand to shield her eyes as she faces the young man, the medical student, behind the camera.

What did she hope for her future?

She lived in an apartment in Toronto at the corner of College and Dufferin with two other girls. She owned a parrot named Lucy. (Her first parrot, Frieda, she'd bought for herself, over her parents' protests, at thirteen.) Back home in Victoria, she'd proved herself an able birder. She'd even won a New Year's bird count, the year she turned sixteen. She would lecture anyone on the intelligence of parrots. Now, a year out of university, the first in her family ever to attend and graduate, she worked for a distributor of religious books, not because she was particularly religious or even because this was the only job she could find that had any connection to winged creatures, but because it was the best job she could turn up. It was steady. She needed the money. She wanted to be able to look after herself. She recognized, especially given her combination of job and interests, that others might find her odd. She had fallen in love with another English major, blond and sunny, a fellow birder not nearly as good as she was; she had given herself wholly to the dream of their life together when he up and left her for a brassy redhead who wanted to be an actress.

A year later, the wound of this abandonment was still raw. Four years before, when she'd moved east, an acquaintance in Victoria had given her the phone number of her brother in Toronto. Sylvia had written it dutifully into her address book but had never called. When she stumbled upon the number once again, she had no idea if it was current. The male voice that answered still bore a trace of an English accent, but then he had come over later than she had, at sixteen. He seemed at first subdued but roused himself to gregariousness. He mumbled something about having been away, having taken a semester off. He was returning to medical school in the fall. In person she warmed more to him — he entertained her and was clearly smart — although a certain sombreness never left him. He carried Charles Dodgson's books of mathematical puzzles around in his pockets the way other people carried paperback thrillers. One afternoon he went out and bought a car, like that, and picked her up at work in it. She sensed things churning beneath his surface, the pressure of unspoken things, but this didn't frighten her exactly. It felt familiar. He was going to be a doctor, a good career. The past was the past, they both said: whatever it was, you put it behind you. If his attentions towards her had been too dramatic, without some tempering of caution, she might have mistrusted him, for all that she was eager for, was desperate for, love.

*I*n Amsterdam everyone was talking, in excellent English, about soccer. The taxi driver who picked up Claire and her bags at Schiphol was lamenting the heartbreaking loss of the Dutch team to the Italians in the Euro 2000 semifinals the week before and admitting to the bittersweet pleasure of watching the Italians go down to defeat at the hands of the French in the final four days past. All the games had been played in Dutch and Belgian stadiums. The city, as they entered it, was still festooned with orange bunting, the Dutch team's colour. Without prompting, the young, bespectacled man at the reception desk of the Ambassade Hotel regaled Claire with stories of the night the Dutch had routed the Yugoslavs, and their brilliant playing against the Danes. Those nights, there was dancing in the streets and on the bridges over the canals, and young girls and their grandmothers bicycled safely home under a full moon at 3 a.m. All the way up the five narrow and neck-breakingly steep flights of stairs to her sloping attic room, the bellhop talked of nothing but Overmars and Kluivert, the grace of Overmars, the swiftness of Kluivert, until Claire was nearly dizzy. The room struck her as instantly familiar, a mere three paces wide – as diminutive as the rooms in her house in Toronto, which helped ground the part of her that wondered what in heaven's name she was doing here.

The glass in the windows at the front of the room was old, and moved, not quite solid. It had been falling slowly, perhaps for centuries, within its pane, which distorted its translucency and the view ever so slightly. Single-paned, the window opened with a clatter upon a scene that could not have made Claire happier. She was high above one of the city's canals. Steep rooftops, staggered like steps, rose across from her, some with hooks projecting beneath the eaves from which ropes and pulleys hauled goods that would not fit through the narrow doors, but only through the wide frames of the windows.

It was Thursday morning. She was to meet Ariel, the healer, the next day. Until then, she was on her own. Jet-lagged, drugged, she lay down on the bed, on its gold chenille spread, above a royal purple carpet, and listened to the sounds of the street rising up from below. The whirr and rattle of bicycles, the ping of their bells. The bleating of moorhens or – she couldn't yet tell which – the squeaking of boats, and ropes, against their moorings. The sounds that said Amsterdam, that made it clear she was not in Toronto or New York.

It had been a month, four days ago exactly a month, since Brad Arnarson had first called her.

Once before, she'd come to Amsterdam, a brief stopover in the middle of her rite-of-passage backpacking tour through

Europe at twenty-one. She and Gabrielle Rosen, a fellow cartography student from Windsor, Ontario, had arrived late at night on a Sunday train from Bruges, hungry and grimy and confident they'd have no trouble finding a room, an affordable room, only to discover the city booked up. From a phone booth by the information kiosk in the railway station they kept calling, with increasing desperation, hotel after budget hotel until they managed at last to snare, not an expensive room, but one already beyond their means, with floor-length red velvet curtains that drifted down from somewhere near the ceiling and a double mattress that sank into such a valley that there was nothing they could do to stop themselves from toppling towards each other all night. Two sweaty girls in their underwear. They barely slept for laughing. The next day they moved into a hostel and spent the evening stumbling wide-eyed through the red-light district. Yet Claire had no sense then of this being a city of canals, a city built on water.

Once the drugs had kicked in and her head began to clear, she roused herself. She scanned the street map of Amsterdam, which the hotel had provided, then folded it into her shoulder bag. With luck, given her ability to orient herself visually, even in places she'd never been before, and her knack for not getting lost (only London, once, with its ancient curlicues of streets, had got the better of her), she wouldn't need the map again.

Outside the hotel, she turned right and walked a little way beside the waters of the Herengracht until she came to the intersection of Oude Spiegelstraat, on her right, and, running left, over a little bridge, Wolvenstraat. She turned left, crossed the bridge, and walked a block past a row of shops to Kelzersgracht, the next canal. She looked to her left and right, turned left and then, at the intersection of Huidenstraat, left again, entering a row of shops that sold comestibles. Here she found what she was looking for: a greengrocer, cheese shop, bakery. She bought olives, green apples, goat cheese, almond tarts, and in a tearoom-chocolaterie, as a present for Stefan, chocolates flavoured with Earl Grey tea. Dark chocolate, a tart and smoky ganache. She tried one herself, having never tasted tea-flavoured chocolate before. Her head felt light and fine now. Invincible. As if she were meant to be here.

While the paths of arrival that led to a new place – the bus from Newark airport, the Piccadilly line from Heathrow, the van ride into Basseterre – were often seared with pain, the settling in, after that first spasm, could provide sudden release. Sometimes the spell lasted for days, a week, even two weeks. Fourteen days without a twinge or pang of migraine was possible, *and* a kind of miracle. In some sense, Claire surmised, you chemically jump-started your system – cut its ties, cut it loose, cut the familiar treading of certain neural pathways. The brain was forced to recreate itself by breathing different air and eating different food and walking different streets. There was always a point at which you allowed yourself to believe that this time you were home-free, you had liberated yourself from whatever ailed you, a true transformation had taken place. If you stayed, you might remain pain-free forever.

She wondered if Rachel felt this, too. Perhaps it was the lure of the city – any new city or specifically Amsterdam, city of gurus and dope-smokers and asylum-seekers and hidden rooms – that had brought her here, as much as the promise of treatment by a man who spoke to angels. Rachel had arrived in Amsterdam on March 17, four days before seeing Ariel on the twenty-first. What had she been up to during that time, days when she could have been in Toronto visiting Star? Or had she been so ill, so driven to see Ariel that she'd dropped everything and come here as soon as she could?

It was Ariel who had given Claire the name of the Ambassade Hotel – not real luxe, but no budget hotel, either. He had offered to provide the name of a budget hotel or even a hostel if she needed. She'd asked if he knew where Rachel had stayed in Amsterdam – the same hotel? No, he thought she'd stayed with someone. A friend. (Claire had not uncovered any business cards with Amsterdam addresses in Rachel's apartment.)

What if by chance Rachel had called in and picked up the first message from Amy Levin, the one left on her voice mail, which Claire couldn't access? What if she were on her way to Amsterdam even now? And yet if Rachel had set up her own appointment with Ariel, surely Ariel, or Amy, would have let Claire know.

She kept walking.

The transformation a new place afforded was not simply the release from pain. The place itself was transforming. The streets Claire walked along moved from her feet up into her body. At the place where she and the city met, as the city entered her and became part of her, she herself was changed. An orange-canopied bar on the Prinsengracht would remain in her forever. The view from the Leidsegracht across the Keizersgracht through a second-storey window to an abstract painting on a white wall.

A city linked not just by roads but by water offered more fluid possibilities of travel: a city built on blocks not gridded but curved. Her limbs, her brain felt lissome, calmed, now, like the water and tall houses under bright sunlight. In the future, the meeting of the Leidsegracht and the Keizersgracht would surface in her, encoding this calm.

Ariel had given Claire an address. She asked the concierge if she could reach the place on foot or if she needed to take a taxi. He said she could walk if she wished but to follow his directions closely – he pulled out a map of the city and drew a route on it – because all the streets looked the same. She would have to walk *here*, through the red-light district.

The weather was warm and sunny, once again hazy but not too hot.

This morning, once again, Claire was headache-free.

The street she entered at last was narrow, nondescript, not on water. The same tall brick houses rose towards the sky, the old interspersed with the new, all accented with window boxes. The building she wanted was an old one. A male voice greeted her and she was buzzed up. She ascended a white, wooden staircase, passing a woman in a trim red jacket who was descending. On the fourth landing, the door to apartment three stood ajar. Claire knocked, perhaps too softly, waited for a response and, receiving none, pushed the door open. To her left, in a small kitchen, stood a man clothed all in white. White jeans. White T-shirt. Barefoot. A man of perhaps fifty, not tall, neither thin nor plump, solidly built and of middle height, with a suggestion of feline suppleness, waited for a kettle to boil above a ring of blue flame on a gas stove.

"Hello," Claire said, "I'm Claire Barber."

The man swept her, startled, into his arms. "Ariel. I am so happy to see you."

He did not give her now, nor did he ever mention a surname. His accent was as pronounced as on the telephone. He hugged, then released her. Stepping back to the stove, he poured boiling water from the kettle into a white teapot, from which rose an aroma like straw, and asked Claire if she wanted a cup. When she said no, he motioned her out of the kitchen and asked her to take off her shoes. Then, mug in hand, he led her into a room that must ordinarily have been a living room, five by six paces, only all the furniture (sofa, armchair, end tables) had been pushed to the walls and draped in white sheets. In the middle of the room, a futon mattress with a sheet over top of it lay on a rectangle (1.8 by 2.4 metres) of Turkish carpet. Like a bed. It made Claire uneasy. She wondered who the apartment belonged to. A woman. There remained something female about it, decorative touches. The carpet. A mirror over the mantelpiece, and on the mantelpiece, dried flowers in a vase, a china bell. Ariel seated himself cross-legged on the floor in front of a low table covered with small brown dropper bottles. He set his tea on the table, and beckoned Claire to sit in front of him. "Already I see something of Rachel in you," he said. But Claire felt no trace of Rachel, had no intimation that Rachel was about to appear through the door or from anywhere else.

"You haven't heard from her, have you?" she asked. "Since the last time we spoke?"

He shook his head. "I do not think Rachel is coming to see me this time."

He told her that he travelled regularly to New York, to Amsterdam, sometimes to London, Geneva, other places. For fifteen years he had done so. He did not seem to find it unusual that people travelled the world to see him, to heal themselves. For the rest of the year, he lived in Israel, half the time in the desert in El Alat and the other half in Tel Aviv.

"Can you tell me why Rachel first came to you?"

"Sonya Lang told her about my work."

"Who's Sonya Lang?"

"She plays the violin. She has trouble here." He laid a hand over his abdomen — which meant, what, her digestive tract, her uterus, Claire couldn't be sure.

"If she's a friend of Rachel's, do you think you could give me her number?"

"Amy will give it to you."

"What did Rachel say was wrong with her when she came?"

Ah, he said, he did not so much listen to what people told him as to how their bodies spoke. He treated the whole body, and the body and spirit together. When Rachel first came she was like many people he saw, her body and spirit worn and stressed, because her spirit did not have a proper home in her body, and how could the body heal itself if the spirit was not in the body but loose and wandering the world? Most people when they first came were very ill, although their true sickness might not yet have revealed itself. If Rachel had not come to him, twice in New York, the last time in Amsterdam, in the future she would have been very ill. Much worse.

Where other people's gazes skimmed, his lingered. Unabashed, he stared at Claire though his stare did not feel sexual. There was a presumption of intimacy, however. She wondered if Rachel had responded to his gaze as sexual. She had to listen closely because of his accent. He spoke with an authority that bordered on impatience, a self-assurance that doubled as bluntness, but this might also have something to do with his incomplete and idiosyncratic command of English.

"How did she seem when you saw her in March?"

"Better. There is still much work to do."

"She was complaining, before she disappeared, that her migraines kept getting worse."

"This problem goes very deep. These are old wounds."

It was strange, if Rachel really believed that Ariel's treatment was helping her, that she had said nothing about him to Claire, that she had not, for instance, urged Claire to come to New York to see him.

"How exactly do you work with people?"

"I will show you. There is no charge this time." He laid a hand on Claire's shoulder. "This is my gift."

He stood and beckoned Claire towards the futon. He asked if she would mind taking off her clothes. The first thing he had to do, he said, was find her wound. Then he could begin to heal her.

She could, even now, decide that this was not for her, despite having come all this way. And yet surely that would be a failure of nerve. She had tried some unusual things in the name of searching for a cure, if nothing as unusual as this. And she trusted Rachel, who would surely not have returned twice more to see Ariel if she considered him a complete hoax.

Claire removed her cotton dress and, in bra and underwear, seated herself cross-legged on the futon while Ariel crouched in front of her. He asked her to close her eyes. His hands began to move the air around her. He did not touch her, however. For a few moments he was silent, moving. Then he said he had found her wound. Nearly everyone who came to him had a wound, and it was his job to locate it. Then he had to find the wandering spirit in the world and bring it home to the body. When the body and spirit are separated, the body calls out for attention. He must show the spirit how to enter and inhabit the body. Heal the wound. Her wound was at the back of her head. (Where was Rachel's?) Her blood did not flow properly. Not in her head, not to her organs or muscles. Her liver was tired from overwork. She suffered from a problem of circulation. Of energy. Energy did not flow smoothly through her body. There was a block. The energy was blocked because she was frightened. Once the spirit was back in her body true healing could begin. Before the wound was closed, nothing would stay in her body. The spirit was lost. He cupped the back of her head and her forehead in his firm hands, his very warm hands, and held her like that, supported for a moment, before lowering her, slowly, to the mattress.

Claire opened her eyes. He pointed to her bra and asked her to remove this, then to lie on her stomach. She surrendered to his requests, lay down, head turned to the right, cheek to the sheet, facing the empty fireplace across the room. It was all very strange but she tried not to think too much about the oddness. She floated. It was strange to be almost naked in front of this man but she did not feel violated. She did not know what Stefan would think when she told him about this — if she told him about this. Maybe Rachel had not spoken to her of Ariel because she did not think Claire would want to undergo such an experience. Sometimes the healer laid his hands on her and sometimes he didn't. His touch could be a fleck, an adjustment, a vibrating manipulation. The points that he touched on her body and her scalp were all piercingly tender. Her hands grew very warm. This, without him touching them. Her body began to vibrate — it simply happened, there was no volition involved. "Breathe," he instructed her, nearly shouting, "breathe."

At one point she began to cry. She could not stop herself. She shuddered. She was frightened by her vulnerability, by what was being called up out of her. "You must stop being so frightened," Ariel shouted. "Welcome the spirit."

Something happened, she would tell Stefan later, even if she could not have said what. Some kind of energetic exchange. She was convinced of this much. Whatever the experience was, it was not nothing. In the moments in which Claire was most exposed to Ariel, she opened herself to an intense physical trust. The world opened. She opened. At the same time, she wanted to resist him, to make of her body a tougher membrane not a thinner one, and grew almost angry.

He spoke to her as he worked although she couldn't altogether remember or make sense of what he was saying. Partly it was his accent. At one point, he asked her how she was feeling and she said fine, now, and if he meant generally then good except that, like Rachel, she got a lot of migraines. He asked her to turn over, onto her back. He laid one hand on her chest, on top of her collarbone, between her breasts, and peered down at her. "You must ask, 'What is the place of pain?'" Those were his exact words. He did not say, what does the pain mean, or, what do you think is the source of the pain. His phrasing was odd. She wondered if he used this phrase with others, if it was a characteristic of his non-native English, or if it was a phrase chosen specifically for her. He did not know (she had not told him) that she was a cartographer.

Afterwards, warm and exhausted, Claire was wrung out in the way you are after going through something inexplicably fraught, yet her body felt simultaneously full and limber. Embarrassed, her cheeks still flushed, she dressed and sat re-collecting herself, hugging her knees to her chest (maybe she *had* been helped), while Ariel, cross-legged at the low table, surrounded by small brown bottles, nursed the remains of his tea. Perhaps an hour had passed. He said she should begin right away to notice some difference.

"With the headaches?"

"All of you."

(The difference she noticed was not one she would have predicted.

For days afterwards, people, men in particular, would come up to her in public places and begin to talk about themselves. That night, in a restaurant on Spuistraat, a red-haired Dutch-Canadian doctor, seated alone at the table next to Claire, launched with almost no warning (what was the precipitating comment – something about travel, their shared country, being far from home?), into the story of how he'd once been captured by Zairian rebels and forced in front of a dummy firing squad. He was, she realized, a missionary doctor. Something evangelical. Soon after the faux execution, he was commanded to operate on the wounded rebel leader, an order which provoked a great struggle in him, perhaps the most acute of his life, so deep as to shake his sense of faith, since the idea of aiding those who'd captured him repelled him, while the Hippocratic oath compelled him to do so. He surrendered to God's will. He saved the man, who then helped spirit the doctor and his colleagues to safety. The doctor looked at Claire in puzzlement and said he had not talked about this episode in years and had no idea what made him speak of it now; then his expression turned to something closer to humiliation, as if his confession, his lurch into self-exposure were all Claire's doing. She remained astonished, past the point when he paid his bill, without addressing her again, and left.

Then there was the Indian man the next day in the coffee bar at Schiphol, who, with no coaxing, launched with effusive mania into a paean to the wonders of his patented electric bug zapper, regaling her with his dream of making his bug zapper the number one choice of all Indian households within the year, so enthused, so ardent in his mission that Claire was convinced, unless she made a run for it (she made a run for it), he would never stop.

And the man −)

Of course, Ariel went on, he did not like to work on someone just once. It left so much undone. Regularly his sessions cost $150 US. Claire should think about coming back. To New York. It was not so far from Toronto. In the meantime, regular doctors would not be necessary now that she had begun to work with him.

"Rachel didn't say anything when she was here about not getting in touch with anyone. You didn't −"

"No. I believe there is a reason for her silence. She is on a journey, but if you see her, tell her we need to continue our work together. It is very important, for the sake of her health."

Well, maybe, Claire thought. "She didn't say anything about what else she was doing in Amsterdam or where she was going afterwards? She was supposed to fly back on March 23 and she didn't."

"In March she was very tired. I say to her, rest, let the body and spirit recover, but she says she cannot. I tell her about a woman I know in Italy. She does very good work, with her hands. I tell her, Rachel, you are here in Europe, go to see her. I did not think she listened, but I have talked to my angels and now I think she went there."

"Went where —?"

"Hannah di Castro." The buzzer rang. "Her work will be good for you, also. At Terme di Saturnia. Near Grosseto. You take the train to Grosseto. Someone will show you the road."

After a lunch of chicken baguette, Claire tried calling Stefan from a public phone near the Nieuwmarkt, but at a little after eight in the morning in Toronto, he must have been somewhere between home and work because she couldn't reach him at either number. Neither of them had a cellphone, nor had ever yet seen the need to own one. She found an Internet café and looked up the Terme di Saturnia on-line. It appeared to be a spa, a resort hotel known for its healing waters, in southern Tuscany, north-west of Rome, not far from the coast and Isola d'Elba. Not the sort of place she would have predicted that Ariel would recommend, but at this distance, and given her limited knowledge of him or the place, she was without the proper means to judge. She wrote down the Terme's phone number.

She kept testing, internally, to see how she felt: did anything seem deeply different?

Back in her hotel room, she called the Terme, where the phone was answered by a young man who seemed to speak fluent English. She said she was looking for a Hannah di Castro and wished to speak to her. The young man put her on hold and when he returned said that Hannah was not available but he could leave a message for her. What kind of work does Hannah do? A kind of hydrotherapy. Hannah is amazing, fantastical. The spa was expensive, but had space for her this weekend, if she wanted.

She called Charlie Gorjup in Toronto.

"Hey, Claire, how's it going over there?"

"Charlie, I have another lead. In Italy. Would you kill me if I took another couple of days?"

"It's getting a little hard, Claire. Staff-wise, we're cut to the bone."

"I'm not asking for paid days. I know I'm a little behind on the wetlands survey but I'll work around the clock, I promise, as soon as I get home."

Why did she feel the need to keep searching for Rachel? She could just turn around and head back to Toronto. Only there was something she needed to discover, not simply by looking for Rachel but by following in her footsteps.

She tried Stefan again. This time, according to his lab-mate Maria, he was in with the mice. Suited head-to-toe in white, he would be behind an airlock, in what was known as the dirty room, where the researchers handled the genetically altered mice, and which was distinguished from the clean room, where the mice lived and were bred, and which only the mouse attendants were allowed to enter. He'd received her message, Maria said, and knew Claire was trying to reach him. Could she call back in like half an hour?

"How was your session?" he asked when she finally got through to him.

"Odd. Intense." Hard to explain. "He barely touches you. It's more like tweaks than anything and sometimes not even but something is called up out of you. You respond. It made me cry." Her still-perplexed face was reflected, along with her gesticulating arm, in a large, gilt-framed mirror on the far side of the room.

"Do you think it helped?" Claire couldn't tell if he was just being polite, or if he really believed that something like this could make a difference. Maybe his questing mind was still taken up with tumours and genetically altered mice.

"Hard to tell yet. My head feels fine. We'll see. He thinks Rachel went to Italy to see this woman he told her about who works at a spa in Tuscany."

"Claire, you're not thinking of going to Italy."

"I'm so close."

"Amsterdam is not all that close to Italy."

"It's closer than Toronto."

"I don't see how this helps you figure out where Rachel is now, or why, if she's just bumming around Europe, you need to find her."

"Maybe there's something in Italy that will help *me*."

She wished she had some access to Rachel's state of mind after her session with Ariel in March. Perhaps Rachel had felt so buoyed, so enlivened by his treatment that she had been more than ready to take his advice, to rest, to seek out Hannah di

Castro. Or perhaps she'd only been more desperate and taken off for Saturnia because she desired to throw herself at anything to get rid of a pain that would not leave her, ready to gamble wildly as you did when you had nothing left to lose, as a young woman in England had done – her agony so deep that she had bought a cordless drill, borrowed some local anesthetic, and, standing in front of her bathroom mirror, drilled a hole in her forehead. Trepanning has a long history as a remedy for headaches (Prince Rupert of the Rhine, cavalry commander to the English King Charles II, had a hole drilled in his head by the Duke of York's physician and went on to help found the Hudson's Bay Company) but is not usually recommended as a do-it-yourself activity. Although Laetitia Totter drilled a little too far and punctured the membrane surrounding her brain, she suffered no long-lasting ill effects and in fact claimed to have reduced the chronic pain that plagued her. Claire had passed this story on to Rachel.

In return, Rachel told her about a girl whose migraines were cured by waltzing. Two years ago, Rachel had in fact flown to Vienna to write an article about Therese Krutz, who was fourteen and lived with her mother, her existence nearly reduced to that of an invalid because her headaches were so frequent and severe, until the day that her mother enrolled her in the Feltzer Academy of Therapeutic Waltz. The academy operated like almost any other school of dance: the girls wore dresses and their partners white gloves when they paired up. The school was run by a former doctor who claimed to have stumbled upon the curative powers of waltzing, and indeed the school had a reputation for easing a variety of ailments. Its students were never called patients. In fifty-minute sessions, they did nothing but waltz to the music of Johann Strauss, Jr. For beginners, instruction was provided. After her first class, Therese began to notice a lessening of her headaches. Over two months of instruction and weekly waltzing, her migraines almost completely vanished, although it seemed that she had to keep waltzing in order to maintain this effect. Rachel had visited the academy and interviewed the director and Therese, as well as doctors who poohpoohed the waltz's miraculous powers and put Therese's recovery down to the mere increase in physical activity (any sort would have done the trick) plus the simultaneous social life (in particular, the regular contact with young men). Pain is idiosyncratic, Rachel wrote. Perhaps waltzing is a culturally specific response to a culturally specific pain and works only for the Viennese. Yet she had tried waltz lessons herself, three in one week. At the time, Claire had thought Rachel was doing this as research, and as a bit of a lark. Perhaps she was more serious, more drawn to believe in the possibility of such a cure than Claire was giving her credit for. She'd thought, then, that Rachel was coping with her headaches. Perhaps within all of Rachel's assignments (the trips to Budapest, to Morocco) lurked a private, and increasingly frantic, mission to find a cure for herself.

The night was warm. Claire left the restaurant where the Dutch-Canadian missionary doctor had run from her, his bewildered face hovering before her as she walked south along Spuistraat. She was thinking not only of his face but of his story, which was a tale both of a gamble and of faith. She understood the gamble but was not prepared to discount the faith, even if she was uncertain how to define it. When it came to healing, faith counted. There was statistical proof for the power of the placebo effect and even for prayer, not just a patient's prayers but of those who prayed for the patient. She did not know if you had to believe in God to make your prayer effective or if it was enough to believe in the power of prayer itself, the strength of your conviction that someone could be healed, however this occurred – faith in the healing rather than the healer. The ways in which people were freed from pain sometimes seemed as mysterious as their pains themselves. Did she need to believe in the powers of a man such as Ariel for his healing to work on her?

Just before the bottom of Spui, where a little street turning off to the right would lead her back to the hotel, there was a bar, like many still strung with orange streamers, its windows open. From inside came the sound of men and women singing. Claire stepped through the door. On impulse, she made her way to the counter and, in English, ordered a small bottle of mineral water.

"American?" asked the young man standing next to her at the bar.

"Canadian."

"Nothing stronger?" He indicated her glass.

"I can't drink alcohol," she said.

He was American. Tall. From Boston. He was in town for an ultimate frisbee competition. He travelled the world as a competitive ultimate frisbee player. Had she seen any of the soccer? No, she said, she'd arrived too late. She was sorry she hadn't. She was here looking for her sister. They stepped outside where the noise was less ferocious and it was easier to talk. She described Rachel to him. He looked at her with a directness that was not immediately off-putting, different again from the blunt gaze of Ariel, and said, "I can see you thinking before you speak." This was startling. It was startling because it was as if, without preamble, he'd looked inside her and recognized something true about her. He was not making fun of her but demanding her attention in return. He walked her to the banks of the Singel, the canal next to the Herengracht, where her hotel stood. He kissed her — on one cheek, then the other, then, leaning further over her, buried his nose against her neck and under the lobe of her right ear, as if to inhale her scent.

Breathless, Claire stopped running only when she reached the doorway of the Ambassade Hotel.

Upstairs, still breathless, she leaned against the back of a chair. What exactly had happened? Had she done anything to feel guilty about? She stepped in front of the gilt-framed mirror, her hair still askew from where, earlier in the day, Ariel had worked his hands against her scalp. What had changed — had Ariel done something to her, or had the city infiltrated her in some fashion, or had she done something to herself?

The hills rose and fell, rearing out of the golden land that Claire drove through. She zigzagged up ascents towards the Tuscan villages that clutched the peaks, their stone walls and the jut of roofs and church towers forming jagged jigsaw lines.

Above her, swallows flew like arrowheads, strafing the air.

Up or down, the hills afforded such views that she grew dizzy at the sight: the sweep of fields below, and other hills, banks of olive trees, the silhouettes of cypresses and ilexes along the rises, rocky cliffs that fell away into gorges so steep that your stomach dropped when you looked at them. From far in the distance came a glimpse of the sea.

Ever since the morning's flight from Schiphol to Rome, Claire had been in transit: by train from Roma Fiumicino to Roma Termini, from Roma Termini to Grosseto, where she'd rented the car. In Grosseto, on her short walk from the train station to the car rental office, three people had stopped to ask her for directions, two men and an old English woman who confided that she was on her way to visit the cathedral, a level of attention that Claire, with her bags and nearly helpless Italian, could only think of as the Ariel effect. Not that people weren't generally friendly to her or she to them, but this was something else, something more. Her head was holding up, shaky at moments, the shakiness then subsiding. Now elongated evening sunlight flushed the olive trees that grew in rows on either side of the road and turned the tops of their leaves silver. The swallows banked and darted. Crickets sawed in the grass. For the last hour, there had been no other car behind hers as she followed the signs for Saturnia.

She passed a waterfall. On her right appeared a sign for the hotel at the Terme and another indicating that the town of Saturnia lay two kilometres farther on. Although her destination was the Terme, she took the route that led to the town, approaching up a slope and along a crest of hill until she found herself, first among houses, then entering a piazza where sweetly scented linden trees were strung with white lights, and outdoor tables were set in front of the restaurants that bordered the square. Already people had begun to fill these tables. A crowd clustered outside a gelateria. The sight drew her on. Perhaps she should have stayed here.

She wondered if Rachel had passed this way. Claire roused herself and nosed the car out of the town again. Below her lay what must be the Terme: a complex of white rectangular buildings, one larger than the rest, set regimentally in a green swathe of field. She approached at last at dusk through a long *allée* of trees.

At the front desk she asked for Hannah di Castro. The young man uniformed in a black suit who was attending to her appeared, like the young man to whom she had spoken by phone, to speak perfect English. He ran his finger down a list of names and phone extensions. He searched through a large appointment book. He asked Claire what sort of therapy Hannah di Castro performed and Claire said she wasn't sure but the day before she had spoken by phone to another young man, who clearly knew of Hannah's work and told her he would leave a message for Hannah. To whom did she speak? She didn't know. She swallowed her frustration. This young man gave a neat little frown. He consulted in Italian with all the other elegant young men in uniform hovering around the reception desk (none of them seemed to be the one to whom she had spoken yesterday). They agreed, in English, that Hannah's name was familiar, she had certainly worked at the Terme, in fact until very recently, they just didn't think she worked here now. They did not know what had happened to her. Claire's best recourse was to inquire – the first young man pointed behind her to an open doorway, beyond which, as she later discovered, was a dim and aqueously lit room containing a single desk – tomorrow between nine and seventeen hundred hours. There were so many other therapists, all marvellous. She must not let this little problem spoil her time at Terme di Saturnia.

Claire persisted. Did they ever release the names of guests or former guests? The young man mimed zipping his lips. Never, signorina. He winked at her. Sometimes people bring illegal girl-friends here. For such information you would have to corrupt someone. He was kidding, being flirtatious even, but not, as far as Claire could tell, offering himself as someone to be corrupted.

The hotel corridor stretched so far into the distance that Claire gave up counting steps. Although she found her room without difficulty, the walk from the room back to the elevator seemed to take even longer than she remembered and she, who never got lost, kept feeling on the verge of becoming so. She was tired. The air in the hallway smelled faintly but distractingly of sulphur. There were no visible speakers yet the tremble of a string quartet was carried distantly but constantly towards her. For a moment, she thought she saw a young girl up ahead.

Downstairs, the floor tiles were large blocks of watery marble. To the right of the corner reception area, another hallway opened. A few metres along, where the hall turned left, through a glass wall and murkily floodlit, the thermal pools beckoned. At the end of the hall was a bar, also glass-walled, as was the restaurant beside the bar, the grounds outside growing inky as the last rays of light dispersed beyond the hills.

Claire found herself looking for children in a place where there didn't seem to be any. In the bar, men and women sat smoking cigarettes and slim dark cigarillos, despite the discrete *Vietate Fumare* signs. She did not hear much English spoken, mostly Italian. In a corner, a string quartet, three men and one woman dressed in black and white, were playing a disturbingly jaunty tune, a waltz, although most people appeared to be ignoring them. Everyone who wore jewellery — rings, necklaces, ankle bracelets — wore gold. Claire sniffed the air, well-ventilated but faintly acrid with smoke, wondered what she would be able to eat, and how she was going to manage to corrupt someone.

As children, they would not have been brought to a place like this. Their parents would never have come to a place like this. (Claire had never before been to a spa. Rachel had. She wrote about such places in travel articles and for the health sections of women's magazines. She believed a woman should have at least one facial a year, to which Allison had replied that the only facial she was likely to get was a spattering of orangutan spit, but maybe that had undiscovered anti-aging properties.)

The summer Claire was nine, while they were visiting their parents' relatives in England, they'd spent a week as a family by the sea in Norfolk. They'd stayed in a dilapidated manor house owned by an English man and his Finnish wife, where, in a back room, deep within the maze of the house, there was a home-built sauna, which their mother had tried out one rainy afternoon. Claire had wandered by herself back through the warren of rooms and found Sylvia, shiny and flushed, in the room beside the sauna, lying on a cot wrapped in a towel, drinking a cup of tea and eating cold triangles of toast in the company of the Finnish woman.

On the days when it wasn't too cold they'd gone to the beach. Two days, Claire remembered, were blazingly bright. On the first, their father had taken off his shoes and socks and rolled up his trouser legs, before immersing himself in a book of mathematical puzzles, oblivious to the fact that by the end of the afternoon the bottoms of both his feet would be sunburned. From under her hat, their mother watched them play, Allison in the brisk sea water, whose frigidity didn't seem to bother her, Claire at the shore, building inlets of sand to channel the tide. Not far from Allison, Rachel lay on a beach towel, in sunglasses and a bikini (a bikini, in England), reading magazines and eyeing boys.

Later, they would all walk along the beach together (this was before their father realized how badly burned his feet were). They made their way towards the boardwalk and the Hunstanton pier and stopped at the low-roofed penny arcades where Hugh gave them each a handful of one-pence coins and Claire watched hers be carried relentlessly one by one across the geometric black and white backdrops of the machines, her gaze gripped not by the tantalizing mounds of money into which her coins eventually dropped but by the backdrops' dizzying swirls.

(Only once had she been to a beach with Stefan, on St. Kitts, where they'd lain in the shade of a palm tree, taking turns to trace messages letter by letter on each other's back, the one who wrote waiting for the other to guess the secret words.)

The next morning, the elegant woman behind the single desk in the dimly lit room said that Hannah di Castro had departed Saturnia in April without leaving a forwarding number. She thought Signorina di Castro had gone travelling. She did not believe she was currently practising massage. She was sorry there had been this confusion. Perhaps one of the doctors knew more. They could be identified by their white coats. She could ring for someone, but if they were in their offices, they were likely with clients, and if not, they were most likely to be somewhere about the grounds.

In daylight, most of the spa guests had donned white terry cloth robes, belted at the waist and thus distinguishable even at a distance from a doctor's white coat. Also, the spa-goers' legs were bare. Something about the robes made people appear even more *déshabillé* than if they had simply been in swimsuits, perhaps because swimsuits proclaimed a function – bathing whether in sunlight or water – and were so emphatically exposing, while the robes suggested a disguise or some unsettled state between being undressed and being clothed.

Ahead of Claire, a white-robed woman clicked along the hallway that led to the bar and thermal pools, her feet clad in small scarlet sandals, her skin darkly and cracklingly tanned.

Outside, people swam slowly through the water or rested, submerged, supine along the edges of the thermal pool, many with their eyes shielded behind dark glasses. Even in daylight, the water, which surged out of the earth below, was murky green and nearly hot and sulphurically pungent. Blobs of slimy algae floated on its surface, which some of the bathers scooped up and smeared over their skin. She could not see any doctors out here.

Somewhat discouraged, Claire returned to her room. She changed into the bathing suit that she had borrowed from the spa – a black one-piece cut high at the thigh and low in the back, which fit her, more or less. There was a sign on her dressing table noting that all silver jewellery should be removed because the mineral content of the water tarnished it; the water had no effect on gold. Wrapped in her own white robe, she descended once again.

At the far end of the pool were two doors that led back into a wing of the hotel, each bearing a sign. *Consulenza Idrologica* said the first, the second, *Consulenza Cosmetologica*. Claire entered through the first door, stepping out of the pounding brightness into an interior of pale aqua where young women in starched white uniforms hovered around a reception desk, and a long hallway lined with white doors stretched away to her left, the doors all closed except for the one to the room at the very end, lined, like a lab, with shelves of bottles. One doctor of hydrology was with a patient. Another was already at lunch. The others were elsewhere. Any of the doctors will be happy to help you, one of the young women told her. In the meantime, you must take the waters.

Inside the second doorway, a peach-coloured corridor led into a large room through which extended a row of golden doors each set within a plaster arch, and more young women in the same white uniforms clustered about a similar reception desk and looked up expectantly as Claire entered. Here, as everywhere, the air was tinged with sulphur. Signora Forconi per la fangoterapia, one attendant asked her.

It was possible that Rachel had stayed on in Italy. She might be here, among the sunglass-shielded, white-robed spa-goers, difficult to recognize beneath this disguise. Perhaps she had met a man, an Italian man, and decided to throw in her luck with him. Perhaps Italy, the land itself, had worked some languorous seduction upon her.

Outside once more, Claire scanned for doctors. Beyond the three gold spigots set in a marble wall from which you could drink the water (no more than three cups in twenty-four hours, preferably on an empty stomach), beyond a shallow, narrow ambulatory pool, where from the foot of a small artificial waterfall women set out to walk up and down to tone their thighs and benefit their circulation, near a large stone toadstool which pounded water from its cap upon the heads and backs of those beneath and lacked only a caterpillar with a hookah seated upon it, a doctor in a white coat, deep in conversation, gestured and nodded.

The doctor poured a bottle of aqua minerale into a glass for Claire and then did the same for himself. They were seated in a triangle of shade. The frolicking notes of the string quartet tripped out of an open door towards them. His name was Dottore Nicolo Maggiorelli. He was evenly tanned, the smoothness of his manners and appearance offset only by the extraordinary length of his very black eyelashes. In English, as they walked towards the bar, he'd asked Claire where she came from. Canada, she said, a response that seemed to delight him, although perhaps he would have reacted similarly no matter what she'd said.

Now he asked courteously and in fluent English if there was a particular ailment or condition she wished to discuss.

"Do you get many visitors who suffer from migraines and is there anything in the water that's particularly good for them?"

He came close to touching the back of her hand with his fingers: the gesture hovered in the air. Claire crossed one leg over the other, her pale right calf protruding beneath the hem of her robe. She felt swallowed up by the robe, the bathing suit riding up in places where she didn't wish it to. She tried to loosen her belt and part the sides of her robe in a manner she hoped would be alluring yet feared was ridiculous.

"Let me tell you a little how we work here," Dottore Maggiorelli said. "Do you know what the word *spa* means?"

Claire didn't.

"A Roman acronym. Salus per aquam. For three thousand years people have been coming to visit these waters, fantastic, isn't it?"

She agreed it was.

"Now the nature of most illness is complicated, and much lies deep in the unconscious. So not only do the chemical and mineral characteristics of the water and the presence of these two gases, hydrogen sulfate and carbon dioxide, have their healing properties, but – this is very important – there is the symbolic value of the water. We bathe in the water. It soothes us. This is also therapeutic. We ask people not to think of their illness as a separate thing but of their global well-being."

Claire kept being distracted by the twenty-two centimetres between her hand and the doctor's, now thirty-eight, nineteen between their feet. By his eyelashes and the liquidity of the sunlight beyond him. She drank some water.

"If you suffer from migraine, what are the specific qualities of the water that help?"

"Eh – It is very good for the circulation and has strong anti-inflammatory effects on the muscles. It may not work directly on the neural system but overall it is a powerful relaxant. Think of the global organism."

"Do you go in the water?"

"Of course. It is also detoxifying, good for the liver." He smiled, which did something odd but not inelegant to his chin. "When I was a medical student in Rome, we used to visit for the weekend. Pleasure is also part of the therapy. This can be a very good place to cure a broken heart." He glanced down, eyes shielded by those lashes. He had small, neat knuckles. "I have worked here for five years, and before that, for many years, at a hospital in Rome, and while there is a great hope in a hospital, there is also great hopelessness. Here, people come because they want to be here. They are trying to help themselves and the doctor aids them in this process whereas in a hospital the doctor is the source of the cure, he is the source, one could say, of the magic —"

Something distracted him. A female doctor, outside the door marked *Consulenza Idrologica* was waving one white arm at him, a black shadow thrown across the wall behind her. His fingers touched Claire's knee. "We must continue, I apologize. You will be here in the morning?"

Once he'd left, she sank back in her chair, eyes closed, convinced she'd blown it.

She took the waters. What was the point of being at a Terme if you didn't? The Terme's water, sour and eggy to drink, was heavy and thick to swim in, something about its mineral content slowing the body down. Like others, Claire kept her sunglasses on as she swam and settled into an empty spot along the side of the pool and tried to soothe her global organism.

There were, she now realized, families here, not staying at the Terme but day visitors, who arrived through a separate entrance on the far side of the grounds. They did not languidly peel themselves from robes, but launched themselves through the doors of change rooms in bathing suits, already disrobed. Families, generations' worth of families, raucous and high-spirited, boys teasing girls.

Perhaps Rachel had attached herself to a man and his family, had decided to reinvent herself as a slim Roman matron, step-mother to someone else's motherless children — this was as radical a prospect as anything else Claire could imagine. Perhaps Rachel was not only trying to escape her life but jettison her family, or what remained of it, its awkward tugs and lingering ghosts. Although the desire for a new family, a different family, was surely more of an adolescent desire. Years ago, Claire had watched Rachel as she walked along the Hunstanton beach, staring at other families with a curious, lingering gaze. Yet this was normal, at thirteen.

Did she want a child? Of course this was a different question than whether she felt she could manage with a child. A family was by its nature chaotic, even if hers had not particularly seemed so, apart from the chaos brought on by their migraines.

Migraines had not stopped their mother having children, three children in six years. Sylvia had told them explicitly how much she wanted a family, the family she'd never had — siblings gathered around a kitchen table. No doubt her desire had been strong enough to outweigh whatever pain the desire had cost her. With a toddler underfoot, she had become pregnant a second time, and spent that pregnancy on the road in Africa. And became pregnant again with Claire, a little over a year after their return to Canada, while they were all still squashed into a two-bedroom apartment. It was never mentioned whether or not their father had wanted three children.

Perhaps Sylvia was simply tougher than either Rachel or Claire. Also, her migraines were not as frequent. It was not until she was an adolescent that Claire remembered her mother taking to her bed with a headache (and her father's disquiet in the face of this). Perhaps Sylvia had not needed to do so earlier, or she had simply hidden her symptoms and managed to keep on her feet. Perhaps Claire simply did not remember her mother being bedridden.

What she did remember from her childhood was a sense of her mother holding something back or overcoming something. All that ferrying them about, to ballet classes and skating classes and piano lessons, was not effortless. At seven, sitting beside her mother in the car, waiting for Allison to finish a skating lesson, Claire was aware that what her mother was doing wasn't easy. She had no sense that Sylvia wanted her to feel this, wanted to place any burden of knowledge or responsibility upon her, yet Claire couldn't help feeling the undernote of strain beneath her mother's selflessness.

What if she had a child, a daughter, who had migraines even worse than hers? Had Sylvia worried about this? Later she would helplessly apologize and say openly that she felt guilty for the intensity of her daughters' headaches. Not that either Claire or

Rachel had ever behaved as though they considered her at fault. Well, Sylvia said, it's obviously my genes you've inherited. Actually, Rachel replied, it's not clear what we've inherited, whether the migraines are genetic or if it's some neurological predisposition, something in your physical makeup that's been passed on, and the headaches themselves are a kind of learned behaviour, a body language. Great, Sylvia said, I taught you to have headaches. Or, Rachel said, or are they worse for us because of something Dad introduced into the mix, physiologically or behaviourally? Perhaps, Sylvia said, it's better not to pursue that line of thought.

Rachel had worried about passing on her migraines. This was why she claimed to have searched for someone genetically unlike herself as the father of her child. Genetic hybridity would lessen the chance of passing on the damn headaches, and so far there'd been no sign of migraines in any of the three girls, although they did have more headaches than many children.

The waters left Claire feeling sleepy rather than refreshed. Even a shower didn't shake her back to alertness and the smell of sulphur still breathed from her skin and lurked at the back of her mouth, but the wide bed awaited and she sank into its embrace and slept. She awoke, still groggy, to the ringing of the telephone. It was Stefan, for whom it was lunchtime, while the sun in the sky above her was already well into its fall.

"Claire? Your voice sounds funny."

"I'm fine. My head's fine."

"Have you found anything?"

"Not yet. I'm supposed to meet this woman in the morning." It wasn't entirely a lie, it was what she hoped to do, even if she'd got no further in her attempt to find Hannah di Castro. How could she tell him she'd spent all day lolling in a sulphur-scented pool and idling under a toadstool-shaped fountain?

"No other word?" she asked him.

"No word."

What did a spa offer someone who was in pain? Distraction. Hope. The balm of a place where you did not have to worry about other people's suffering. Where you surrendered to your body, to a world of sensation, without feeling guilty about it. Pleasure was good. The head became nothing more than a part of the body. There was the possibility of transforming a life in a weekend or a week, a cure that seemed both medicinal and magic. Drink this. Bathe in this and you will be healed. Which was not unlike the allure of swallowing pills. Eat this and you will be well. Eat this and you will be changed. A child's wish.

The next morning, the taste of sulphur was still in Claire's mouth, the dull odour of it now released not only by her skin but her clothes. Her silver jewellery — the necklace and earrings she'd worn only briefly the night before — had turned black. Her head was still all right.

Down on the green lawns below her window, groups of people in white were jumping up and down or setting off in a wavy line, six, seven, eight, along a path into the fields.

This morning she had no time to waste. Downstairs, she hurried along a hallway, unremembered from the day before, empty, lined with columns, her shoes thwacking against the marble floor. She had to find a doctor, any doctor, and no more coyness, today she simply had to throw herself at someone.

Not before breakfast, though. Once she found the restaurant, the quest for protein at breakfast again proved a bit of an issue. There were no eggs to be had: they were not an Italian breakfast food. There was yogurt and milk and cheese and prosciutto and various cereals and fresh fruit and bread rolls and cornetti and rusks. She'd had cheese the day before despite feeling a little nervous about dairy ever since Rachel's recent bad experiences with it. Claire didn't have the stomach for prosciutto first thing in the morning. Since no protein at all would definitely bring on a migraine, she ordered a smoothie: strawberries and bananas blended with milk. How bad could that be? As soon as the brimming glass arrived, she drank it down.

For thirty seconds nothing happened.

A salt taste like the sea welled from the back of her throat and she had to keep swallowing it, salt mixing with sulphur, in order not to throw up. Her toilet bag with all her medications in it was in the bathroom and she was not. She was on the bed. The pain had come on so fast. It shook her in its jaws like a dog. It gripped her throat, it squeezed her eyeballs. Now the room pressed in and withdrew simultaneously. First there was silence and then the faint, blithe melodies of the string quartet started up, drifting through the window through the walls through the floor, the notes prancing across the carpet towards her.

Shellfish. Please help.

Was it the milk? Or possibly the strawberries, or the bananas? Was it something in the water? Was she made more susceptible by frustration or despair at the hopelessness of her search for Rachel, her worry or her torpor of the day before? Was the Ariel effect over? Stress or release? Something obvious or hidden? Had the indulgence of allowing herself to feel well, capable of being healed, set her up for a fall? Had she lacked faith? Had her spirit gone into shock at its re-entry into her body? Surely part of the pain was its apparent randomness, the state of not knowing what had tossed her overboard, yet the part of her brain not wholly occupied with sensation searched for meaning, to draw a line between pain and trigger. When she closed her eyes against the light, the white white light pouring in on her, Claire saw hills, the Tuscan hills rising and falling.

She opened her eyes. She sat up and edged her legs over the bed. The sea, the sea. Made it to the bathroom. Lay down on the floor. Struggled to stand and pour herself a glass of water.

One pill. Another pill. Another.

Made it back. The phone rang. All the way across the sea, in the early hours of the morning, Stefan had woken, heard her calling out for him.

"Signorina Barber," a voice said.

"Who is this?" Claire rasped.

"Dottore Maggiorelli, Signorina Barber. You have not been seen today. Are you all right?"

"I have a headache." According to the bedside clock, it was nearly noon.

"Did you spend a lot of time in the waters yesterday?"

"Not a lot."

"It is unfortunate but not uncommon for our guests to suffer what we call a thermal crisis, often on the second or third day of their visit. Do not be alarmed. Think of it as a sign that the body responds. However, we would like to send someone to make certain you are all right."

"Doctor Maggiorelli —"

"Miss Barber, I insist."

The first knock on the door was housekeeping. Permesso, permesso? A woman in a housecoat, carrying a duster, let herself in, saw Claire, began apologizing, Scusi, scusi, and backed out. Along with the second set of knocks came voices. If she did not answer the door, would they go away? (Whatever happened, she had to be well enough to check out of her room in just over an hour.) She could not get off the bed to answer the door.

There was the chirr of a lock turning, the door handle depressed, and the door opened upon an attendant in a white uniform holding a tray, Dottore Maggiorelli, in his white coat, propping open the door behind her.

Claire pulled herself up. At least her nausea had lessened a little. She inhaled the alcoholic note of Maggiorelli's cologne or aftershave. On the tray, which the attendant laid atop the hotel room's desk, against the wall opposite, was a glass of ice water, some slices of cucumber, and a basket of bread sticks.

"How are you feeling?" Maggiorelli asked.

"Not well," Claire replied.

"Quite possibly you are suffering a thermally induced migraine. Which is unpleasant but you will undoubtedly feel even better than usual once it passes. This is not an uncommon experience. I hope it will not dissuade you from the benefits of our waters."

"It isn't fair," she said ruefully.

"It isn't," he agreed. "You have the medication you require?"

She nodded, though, in truth, apart from the release from nausea, the Zomig, even now, didn't seem to be doing much.

"I have to check out by one."

"We shall arrange a late checkout for you. Or if you must stay, you must stay."

"I can't."

He rested his palm against her forehead. "No fever."

"Do you have any idea where Hannah di Castro is? She used to work here."

If he was caught off guard, he didn't show it. "Hannah, yes, Hannah left us in April. She specialized in idrofisiochinesiterapia. She was very good, but has gone now to work for the world wildlife refuge. No more people, she told me, just animals."

"What's idrofisio —"

"It is a form of muscle therapy that takes place in the water."

"Is the animal refuge near here? Can I get there?"

"Oh, maybe fifteen minutes. Ten kilometres?" He conferred with the attendant in Italian (diece, she said, vente?). "No more than twenty minutes."

"Do you think she's there now?"

"Honestly, I have no idea. You might try calling. But you cannot go now, like this."

"I think my sister Rachel came here in March. She also gets migraines." The xeroxed photograph of Rachel was in her bag on the floor. She couldn't reach it. "She doesn't look like me but there's a family resemblance. Is there any chance you remember her? Or could you help me find out for certain if she was here?"

"In March?" The doctor looked at Claire. She had no idea what he saw. "I'm sorry, there are too many guests."

She could not afford to stay in bed. She had until mid-afternoon to meet Hannah di Castro before she had to begin the drive back to Grosseto, before her return to Rome and evening flight back to Amsterdam. Pain was simply a form of consciousness, a quality of awareness (if we are not aware of it, it does not exist); therefore, she simply had to get herself out of the state in which the migraine filled her consciousness completely and make some room for other things. As long as her nausea stayed in retreat, she would manage.

Woozily Claire waited for a porter to bring her rental car around to the front steps of the Terme. She would drive, whatever the dangers (two Tylenol 3s had dulled the pulsing sensation after the Zomig failed to do much good). Luckily, there was no other traffic on the road. She canted forward over the steering wheel. What was the place of pain? She should have asked Ariel exactly what he meant by this. Did he mean "place" literally, as in she had to figure out where in her body the pain came from (somewhere in her head) or was he referring to the role it played, its importance to her? Had she somehow put the pain in her head (as opposed to elsewhere)? Was putting it in her head, which was and was not part of the body, different than putting it in her brain? Or was he suggesting that there were places out in the world where her pain lived and which she had to find?

It was as if she were driving with the top of her head. Up hill and down. The hills were rising and falling inside her. All she had to do was fix on this task, follow the line of the road. Take the left turn at the junction.

Hannah di Castro had a monkey clinging to her hair, so that, stepping out of a doorway as Claire climbed out of her car, she immediately called to mind not Rachel, but Allison. Claire had eased her way to a stop at the end of a dirt track, between two stuccoed buildings, as Hannah had told her to do when they spoke briefly by phone. Her headache began to recede a little.

Holding out her hand, slender but muscular, not as tall as Allison, jeans riding her boyish hips, Hannah said, in English, that she and Piero, the vet at the refuge, were nursing the infant monkey, and no matter how often she settled it on her back, it would climb into her hair, because her head — she lifted a handful of her long, black hair — most resembled its mother.

Above them, the swallows shrieked and darted, diving around the tops of a stand of cypresses.

She and Piero cared for abandoned animals and injured wild animals, Hannah said, hands reaching for her neck to steady the monkey, as she led Claire into a house lined with reddish tiled floors, past a living room in which a metre-long lizard snoozed in front of an electric heater. The heater filled the room and the hallway with gusts of preternatural heat.

They settled on chairs in a similarly red-tiled kitchen where Hannah offered Claire a glass of bottled water and motioned to a bowl of figs sitting on the table. She apologized for the confusion at the Terme about her whereabouts. She *had* gone travelling after ending her contract there, before coming back to live and work with Piero. She believed she'd left a forwarding number. She had not spoken to Ariel in close to a year.

In the spring, she had in fact gone back to Israel to visit a favourite aunt who lived in Tel Aviv, the same aunt through whom she had first met Ariel, ten years before, when her aunt was being treated by him. She herself had first gone to him as a patient but he was also the one who had sensed that she had a gift. Up until then she had had some standard kinesthesiology training, and she had specialized in treating very deep muscle injuries, not superficial strains but damage to the very quality of the tissue that did not show up on X-rays. But she learned, through Ariel, that she did not always need to touch the body to affect the tissue.

She had worked for some years in a clinic in Rome and also on her own. The work she had done at the Terme was again a little different — she had come out here because she loved the country and took what work she could find.

The monkey watched Claire over the top of Hannah's head, pressing first one cheek, then the other against Hannah's scalp — like a child, but not a child. When Claire picked a fig from the bowl and began to peel and eat it, the monkey watched her fixedly until Hannah, too, picked up a fig and fed tiny pinches of fruit to the creature.

"Why did you give up working at the Terme?"

"I grew tired," Hannah said. "All those people. And I met Piero. Perhaps the animals deserve this care also. But your sister, yes, she came here from Amsterdam. She had seen Ariel. Her muscles were very sore, very stiff and hard. Blood did not circulate well through the tissue. The tone of the muscle was very bad. She was losing strength. She was having a lot of trouble writing. She could not write much at all any more. And of course this is a big problem because of how she earns a living." She stroked the monkey's fur.

"Did she talk about her headaches?"

"Only a little. I said she should stay here for a while, not at the Terme, we would find another place for her to stay and we would do some more work together. Four, five days is not long, not long at all. But she said she could not stay any longer."

"Did she say where she was going?"

"No."

"Did she mention Naples or anywhere else in Italy or Europe?"

"No, no, I am afraid not."

"Was she travelling with anyone?"

"No, by herself. If I hear anything from her, any time, any time, I will let you know."

Claire had told Stefan when her flight from Amsterdam was getting in but did not expect to see him waving at her when, a little after four, she exited through the security barrier in Toronto, on the far side of the baggage claim and customs control. She fell into his arms, nearly crushed against him. She was glad to be home. She'd been a fool to head off to Europe, to Italy anyway. A wild goose chase. (All she had to show for her efforts were the remnants of a really bad headache.) They kissed. Stefan seemed both effervescently relieved to see her and distracted. Taking her bag, he paused, then, in a rush, said that Brad Arnarson had left a message at the house that morning — he hadn't been able to get hold of her before this, of course, since she'd been in transit, but Brad had heard from Rachel.

"What?" Claire's shriek bounced off the walls, her voice so loud people turned. Every filament of fatigue and discomfort was flung to the back of her head. "When?"

"She sent him a postcard."

"When? From where?" *Him?* She wrote to *him.*

"From Las Vegas. Claire, I'm not kidding. He said it just arrived but it looks like it took a long time to reach him." Outside now, they made their way along a cement walkway towards the parking garage.

"What did it say?" she asked dizzily.

"He didn't leave that in his message."

"Couldn't you have called him back?"

"I assumed you'd call him as soon as you got in or, if you felt too wrecked, in the morning." Even when she slowed, Stefan kept walking.

"But you knew I'd want to know."

There was a moment of awkwardness between them as Stefan settled her bags in the trunk and Claire fumbled her way towards the passenger door. He hadn't wanted to tell her, she realized. He simply wanted her home. Then they were in the car, winding their way towards the exit, slowing in one of the lines to pay, decelerating in inverse proportion to the acceleration of Claire's thoughts. What was Rachel doing in Las Vegas? *Las Vegas?* What exactly had the postcard said? How could she have done this – got in touch with him and not any of them? Claire reached out and brushed Stefan's thigh – the last thing she wanted was to get angry at him – as they were released into open air, along a ramp that fed them through a tricky merge into traffic speeding south along arterial Airport Road and from there along another artery onto the 427.

"How are you?" she asked, trying to observe him through her haze.

He kept his eyes on the road. "Some great results coming in on these arrays."

"I'm glad." Although it was hard, just at this moment, to share his excitement about lab results. What Hannah di Castro had said about Rachel being unable to write might have explained why they'd had no e-mails but not why she hadn't called – and yet she was able to write a postcard, at least to Brad Arnarson. When had she travelled from Italy to Las Vegas? They exited the 427 on the long curved ramp that led down to the Gardiner Expressway, which would carry them east along the lakeshore into the city.

Claire was surrounded once again by Toronto, a city she knew in how many different ways, as map, as data, as home, a city that had always been central to the way she oriented herself in the world, so internalized as to be like the pathways of her brain, only now she felt cut off from it.

"I called Allison and left a message for her," Stefan said.

"Thanks."

"It's just a postcard. It doesn't mean she's there now."

"Stef, I know that."

Claire called Brad as soon as she got to the house, but he wasn't in and his cellphone appeared to be switched off. She told him to call whenever, however late, it didn't matter. It was not even 6 p.m. It felt like midnight. She was practically dancing from one foot to the other. If she was hungry, Stefan said, he could run up to Queen Street and pick up a couple of rotis. Claire nodded.

Stefan went out and Claire stayed home, unwilling to leave the telephone. She called Allison's house, but no one answered. She climbed the twenty-one stairs and, in the bedroom, made a stab at unpacking. The duvet was pulled up over their bed, the room tidy, apart from a plastic laundry basket of dirty clothes dropped between bed and closet door. The house had a slightly fusty, unfamiliar smell, which took Claire by surprise (did it always smell like this and she was only now recognizing it?). Her gaze travelled over details of the room, the baseboards, wrought-iron curtain railings, gauze curtains, the bed. She couldn't help noticing, with the clear-eyed vigour of one who has been away, the dust gathering on the top of baseboards and on windowsills, signs that in the past month neither she nor Stefan had had time to do much cleaning.

When Stefan returned, Claire hurried downstairs, pulled him into the backyard, away from the redolence of West Indian curry, and held out an arm to him to sniff, the only bit of Italy, she joked, that she'd brought back for him. The phone didn't ring. Neither of them commented on this. After dinner, she brought out the chocolate that she'd bought for him in Amsterdam and fed him a piece. When Stefan offered her one hesitantly, she ate it, whatever its dangers to her, for these hardly mattered when she was already on the verge of getting a headache. They made their way upstairs, not arm in arm, since the stairs were so narrow that they would have tripped to their deaths that way, but Stefan practically pushing Claire. Upstairs, he kicked the basket of laundry from the bedroom into his study. It was still light outside, not quite nine o'clock. Claire laid the phone on the floor beside the bed. Her head hurt more now, the pain of travel and dislocation catching up to her. She yanked open her bedside drawer and stared at the pile of plastic bottles: her vile pharmacopoeia. In the doorway, Stefan stood watching as she swallowed her pills.

"Why is it essential that we have a child?" she asked him. He would make a good father, she knew that.

He leaned against the lintel, frowning. "As a sign of our love."

"And our love doesn't go on without a child? What if I couldn't have a child, or we couldn't."

"We don't know that yet."

"But what if I couldn't, if I decided I couldn't."

"You're just frightened."

"What if it isn't simply a matter of fear, if it doesn't feel like the right thing."

"Claire, why are we talking about this now?" He switched off the light. "Go to sleep."

At 5 a.m. she was wide awake, as suddenly as a light bulb flicked on. She could not call Brad Arnarson at five. If there'd been any urgency in Rachel's message, any emergency — well, people didn't tend to send postcards in emergencies, did they? And yet now Claire was also most aware of being home, her body nested against Stefan's, heat rising from the small of his back, her fingers pressed to the swell of his ribs, seeking comfort, seeking the pulse of his heart beneath them. She was struggling to feel at home, aware of Stefan as someone utterly familiar and yet made briefly new by her absence, his brown hair flattened by the pillow, the pillow's whiteness accentuating the line of his nose, the slender sculpting of the bones beneath the darkened skin around his closed eyes. He'd shaved. He must have done so at night, before coming to bed, after she'd fallen asleep. As she leaned gently over him, he murmured something that sounded like pickup (pick up?) but did not wake, not until, at five to six, eyes wide open, he rolled into Claire's arms.

It was a little after eight-thirty, just after Stefan dashed off to work on his bicycle, when Claire checked the phone and discovered there were messages waiting. Brad's voice: Hey, Claire, Stefan, are you there? Pick up if you're there. I'm at Rachel's. From Allison: Hey guys, it's me calling you back. Brad again: Okay, I know it's late and you're probably asleep. I'm at home now. Call me whenever. I've got something else Claire will want to see. I'll be at work tomorrow. He left a work number. His first message had been recorded – Claire checked – at 9:39 p.m. The second at 11:50 p.m. She turned the portable phone on its side. The ringer had been switched off. She'd picked up the phone from where she'd stowed it the night before, at her bedside. She settled back on her heels, on the floor, cradling the receiver. Then she called Brad Arnarson, first on his cell, which he didn't answer, then at work.

"Pure," said a woman, her voice as soft and smooth as an emollient. The woman said Brad was already with a client.

"Tell him Claire called. Do you know when he'll be free?"

The woman clattered at a keyboard, before returning to pour a new syrup of sound into the telephone. "He's doing an hour-and-a-half, so maybe like a little after ten?"

Claire thanked her and hung up. She took the phone with her downstairs to the kitchen. She sat for a moment, the woman's melodizing voice — Pure, Pure? — ringing through her head. She stared at the phone, then switched the ringer back on. She called Pure back. This time she got shunted into a holding zone, through which another woman's similarly timbred voice led her, detailing the services that Pure offered, facials, manicures, pedicures, massages, wraps, scrubs, detoxifications, press two to make an appointment. Another spa. Brad Arnarson worked at some kind of spa, how bizarre. She'd never imagined it. Nor had she predicted how far searching for Rachel would lead her into the land of upscale beauty treatments.

Call three: a different woman picked up.

"How late is Brad Arnarson working today?"

"Until five. But if you want an appointment with Brad, we're booking four months from now." How familiar and proprietorial that *Brad*.

"I just need directions and the address." Four months meant November.

"Where are you?"

"Coming from the north."

"From the East Side, take a Number Six to Bleeker and come out the Houston Street exit, or take the Broadway line to Prince. We're south on Broadway, east side of the street, just above Prince."

Claire did not call Stefan at work on the morning of Wednesday, July 12. She travelled on points, her intention being to return that night. She didn't call Charlie Gorjup either, although the wetland survey a.k.a. the mosquito map was so far overdue it really wasn't funny, because it was Charlie who had instilled in her that mapping was an investigative calling and wasn't she, in the end, just taking his dictum to heart?

At 2:16 p.m., she was climbing the subway stairs to Houston Street, just east of Broadway, and once she stepped out of the subterranean heat into the even moister, denser, dirtier New York air, nothing seemed surprising, least of all the fact that she'd travelled through three cities in three days, or six cities (well, four cities, a town, and a terme) in five days, or that she'd had breakfast in Toronto and found herself, just after lunch, at the corner of Houston and Broadway, and now these taxi horns these fumes these throngs these skimpy-clothed bustlers these three old women in flowered dresses on their lawn chairs at their card tables hawking what might, as far as Claire knew, be the same sad ancient issues of *Reader's Digest* and individual packages of instant soup as she had seen when she'd passed this way a month before, all the jangle of New York slipped around her as easily and pressingly as a skin-tight dress, and carried her forward, making its own urgent and unignorable claims upon her.

Claire hurried down Broadway. The heat was terrific and odorous, anything but pure. What she was looking for turned out to be an older office building, with glass doors, a light-filled vestibule, and a security guard at a desk. In an alcove, to his left, stood a bank of elevators. Upstairs, on the fifth floor, she stepped out into a wide, high-ceilinged hallway larger than many

New York apartments. As she rounded the first corner, a young woman in grey track pants and a white tank top, as lean and clear-skinned as a sylph, stepped through a pair of frosted glass doors, on which the word Pure was etched.

The room that Claire entered, just over twenty feet by thirty, appeared to be made entirely of greenish glass. It brought to mind not only an aquarium but also the interior of a spaceship. So much minimalist elegance (such cool beauty) surprised Claire, and seduced her, even as she scrambled to take in the fact that somewhere in here scruffy Brad Arnarson apparently was. The walls shone, as if some spectral sun hovered beyond them, illuminating the tinted glass bottles of potions – pink, yellow, blue – set alluringly on shelves at different heights along the walls.

At a translucent desk, her hands poised over her clear plastic keyboard, a honey-haired young woman asked how she might help. Claire gave Brad's name. She sensed some reluctance on the part of the young woman to entertain her unorthodox request to wait and speak to him, without an appointment or desire for service, as if she might burst Pure's bubble with her over-eager demands from the outer world. "I guess you can sit in the clients' lounge. When he's finished he usually goes into the staff room. It's across the hall. I'll leave him a message."

The young woman led her down a greenish hall into a room where she directed Claire to take a seat on one of three six-foot, off-white sofas. Two other women were already seated, both wearing unbleached terry cloth robes and plastic thongs on their feet and flipping through books of black-and-white photography. Both glanced up, took in Claire's streetwear, looked away. There were sixteen-foot windows covered in sheer drapes behind her. Here, too, the glass was frosted: light poured in upon the whitish walls but it was impossible to see out. There was a tall vase of flowers on the low table in front of her and beyond, to her left, on a linen-covered sideboard, bottles of water and juice, a pot of boiling water on an electric hot plate, a saucer of lemon slices and, in a small basket, six packets of instant hot chocolate.

A woman in a white T-shirt and jeans called, "Corinne?" from the doorway and one of the women went away.

Of course Rachel had been here. Claire didn't doubt it. This was where she'd met Brad. Of this Claire was suddenly convinced. Once she herself might have found a place like Pure too much, but she was beginning to see its appeal. The piped-in flute music continued, annihilating any vestigial roar of the city. The sweat had already dried on Claire's skin. Pure felt like a lung, a filtering organ that breathed for you, that circulated its own citrusy, astringent air. Escapist and vaguely puritanical. Perhaps the other woman was here to see Brad, and Claire was intruding on their private sphere, breaking the unspoken contract between therapist and client that maintains that in a certain space for a certain span of time you two are the only people in the world.

A figure passed down the hall – blond, a blur of brown and white. Claire leaped to her feet as Brad stuck his head through the doorway.

He bounded across the room, arms outstretched, hugged and kissed her like an old friend, not someone he'd met only once before, while peppering her with questions: what was she doing here, when did she get in, of course she'd got his messages?

At the same time he did not seem *so* astonished by her arrival, as if it were almost natural for her to have shown up.

He was chewing mint gum. His shirt, untucked, was of a garish brown and white paisley, sleeves rolled high on his biceps. His uncombed hair was longer and therefore more dishevelled than a month ago, although now Claire had the sneaking suspicion that there was something a little more cultivated about his appearance than she'd originally thought. He beckoned her across the hall towards the staff room. She'd missed, on first meeting him, any impression of his professionalism. He was at home here, offhand because he could afford to be. He had rank, even seniority. The voice of the woman she'd spoken to that morning by phone returned to her, the almost possessive tone in which she'd spoken his name. He must be good (four months to get an appointment). It would cost many dollars per hour, dollars per minute, to be worked on by those hands, those clean, citrus-scented hands. Imagine those hands on Rachel. On herself. Try not to.

In the staff room, a couple of women — other massage therapists? — were chatting. Brad introduced Claire to them. Mel and Rae. From a mini-fridge, he hauled a carton of vanilla soy milk, swallowed a mouthful, then handed the carton to Claire. She took it, a little nonplussed, as he grabbed a black nylon knapsack out of a metal locker and hoisted it over his shoulders, before taking the carton back.

As they passed the front desk, the young woman sang out, "Brad, your three o'clock just phoned, she's going to be a little late" — again that proprietorial note of intimacy, now affronted, as if Claire, an interloper, were stealing Brad away.

It was 2:35 by Claire's watch. "We have to run a little errand." Brad nodded in Claire's direction. "I won't be late, but if I'm like five minutes, don't panic, I'll be back, okay?"

As soon as they were through Pure's doors, Claire turned to him.

"What did you find?" she asked.

"Wait." When he pressed the elevator button, the doors sprang open and they stepped inside.

"You were in Rachel's apartment." The elevator sucked them towards the ground.

"In her postcard she asked me to check up on things and so I went over last night to take a look around." Disgorged into the lobby, they came face to face with a herd of bicycle couriers, all wearing helmets and ready to surge.

Out in the street, the air was hotter than ever. Brad waved his arm and dragged Claire towards a cab pulled up half a block away.

"Where are we going?" she asked breathlessly.

"Back to my place."

In the cab, an automated voice asked her to fasten her seat belt, so she did. (South on Broadway to Spring, east on Spring, north on Lafayette.) Brad swigged from his carton of soy milk. Finished, he squashed the carton flat and wiped his mouth with his fist, then his hand across his forehead, beginning to flush from the heat (the cab wasn't air-conditioned). So what was the story, she was just back from Europe? Had Rachel ever told him about Ariel, Claire asked. She hadn't. So Claire did.

The gunmetal grey door to Brad's building on East 12th Street was more modest than Rachel's, only a single step leading up to it from the sidewalk, the vestibule dark and cramped, wire mesh over the small, square window. Despite their rush, Brad stopped, as if it were a reflex, to check for mail, pulling a key from the clump on a chain attached to his belt loop. In contrast, the door to his apartment, three floors up and at the back, was painted glossy scarlet, its interior once again nothing Claire would have predicted, so white, so spartan in its furnishings (despite the used cartons of soy milk on the counter and the clothes strewn on the floor) as to appear almost monkish. In the middle of the kitchen, through which they entered, a metal office desk was in use as a table, two small wooden chairs to either side of it. On the table, in a large bag of thick, clear plastic with the words United States Postal Service embossed repeatedly in blue, was the postcard. Brad handed it to Claire. Inside the bag, the card was ripped almost in half. It looked like a piece of forensic evidence. On the front: the photograph of a hotel at night, a flourish, now bisected, of floral neon. The Fla mingo. On the back, Rachel's writing, or an eerily good facsimile of it.

Dear Brad, It was very bad of me to leave like that. In a bad way. No excuse. Strange place, isn't it? Everything you said and more. Desert's a balm. Would you mind keeping an eye on the apartment for a while? love, R.

The diction was a bit odd but credibly like Rachel. *A while.* She had not, but this was typical of Rachel, dated the card.

"When did it arrive?" Even the plastic felt hot, steamy in Claire's hands. Rachel's words — so much left out of them.

"What's today? Tuesday, yesterday. I called you guys as soon as I got it. I can't tell when it was sent, though. Look." He pointed. The postmark was smudged and the rip went through the middle of it. "What do you think?"

Claire peered. "April? May?" Definitely not JUN or JUL. "The fifteenth or the sixteenth."

"I think it took so long because it got ripped. It probably sat in some vault of lost postcards for a couple of months. Anyway, I went back to the apartment last night." He was walking away from her as he spoke, to the left, stepping over a pair of jeans and into the small room that she surmised was his bedroom, since, in addition to bare walls, a corner of mattress was visible through the doorway. (On the far side of the other room, to the right of the kitchen, the white drapes were drawn, and the wooden frame of a massage table projected into the doorway, a bundle of sheets at its feet.) "Just to check on things. And I found this." He reappeared, holding out a notebook. "You didn't know this was there, did you?" Claire shook her head. She took the notebook, a blue Hilroy two-hundred-page 5 x 8 inch spiral-bound pad, and flipped through its pages. A diary of some sort. The notebook had been mostly but not entirely filled. The entries broke off in February, it appeared, although not all the entries, especially the final ones, were dated. All those that Claire glanced at seemed to be about pain.

"Where did you find this?" she asked dizzily.

"Underneath the mattress. Between the mattress and the box spring. Slipped right into the middle." She hadn't looked there. She'd slept on the bed and hadn't felt a thing.

"You were going through stuff in her apartment?"

"Only a little."

Had Rachel abandoned the notebook or hidden it? Between mattress and box spring seemed an odd place to abandon anything. If she had hidden it, had she done so trusting that no one would find it or in the hope that someone would? Perhaps Brad, in the past, had seen her tuck it there. Whether or not Rachel had wanted someone to find the diary, she must have realized there was a chance that someone would stumble upon it – that, after a while, they were going to make an effort to look for her.

"Did you read it?"

He nodded. "I thought – I thought maybe there was something in there that would, you know, help."

"And?"

"Well, I worry about her. I worry about her more now than before. I know she lives close to the edge but, Claire –" He glanced at her – "have you ever worried if the pain got bad enough she would do real damage to herself? She's tough, on the whole, there's that, but there's the headaches, and her kid." His gaze shifted to the clock above the stove. "I've got to go. I'm sorry. I can't –" He shrugged helplessly. "As soon as I'm through, I'll meet you at Rachel's. Take the notebook. Read it and tell me what you think."

Rachel's House of Pain

Aug 15

Keep a record of them, Dr. D. says. A diary. Look for patterns. Any pattern. Keep track of everything you eat, any unusual environments, stresses. I feel like the frog in the pot of water beginning to boil who doesn't know what awaits it but unlike the frog, I'm aware that things didn't use to be like this. I can look back ten or eleven years and although I suffered terrible migraines then, I also know I went out to clubs. I hung out, danced. People smoked. I smoked. I spent hours in bars and didn't think about it. I couldn't have been in constant pain. I couldn't do this now. I remember one night sitting on a bench near the edge of Tompkins Square with Lorrie G., both of us in our little black leather jackets, sharing a flask of brandy (M. must have been away or didn't want to come out) and getting happily drunk. If there was a headache, it came later, and if anything came that night, it must have been something I could toss some codeine at and go on.

Aug 16

2.2 BPS. Right side. Z + Tyl 3 (3 a.m.)

I took a lot pills, it's true. More than now? Possibly. I used pills to help me forget the pain, shut it off, so I could go on functioning normally, as if everything were fine. The illusion was that they dissolved the pain but probably they just covered it up. Drugs repress a pain that doesn't want to be repressed.

2.1 Right side. Z + Tyl 3. (10 a.m.)

Aug 18

How were things when I was with M.? Before we lived together, I hid things pretty well. Often in the morning, when I got up there would be something so I would down a couple of codeine (222s smuggled from Canada) and eat some breakfast and have a cup of coffee and sometimes the coffee and codeine would act together and I would be fine and sometimes I wouldn't. M. had lost his father when he was fourteen. A heart attack. I wonder if I needed to feel he had access to some sort of pain to feel attraction (I wonder this now, don't think I wondered then). I remember wanting to seem fearless. I did not want to be the kind of woman who uses pain as an excuse for not doing things. M. used to make fun of what he called an organ recital: old ladies (anyone) sitting around rehearsing their health problems. So, on the whole, I shut up and kept things to myself. And yet he was not unsympathetic. I think he felt his own presence ought to be curative and it was a peculiar kind of insult (he would never have said or even thought this explicitly) when it wasn't.

The first time we met, I felt nothing much. The second time, my heart dropped to my knees. We were at that gallery opening arguing about minimal consciousness, can a rock be said to experience any form of consciousness, if not a rock then a plant, if not a plant then what. His brother was a philosophy professor who studied this. What are the conditions of minimal consciousness? I argued for plants, that minimal consciousness must include some awareness of pain, and the awareness of pain requires consciousness and plants (unlike a rock) are, in some rudimentary way, aware of pain. He started defending rocks. Something about his laugh reminded me of Dad (Of course D was still alive then)

— this shook me. If I had a headache that night, I was able to act as if I didn't. He sang. He was taking singing lessons. What son of an Irishman needs singing lessons, he said. He sang Leonard Cohen's "Hallelujah." Because I was Canadian. I have never felt so overtaken by longing as when he walked from one room of my apartment into the other singing in the dark.

If I think back to the headaches then, I was aware there had to be triggers but I didn't know what they were. Sometimes it seemed to be one thing, sometimes another. So I ended up careening about. Anything that seemed to help once — a glass of orange juice, a bottle of Coke — had an almost mystical power. There's a lot of frustration, the sense that you never know how much time you'll have before it begins again. I read with a kind of fury because I never knew how long I had — that probably induced a tension that made everything worse.

Migraines, says Dr. S., are more overdetermined than dreams.

Sept 21
Today, nothing. Finally. How long will it last? Last week, four days at 2.75 (Barber Pain Scale). (M, T, W, Th) Drugs? (Z + Tyl 3 x 5)

I was trying to finish a piece, past deadline. On how we appear to do, believe we're doing two things at once but on a neurological level, we can't, we switch between them. Only my own crazy brain kept interfering. I'd medicate every four or five hours, but I couldn't get the migraine to cut out, and I had to keep working because they were holding space for me. So sleepy and nauseated, every relevant thought just out of reach, but I had to keep going. I got to the end. Then their e-mail system shuts down or something goes wrong and no matter how many times I send the piece, F. H. doesn't receive it. I don't have a fax machine. I did but it broke. They could have sent a courier but there was worry that the courier wouldn't complete the delivery before the end of the afternoon, and the fact is, I was late and F. was getting pissed off. So I told her I'd bring it in. It's just a subway, a taxi ride uptown and back. I took some Dramamine. If the cab driver or receptionist stared at me strangely I didn't notice. F. doesn't just stare, she asks me if I'm okay in such a way that it's clear something is not okay. At first I think I've slipped professionally. Also, I figure I am nearly green. I touch my hair and scan my clothes but everything seems buttoned right. I tell her I'm fine, just a little tired. This response does not seem to satisfy her. Before leaving the office, I ask for the key to the women's room and check myself out in the mirror. All afternoon, I'd been rubbing the place where the pain was concentrated. I'd rubbed the skin right off. There was a raw, bloody spot in the middle of my forehead.

Nov 2

Woke in night, 3 a.m. After dinner party. 2.25. Z + Tyl 3. Hate explaining to people I barely know why I won't eat something or don't drink. Most people assume you're on a diet or intuit a note of moral superiority. "Don't you have any vices?" a man asked last night.

And then begins a strange, collective, nearly tribal effort to break you down.

Enemas. No vices I will admit to. Okay, it was a wickedly fine Amarone so I broke down, half an inch, that was all it took, half an inch.

Nov 7

Okay today. After that bad day in September, I bought myself a pair of tinted glasses, rose-coloured, since this particular tint is supposed to reduce visually provoked activity in the brain (from fluorescent lights, etc.). Have been wearing them. B. makes no stupid jokes. I did. Yet there's something soothing about the tint, taxis turn to pumpkin, and in no time you forget there ever existed any other colour field. Some days I leave them on until bedtime. Taking them off is a neurological jolt in its own right. Forgot them in a cab today. Trying to decide whether to replace them. Not sure if they work, if they really help, or if I just like them.

Fact o' the Day

Dr. Albert Hofmann was working in his lab in 1943 on the ergot fungus, searching for a more effective treatment for migraine, when he first synthesized LSD. No migraine, no LSD. Dr. Hofmann called LSD his problem child, but migraine's mine.

Nov 8

Tension/tension-type headache; chronic daily (mixed, combination headache, transformed migraine, transformational migraine, rebound headache); analgesic-induced; cluster; chronic paroxysmal; hemicrania; hemicrania continua; post-traumatic; sinus headache; allergic; eyestrain h'ache; benign exertional; wind in your face h'ache; sex h'ache; ice-cream h'ache; idiopathic stabbing (formerly ice-pick pains); hangover; substance-abuse h'ache; Lupus h'ache; benign cough, external compression h'ache; life-threatening h'ache; fever h'ache; headache caused by malformation of blood vessels; headache caused by lesions; migraine [migraine without aura; migraine with aura (migraine with typical aura; migraine with prolonged aura; familial hemiplegic migraine; basilar migraine; migraine aura without headache; migraine with acute onset of aura); ophthalmoplegic migraine; retinal migraine; childhood periodic syndromes that may be precursors or associated with migraine (benign paroxysmal vertigo of childhood; alternating hemiplegia of childhood); complications of migraine (status migrainosus; migrainous infarction); migraine disorder (migraines not fulfilling the above criteria)]. Okay, that's enough. This was supposed to be for comfort, i.e., thank God, I don't have all of these.

Nov 10
Bad day yest. Walking up First Avenue when a bus went by. All it took. Exhaust, traffic already heavy, air thick. Impossible not to swallow some of it. Pain came on fast. 2.85 on the BPS. Leaned against a lamppost, threw up. Made it home. Usual drugs. Did not used to be like this. Or else the city's getting worse. It makes travel hard but to stop travelling might be the death of me.

Nov 13

Sometimes I rue the day that I ended up in a six-floor walk-up.
I could have moved. Seemed like too much trouble. And it's
quiet up here. Things would have been so much easier with Star.
Now I think: why didn't I? There were lovers who hated climbing stairs and used this as an excuse for our ending up at their
place. This was not always a bad thing. And the migraines, so
much slamming of the brain with every step.

What if I'd stayed in Toronto? Couldn't have. Stayed with
Michael? He wouldn't have stayed with me. Kept Star with me?
It would have been worse.

Nov 14

B. asks me if I ever dream about them, a question I have never
considered. I said I didn't think I had. I have dreamed about pain.
I have dreamed of knife wounds, being stabbed. The dreams of
being shot are more about fear than pain. I have dreamed of
losing babies, repeatedly. Pregnancies ending in a purge of
blood. I have dreamed I am walking through the world with my
eyes half-closed and there is nothing I can do to open them. But
I've never dreamed of having a headache. (Of sleeplessness, yes,
of lying awake, being unable to sleep, and then waking out of
this.) Nor can I think immediately of something that would be
an obvious stand-in for such pain. Nor do I know, now that I
think about it, if it would be possible to dream about pain
directly, although I have been hungry in dreams, and woken
myself, out of dreams, to terrible pain.

Always the hunger. When the pain is still small, and before the nausea sets in, the hunger begins, it rumbles up, and when I eat, I'm soothed a little, though this, too, is a chemical reaction, and the hunger returns and grows until I feel insatiable, and then the sole of my right foot begins to ache, like a warning, a bell tolling, the sensation travelling all the way up the interior of my leg into my back and into my neck.

Yet the hunger is also a kind of ecstasy. It leads to sex. Claire says she can't have sex when she has a migraine but sometimes what better way to forget, find release, be desired, convince yourself the body is something other than a conduit for pain. There is a difference. I mean, when it gets really bad, there's no point, obviously.

The difference between migraines and sex. At the heart of a headache, when pain overwhelms you, is the desire for stillness, internal and external, whereas sex is about motion, sensation through motion, sensation existing along a spectrum of pleasure and pain. There is no way to confuse migraines and sex.

S., always, a little nut inside me.

Nov 18
I have joined a pain support group. In the spirit of trying everything before giving up, I went for a second time to a meeting of a pain support group. You're supposed to describe your pain(s) and talk about what you've been through recently, the theory being that talking about this among people who have some

similar understanding will begin to make it all seem more bearable. The woman who coordinates the group, Nicki Sanchez (assisted by this old arthritic guy named George) drives me crazy. She's very tall and stoops because she obviously thinks herself too tall and half covers her mouth when she speaks. You can practically feel the tension in her muscles, which must at least be part of her problem, so visibly tense I want to shake her. And when she doesn't think you're looking, she's busy pushing her fingers against her body, all over, which of course looks strange, like she's continually poking herself, but I know exactly what she's doing, she's pressing on points that hurt. If nothing else, I tell myself, I'm here for the stories: girl in a car accident, younger than any of us, not obviously hurt, but ever since has suffered terrible ringing in her ears, so loud much other sound is blocked out, which I accept as a form of pain. Met another migraineur, guy, so photosensitive in the midst of an attack that he can read books (not that he feels like reading) in the dark. No mention of higher powers, thankfully. We are simply here to commune with each other.

I have also realized there are no people here on crutches or with obvious wounds. The flyer on the street said nothing but Pain Support Group. Perhaps we with our invisible pain are the most desperate. We sit in a circle (hideous). Tonight, they asked me to stand up and speak about my experience and because I am new everyone was very gentle and supportive. I couldn't do it. I stood and said, Those who don't feel pain are freaks.

Nov 21
Kim Stuckless called. Haven't spoken to him in at least twelve years, since he moved to New Zealand. He said he's coming to NYC in February and wants to get together. I said as far as I know I'll be here. He's bringing his eleven-year-old son, Max, who gets migraines with auras. Whenever the aura begins, Max says to Kim, the men are coming. He sees men. Until a year ago, his migraines had only ever occurred on the left side. The one thing that relieved them without medication was going to really loud rugby matches. Last year Kim brought Max back to Toronto for the summer. When they changed global hemispheres, Max's migraines switched brain hemispheres, left to right. The whole time he was in Canada, they were consistently on the right side, but when he returned to Auckland, the migraines switched sides once again.

Nov 22
2.30 (yest), R side, came back, this a.m. L side. Bad. Usual drugs.

Nov 24
Hildegard von Bingen, Joan of Arc, Julius Caesar, Cervantes, Blaise Pascal, Alexander Pope, Immanuel Kant, Frédéric Chopin, Friedrich Nietzsche, Sigmund Freud, Thomas Jefferson, Lewis Carroll, Virginia Woolf, Joan Didion.

Nov 25

It always strikes me how few women are on these lists, even though statistically far more women get migraines than men, so does this mean, historically, that more men got migraines (unlikely), or (more likely) those few women who figured out how to make productive use of their painful selves (subverting diagnoses of hysteria) kept their mouths shut about their pain. Do men in pain achieve more than men who do not suffer recurrent pain? Freud tried cocaine to treat his.

No men in our family get them – only women. Right down the female line: my great-grandmother, grandmother, mother. Who knows when it began. In evolutionary terms, they must have had some protective value. A strategy. Dr. S.'s theory: a response to external threat. My grandmother called them sick headaches. She had them badly but only occasionally. Like my mother. So what happened to make ours so much worse? Not just me, one freak, but me and Claire.

Sometimes I wonder if we're more aware of pain because we're so inundated by external stimulation and change, which wear our resistance down. We are so overloaded we've lost our filtering mechanisms, or is it the reverse, because we have so many fewer physical distractions we have more space for this kind of pain. We feel more because we suffer less, because we no longer expect to suffer continuously, because we live in the expectation of being pain-free. It's a luxury to be able to complain. Either that or we're doing something really wrong. (Notes towards a philosophy of –)

Nov 27

They're not getting better. Maybe I'm imagining they're getting worse. 2.5 this a.m. In our family, there was no obvious advantage to being sick. You did not get more attention. When I was eight, I was fascinated by nineteenth-century women (Helen Keller, Laura Bridgeman) who were blind, deaf, and mute. Their condition seemed so extreme. I limped for a while, on purpose. I suppose it was a way of making myself more aware of my body.

When I ran, but then it was more about strain, on the way to achieving something, there was payoff, at least until my knee fucked up.

Nov 29

My father wanted me to become a doctor. And in the beginning I did not entirely rule it out, since I was in sciences but it soon became clear to me that I simply wouldn't be able to do it. The day I told him I didn't think I'd ever be able to hold a full-time job, he yelled at me to stop being such a snob and I yelled back that he had no idea, absolutely none, what it was like. He was the one who was supposed to become a doctor. He was the one for whom sacrifices were made. They came to Canada because they believed it would be easier for him to practise here, get him out of the slums of East End London, where of course it had been impossible for his father to become a doctor, however much he wanted to and apparently he did, but he had to stay in the family shop, he had no choice, the youngest, all his brothers killed off in the first war so really there was no choice. Dad was the first one to go to university. He was the first to have a chance to become a doctor, and in the beginning it seems he genuinely wanted this (not that there's anything socially regressive about becoming a teacher). Was it entirely because of J. B., because of the horror of her death and his helplessness in the face of it, that he quit? (But he didn't quit then, he took a term off from school, went back.) So what happened later — why quit after he'd met Mum, after she became pregnant with me? He got sick and had to take more time off school, but if he left simply because he'd gotten behind, why didn't they say that? No, there must have been some kind of crisis, a loss of faith. Was it discovering himself with another woman with a chronic if less debilitating condition? Was his mind already mostly made up and it took only one more trigger, this small thing, this other helplessness, to push him to the brink?

What gets passed on? My parents die a freakish, grisly death but my grandmother watches her mother die in front of her. She's twenty-one. After her mother has a stroke and collapses at the dentist, she manages to get her home by tram, because there are no taxis or ambulances in their town, but the doctor's taken the afternoon off and her father's at lunch, and she can't get her mother upstairs into bed. Somehow she manages to manoeuvre her into an armchair in the living room. Then she dies. They both (M & D) lived through the war. I asked Dad what it was like when the fighter planes flew over his head in Oxted and he said after the first rush of terror he felt a kind of excitement. But there was another time, before this, when he was still in London. There was some kind of metal cage set up in the living room for them to sleep in, to protect them if the house was bombed. And he was put to bed in there one night with a blanket or a table-cloth thrown over top. For some reason Al, the baby, was not inside, he was with their mother. It wasn't late. Granddad B., who was a warden, was around. An air-raid siren goes off and they race for the shelter down the street. Grandma B. must have thought Granddad would bring Hugh. Whatever. In the shelter, she discovers Hugh isn't there and flips out. That night something hits very close to them. When they're finally allowed out, they discover the house next to theirs has been demolished and their house is only partly standing, the front wall with the door still in place, the back a mess, the living room covered in debris but the cage still there (covered in dust, etc.) and when they pull off the cover, there is Hugh, sleeping. He was not, apparently, concussed, he was simply asleep. A reaction to shock, presumably. They had to shake him and shout his name to wake him up. That's trauma but I drink milk and it brings on a headache.

Dec 5

We met for dinner. I had no expectations. The plan was to talk about pain and his photosensitivity, which interested me. It's a strange kind of bonding, but one I respond to and at that moment that was all I wanted. Partway through dinner, he took off his jacket. His arms were bare. Chinese script ran up the inside of both arms from his wrists towards his armpits. He told me it had taken two days to get the tattoos done, one arm one day and the other the next, and on the day in between he almost decided not to go back, although the whole point of this pain was that it was consensual. He got them done after he ended up in hospital once – status migrainosus. Days and days with absolutely no break at all. He was ready to kill himself. They threw narcotics at him, doped him to sleep. He said, it's true, you don't get high. I said I'd ended up in hospital once or twice but not for years and these days I wasn't sure I saw the point, but we had this between us now, the awareness of what it's like to be so close to the edge that there is almost nothing else of the self left. There's something arousing and sensual about recognizing that state when you are not in it (been there and returned), recognizing it in someone else (empathy without pity or indulgence). Then it is possible to feel vulnerable. I wanted, I needed to feel those arms around me. He said (we were in bed by then) that when the pain is terrible, he holds up his arms in the dark (he held up his arms) and reads from them, and I can't repeat the characters or how they sounded, but these were the phrases, he said, that kept him from killing himself.

Have retreated from B., but also from everyone, from everything.

Dec 9
If he called me and said, come to me, it will help, I would go – but no matter how awful I feel, I cannot call him.

The world feels so distant, the sky, the water towers on rooftops, the pigeons, the guy playing the trumpet on another rooftop (an oddly warm day), the sound of buses. Bad but a little better now. 2.whatever. Still bad. Things fall away, the deadline for that article, the desperate need to eat in that restaurant on First Street, whether B. will drop by, the gnawing fact that I should call S. It is not only the self that feels fragile but the world, so little holds it together and binds me to it. It would be so easy to disappear. A bad migraine is a little death.

Dec 10
A kind of prescience, because of the way you are forced to think ahead. You are always aware this may trigger that – of course I give up trying to think ahead when the endless attention to chains of events proves too exhausting.

And sometimes you push things to the edge, what you do, what you eat, see how far you can go and what you can get away with, because how is it possible to live without testing, hoping. And then you pay for it.

Sometimes I think if I can describe it, that will help. It is like a fit of depressive mania, or at least a fit of depressive mania is like an inversion of a migraine, a migraine without the pain. First the torpor. Then the loss of appetite (rather than hunger). The disgorging of the body. The catatonia and internal wildness of complete despair. The knowledge that it will pass even as it seems impossible, inexplicable that it will ever pass. Like lost love. You cannot see the way out. You have no idea how you will get out. But the next morning dawns, bright and ordinary again.

Dec 11

2.95 on the BPS. Day three on R side. Muscles hurt. Why so much worse now? They were bad after Star's birth, very bad. There were days when I'd look at her and barely be able to see her. I'd walk towards her and feel like I was walking through a flood, limbs barely part of me. How hard it was to respond to her as a human being when in this state, to do even the ordinary things, lift her, feed her, bathe her.

This offers some comfort. It is chaotic but not random. It begins in instability. It is a complicated, dynamic system of neural behaviour and response. You tip from an unsettled state into illness, and at certain critical times, it takes only the smallest stress to push you from unsettledness into illness. Each thought, each action, everything you eat functions as a neurochemical threshold, you move through thresholds towards the final threshold, the singularity, something so small, possibly infinitesimal, that pushes you over the edge.

But the problem, neurologically speaking, is complex, for how much of the migraine is other and how much is indissolubly, chemically part of the self. For instance, a mathematician who suffered from severe migraines went to a neurologist after many years of agony and somehow he managed to locate her single trigger — cheese, say cheese — and all at once when she stopped eating cheese, her headaches vanished but just as suddenly she lost her ability to do higher mathematics. Something about her mathematical genius was so chemically or structurally connected to whatever created the migraines in her brain that she had to choose, pain plus mathematics or no pain and no math. She took the pain and chose the math.

If you can't feel pain, you die. This offers some consolation, if not exactly comfort.

Sonya calls. We make plans to meet for dinner. We haven't seen each other for months, which is largely my fault because I haven't been returning calls. So it's a little awkward. When we meet it's clear how happy she is, she can't hide it and once we're sitting down in the most smoke-free place we can find, she tells me she's pregnant. She's embarrassed, I think, because she's not sure how I'm going to respond. She knows what I did, giving up S. I don't know if she can forgive me for it. I don't know if I can forgive myself. We don't speak of it but it's there between us. I tell her I'm glad for her, after so long (she's convinced it's partly due to her work with A.), and I am, of course I'm glad.

Perhaps it helps to think of the worst. To place the worst in the past. The day M. and I arrived in Ethiopia (the trip we'd planned for ages – I wanted to take him to the place I'd come to consciousness, so much more meaningful than the place where you're born). We landed at the same time as the Chinese prime minister's Official Delegation, and so were kept on board for hours more after a ten-hour flight while the airport was emptied for their arrival and they were heralded across the tarmac by a military marching band, glimpses of which we could see through our airplane windows, so that I was not in good shape by the time we finally made it into the terminal building and into an interminably long and slow line, and grew worse while we waited and I was so ill and addled by the time we got to the customs official (already vomiting, occasionally racing to a sour but functional toilet and unable to keep any medications down) that he kept asking us more and more questions, which lit the long fuse of M.'s annoyance, (I wasn't sure the customs guy was going to let me in the country), and by the time we made it out to where Mum's friend Eileen was frantically waiting, as she had been for hours, behind a barrier, outside the terminal, because of the reception of the Official Chinese Delegation, and into her white Pajero, I was repeatedly throwing up into the only plastic bag I'd managed to rustle out of my luggage, completely dehydrated, (soldiers everywhere), M. furious, Eileen looking nervous about the state of me (collapsed on the back seat) and M. and her truck, (none of this like what she'd anticipated) as we drove along behind the marching band – in other words a real doozie that lasted about five days out of our ten-day trip, and I remember thinking then, for the first time, it will end, Michael and me, not now, but it will end.

One year, at the opening party for the Whitney Biennial, I

spent most of the evening lying on a small black-cushioned bench in the dark womb of a video exhibit.

Once I had to drive alone into the city in heavy, rush-hour traffic across the George Washington Bridge, drugged, barely able to keep my eyes open, stuck in the outside lane, the river beneath, and I thought, I can't go on like this, it would be so easy to – there was nothing to do but keep driving.

I've survived all this. Such solitude, such humiliation to this kind of pain and, even as you're aware of the humiliation, such detachment.

I remember the hospital visits and I remember so many rooms, so many hotel rooms, by their ceilings. Green hotel ceiling in Shanghai. Light fixtures, ceiling fans. Why travel if it's so hard? Because every time you go somewhere else there's a chance of throwing yourself in the path of something unforeseen. These days I check out the state of bathrooms, of toilets, first thing, given the odds that I may be kneeling in front of them. Some-times even clean them – me – if they're particularly disgusting and it looks likely I'll be sticking my head in.

Sometimes when I lie in bed, it's as if there's a figure at the other end of the bed whispering, what will you give up to be free of it? And I'm convinced, if only I can find the right thing – I have given up so much. How much more can I give up?

Or I think my only hope is a kind of continual neurochemical track-switching, a shape-shifting, go suddenly off medications, change diet, change anything that will allow me to restart, to outsmart, if only temporarily, the pain grooves.

Someone once said, It is like you have a ghost living inside you.

M. once said, You should get a new head.

Is there some essential part of me that isn't touched by pain, or, no matter how many layers you peel away, is it still there, a thought which depresses me, but also comforts, <u>because</u> it makes the pain essential.

B. has a way of asking, Do you have a headache, that is less judg-mental than anyone I have known. He manages to make an observation without any trace of blame or recrimination, not the subtlest nudge of what have you done now?

(And yet I'm frightened of his pity. If this gets worse, it will come.)

I told him about R. H., the man from the pain group. He freaked. Perhaps that's what I wanted. Why are you so cruel, he yelled.

I suppose I wanted to hurt him — perhaps it's all I can bear. I want to feel helpless. I want not to.

The thing is, I sleep better when I'm with B. than almost any other time.

Jan 2, 2000
I feel saturated with her ever since I got back. She's learning to draw Chinese characters, Len's teaching them, he's bought them special exercise books. She showed me hers at Xmas. I made a mistake, though, near the end. I asked her if she wanted to come live with me. I asked out of curiosity just to see how she would respond and her face took on the most peculiar expression. She doesn't want to, she was frightened I was going to take her away, but she also wanted to placate me because she knows I have the power to take her away and she doesn't want to hurt me because she loves me and so felt she should say yes (she wants to want to) but she couldn't honestly. Maybe, she said. I said, Don't worry, I'm not going to. I said I thought she was happier with her cousins. I wanted to walk through a door and vanish. Ravaged. The wind knocked out of me. Whatever I do I have failed her. If I took her back now I could not change my mind ever again. And how could I look after her now, like this? I made an agreement. She doesn't remember living with me. (Sometimes she seems as far away as a dream, sometimes I miss her so much I cannot see what's in front of me.) She says she remembers the bed. I remember her sleeping beside me, how restless she was,

how restless we both were. I remember the smell of her scalp and her ears. I remember lying on the floor of the front room with a headache, for hours, not wanting the weight of her presence beside me. Working at night in the front room, I'd walk past the bed on my way to the toilet and be shocked at the sight of her. For the first year there was such joy in her presence, my little love, and wonder, and I'd think of calling her father to say, look what we've made (the pure gift – the extraordinary openness of those moments on the train), but I didn't (and now I can't call him, because how can I admit what I've done?). What did I dream would happen? I dreamed things could be different. I dreamed the pain would break because it had to. But it didn't. I began to weep at the thought of hauling her down and up the stairs. I'd imagine the two of us leaping out the window just to see if there was an easier way of getting from here to there. That winter, the pain was making me crazy, it makes you crazy, all I could think was what could I give up, I had to give something up, I would have given up anything if it made the pain go away.

Jan 3
S. calls. Mother, she says, listen to our spell. I am so miserable, make me invisible. But she's laughing, they're all laughing, I can hear them.

Jan 15
Have been boiling up herbs like a witch.

Jan 30

There are two places in the world that may offer the migraineur sensitive to meteorological and barometric fluctuations some sustained relief: the middle of the Dead Sea and the bottom of the Grand Canyon.

Feb 6

Dr. D. suggests Botox. Says he has nothing else left to offer. Ladies who use injections of the botulism bacterium to relieve their wrinkles by freezing their muscles have discovered it helps their migraines. They think it works by numbing the area around the trigeminal nerve. Injections last about three months. It costs c. $500 a pop. I ask about side effects. None, he says. Well, your eyebrows may collapse.

Feb 10

Claire said she thought I might go for it.

I cannot eat any dairy products at all now. I am needless to say assigned to write an article on the wrinkle-free wonders of Botox. I try to avoid walking along streets that are bus routes or which have a lot of truck traffic. I suppose I could try wearing a face mask as the Japanese do when sick. Even in Manhattan the prospect daunts me. I can last about five minutes in a dry cleaner's. I wave from outside the door of the place across the street on 9th and hang what clothes I do dry clean in the bathroom with the window open for a day. I stay clear of people wearing strong perfume, especially in movie theatres. Avoid movie theatres. Newspaper ink's a problem, but depends on the newspaper. *Times* still okay. Sugar. Dairy. Smoke. Alcohol. The smell of onions. Carpets, esp. new ones made of petroleum-based substances. Oil paint. Varathane. Bleach. Air on airplanes. Muscles hurt. Worse on days when head's less. Maybe it's New York. Maybe it's the life I lead. Maybe it's the world and I'm a canary in it. Everything feels toxic. Yet I am a lucky woman. I can still afford my health insurance, and the bloody Zomig, which isn't working as well as it used to but soon there'll be a new generation of drugs. I have money, work, nothing to complain about. It's all in my head. In all likelihood I'm not dying any faster than anybody else.

Woke thinking of M & D. Wake at the first signs of pain, fearing it will grow. It will grow. Take drugs. More drugs. Think of them on the escalator, riding up. Let them have been happy together at the end. (How many times have I flown through Frankfurt and yet never been on that escalator.) I hope she didn't have a migraine. I think of the photos he took of her in High Park, the day he asked her to marry him, the ones he loved and she hated because she had a migraine. Did he know this about her then?

I could pray. Try to believe suffering is worth it for its own sake.

What is the opposite of pain? Some other kind of pain?

Think of it as fluid. Think of it as your medium, said A. Works for a while. In the doorway, he kissed me on the lips, which surprised me, but I don't think it was a sexual kiss.

Arms hurt too, not so bad on days when my head aches. What lurks always are the things that cannot be said.

There's no use keeping a headache diary expecting it to reveal patterns of cause and effect.

Is the key, still, to give something up, then what, what is the thing to give up?

Three, okay, three, three, three. Fuck the Barber Pain Scale.

They were on a plane to Las Vegas. Claire kept glancing at the aisle seat, not expecting to see beside her this somewhat shaggy-haired blond man in another garish shirt, this one loud with purple stripes. They were midway across the continent when Brad leaned over her, peered out the window, and said he'd been born down below, in Rochester, Minnesota. She told him she knew where that was, southeast of Minneapolis, just west of the Mississippi, which curved beneath them. That she knew where Rochester, Minnesota, was surprised Brad, until Claire reminded him what she did for a living. There are twelve Rochesters in America, she said, and I know where all of them are.

His father had grown up in Canada, Brad told her. In 1958, Arni Arnarson had come south from Gimli, Manitoba, and was such a mean hand of a mechanic that everyone of Icelandic extraction in Rochester (there were a lot of them) had banded together to find him a wife and wouldn't let him leave.

Did he have brothers, Claire asked. No, only sisters, five of them, all older than he was. What did his father think about having a massage therapist for a son? Well, in his father's presence he called himself a physical therapist and talked about all the ball players he'd worked on, going on about their bum shoulders and elbows and leaving out their manicured hands. Manicured hands? Yes, really.

It was now Friday, a little after midday. On Wednesday night, Brad had tried calling people he knew in Las Vegas. He'd lived there once for some months, he said, back when he was just starting out, and had returned a couple of times since, flown in by someone he wouldn't name, who'd brought him to town for a series of private sessions. Rachel knew all this, of course. At one point, he and Rachel had even talked of going out there together for a weekend. His acquaintances were mostly other massage therapists and people who practised body work of one sort or another, some in spas on the Strip, others in private clinics. It was a good place for people like him to find work, all those burlesque dancers and circus performers who needed his kind of servicing. Maybe something he'd said had spurred Rachel to go to Vegas. Someone he'd mentioned to her. There was also the desert and the fact that Las Vegas was close to the Grand Canyon, which Rachel had referred to in her diary as some kind of migraine sufferer's haven. There was more to the city than the Strip, although as Claire pointed out, Rachel had sent a postcard with a picture on it of a hotel on the Strip; it seemed likely, although it wasn't a given, that she had stayed there.

Claire couldn't figure out why, if Rachel's migraines were worse than ever, she would go to Las Vegas, of all places. She had never been that sort of gambler, but on this point, the postcard was mute. Once, in severe pain, Rachel had given up her child. In her diary, she seemed fixated again on giving something up. If nothing was helping her, how far would she go this time?

As a child, Claire's friend Maura had lived next door to a man who suffered from arthritis so crippling that he was confined to a wheelchair, who spoke matter-of-factly of his pain to Maura's mother but did not complain about it. One morning, he wheeled himself out to his car, drove to the closest mall, doused the car and himself in gasoline, and set himself alight.

Rachel had spoken of thresholds, of how, having exposed yourself to various things that might cause pain, you suddenly reached a point of vulnerability that pushed you over the edge. The more susceptible you were, the less trigger it took.

In March, towards the end of their last phone conversation, Rachel had said, I can't go on like this. She had used such words before, repeatedly in her diary. How did you know when to take them literally?

On Wednesday Claire had cancelled her return ticket to Toronto — she could fly back the next day, or the next. What, by now, did another day or so matter? Brad's cellphone rang. He answered it. It rang again. Someone he knew in Las Vegas had given a massage some weeks back to a woman who said she'd once been treated by Brad at Pure. It didn't sound like she was a regular client, or anything more than a client, and also the woman his friend Rita had seen was blonde. But why didn't they go to Las Vegas for the weekend, cheap package deals were easy to come by, and even if Claire couldn't come, he wanted to go, to see what he could find. "I don't mind doing this. I feel a kind of responsibility to make sure she's all right." It was as if the voice of Rachel's need and suffering was working on him, pulling him back towards her. It was his profession to look after people. "I care about her. She doesn't make it easy and I've tried to pull away but I don't see, especially now, how I could turn my back."

Claire took Rachel's phone into the bathroom and called Stefan.

"Where are you? I thought you were at a yoga class."

She told him she was in New York and wanted to go to Las Vegas with Brad Arnarson. Brad thought Rachel might still be there – someone he knew had possibly seen her. "She left a diary, Stef. She doesn't sound good in it at all. It's pretty disturbing."

"Claire, no, that's going too far. There's no reason for you to follow her around, whatever state she's in. Why are you doing this? She's selfish and manipulative and doesn't care what anyone else thinks. Let him go on his own. She didn't even write to you, she wrote to him."

They were beyond Minnesota now, Stefan falling farther and farther away, and yet distress still clung to Claire, Stefan's distress and her own. It left a chemical residue; commingling with grief, it made invisible furrows through her. When the muscles across her forehead and behind her eyes began to tighten, she took an Anaprox and a Gravol. She could not take a Zomig until they landed. She would only take one if she had some reasonable expectation of its working, which medicating herself in the hostile sensory environment of an airplane didn't offer. The pills were too expensive. You had to calculate carefully, or gamble –

was this one bad enough, was it worth it? – and even though you were instructed to take them as early as possible in the migraine cycle to ensure their efficacy, this warning was counterbalanced by the fear that overuse might render them less effective, and the fear of unnecessarily using a fifteen-dollar pill (did scientists factor in the psychological effect of the cost of a pill when performing drug trials?).

Besides, she only had four Zomig on her, one blister pack of three and one extra, no more than the stash of pills that she carried on her at any time. She'd left home expecting to be gone just a day. Before leaving New York, she had taken the packet of Imitrex and the expired bottle of Elavil from Rachel's kitchen cupboard. On Thursday, after she and Brad had made their travel plans, she had called and left a message for Allison, telling her what she was doing and what she feared Rachel might be capable of. And another for Charlie, asking if he could put her on some kind of leave, medical leave, whatever, but she had to find her sister.

Hours later, it seemed, Brad shook her arm. "Don't miss this." He pressed her towards the window, where, down below, the ancient crevasses, the great red wounds, of the Colorado river valley opened.

A black pyramid flanked by a sphinx swam out of a heat haze just beyond the runway. Yellow smog ringed the brown mountains and spread over the flat terrain in front of them, the Strip – already so close – thrusting up from the flatness in one long, outsized, crenellated line.

Brad asked Claire if she minded waiting for the shuttle to the car rental depot or if she wanted to take a cab straight to the hotel and he'd come back for the car later. Burrowed behind sun hat and sunglasses, she said why not pick up the car. They were exhaled into the heat.

She was sitting in a chair in the car rental office while Brad filled in forms. Next thing, he was honking at her from behind the wheel of a white Dodge Neon. How had he done that? He'd also yanked a black baseball cap down over his head. Once she'd settled herself beside him, he passed her a tube of SPF 35 sunscreen while slathering the white cream over himself. The vents blasted air conditioning. His fluidity behind the wheel surprised her, although no doubt it shouldn't have. The sunscreen smelled raw. As they approached the Strip, every building grew huge. Out of scale. Or they, in their little white car, were shrinking.

They'd managed to find a room in the Flamingo Hotel as part of a package deal. Brad had said he'd be able to stay with his friend Altha, another massage therapist, although now, when he tried her, wanting to drop off his bag, she wasn't around. The room, on the seventh floor, was one of thousands in a great three-sided block. Even though it was a nonsmoking room on a nonsmoking floor, there was a palpable hint of smoke, which must have come drifting through the ventilation system. The window didn't open. As she and Brad stared down into the gardens below, Claire spied, under a cluster of palms, by the shore of an artificial pool, foreshortened by distance, some pink, long-legged croquet mallets — no, flamingos.

It was seven minutes past one, although it felt like late afternoon. Stefan would be nearly through work for the day. Should she call him, but if she did, what would she say? After eating a room-service tuna-salad sandwich, Claire took a Zomig and told Brad she was going to lie down for a while. She stripped off the blue floral bedcover and slid onto the bed in her clothes. The white grill of the air conditioning vent billowed gusts of cold air into the room and made her shiver.

"Want me to turn it off?" Brad asked.

"Down," Claire said, because there was no other way to get any circulating air, smoke or no.

He took a copy of the photograph of Rachel that she'd been carrying around with her for the last month and said he'd see if he could find out if Rachel had actually stayed at the Flamingo, although Claire wasn't holding out much hope of his confirming this.

The medications blunted her headache but it did not vanish. At 4:35, Brad phoned from the lobby, by which point, anxious and restless and hungry, Claire was more than ready to go downstairs to meet him. He was waiting for her in a pink armchair and said that while he'd got no information out of the hotel, he'd spoken to a couple more contacts. He was asking people to check spa records and leaving descriptions of Rachel.

The heat had begun to diminish. They set off south along the Strip, among flocks of people ambling north and south, moving faster than the congested cars. They crossed Flamingo Avenue by means of a raised walkway, reached either by stairs or an escalator, set to the east of the intersection, its upper section flanked by Plexiglas suicide barriers which cut off access to the roadway below. Perhaps it was anonymity that Rachel had sought here, or, perversely, somewhere that might heighten her despair. How large everything seemed, even larger, if possible, than before, as if things had grown while Claire slept.

Outside Paris, café tables and wicker chairs were assembled beneath a red awning, high on a raised dais, so that they, at street level, peered up towards people's feet. One huge gridded leg of the Eiffel Tower descended in front of them while the others vanished out of sight through the roof of the ornamented building the tower straddled. Claire had never spent much time imagining herself in Las Vegas. Until now, she'd had no plans to come here. What struck her, even more than the giant facades of the casinos, were the monstrous hulks of the hotels behind them, those thousands of rooms: she had not anticipated the amount of visual space they occupied, nor the small dark figures (mostly male, probably Mexican), each of whom held a handful of cards and thwacked one against his opposite palm before thrusting it at any man who passed, alone or no, while chanting girls girls girls girls girls. The sidewalk was littered with abandoned pictures of girls.

At 3:06 a.m., Claire turned on her bedside light. Brad, who was sleeping on the sofa since his friend Altha had mysteriously not returned his calls, started up wildly before rolling over and pulling a pillow over his head. Claire tiptoed to the bathroom to pour herself a glass of water and take another Zomig. This was the second of the four she had left, and so she was fervent in the hope that she was simply suffering through an arrival spasm and once out of that transitional zone, she would feel better. After returning to bed, she lay thinking of Stefan, arguing with him and with herself. *Was* Rachel simply being manipulative? Was she wrong to have come here?

At five, both awake, since they were still on East Coast time, she and Brad headed out into the pre-dawn twilight to take advantage of the all-night breakfast, which ended at 6 a.m., at the Barbary Coast next door. Even at this hour there was the visual dazzle of the casinos to contend with and their auditory assault. They could not reach the street without traversing the babble of craps tables, the jangle of slot machines, without passing clusters of short-skirted women, and men clutching bottles of water, either to quench an early-morning thirst or because they were trying desperately to rehydrate themselves after drinking all night.

Brad had showered and raked his wet hair back. The fabric of his turquoise shirt was so thin his pale torso was visible through it. In a restaurant as gloomy as the darkened casino they had passed through to enter it, as shaded from the passage of night into day, they ate eggs and bacon, Brad on the banquette opposite Claire, fork gripped in his fist. He chugged from one of the single-portion cartons of soy milk that he'd brought with him in his carry-on luggage. He didn't consume dairy products, he said, not because he got headaches but because of some diges-tive sensitivity.

He told Claire he was still playing phone tag with Rita, the therapist who'd seen the blonde woman from New York.

"I'll catch up with you later," Claire said, "but first I want to go for a walk."

She would open herself to a place in which she took her bearings as much by the mountains, the sun casting its light from the east upon the flanks of the western mountains above the desert, as by the flimsy buildings in front of her. She was experiencing a great desire to be alone, to explore, yes, but also to shut out the rest of the world, or at least the people in it, as she used to do as a child when her head ached and her surroundings grew too much for her, or, as she lay in her bedroom, before Rachel appeared with her own headaches, when the room used to grow and shrink around her.

Would Rachel kill herself? It was impossible to know if she was running towards or away from something. What would the gambling dens, the circus shows, the pirate galleons and roller-coasters have meant to her? Surely she wasn't after such ordinary pleasures. And yet there was a kind of obliteration the place afforded. Here, the past was blown up and cast away. On the Strip, you were shielded from loss and encouraged to surrender to desire, as long as you didn't go looking for what you'd lost.

Claire crossed the walkway and made her way towards the white, vaguely Italianate heights of the Bellagio complex, drawn by the alley of olive trees that lined the ramp leading up to the hotel-casino's entrance. She wanted to see whether the olive trees were real. Convinced they were fake, she plucked a sprig and sniffed the waxy leaves: no, this was the honest thing, although she was, confusingly, no longer in Tuscany but in a North

American desert. She turned back the way she had come and set off north up the Strip, towards the Venetian, drawn, despite herself it seemed, to things Italian — pseudo-Italian. The gondoliers were warbling, warming up their vocal chords and indulging in mock races across their swimming pool of a canal.

Off the Strip, everything shrank except for the distances between things, which were clearly not meant to be traversed on foot. It was already stupefyingly hot, a dry desert heat that pressed but didn't cling like the mugginess of Toronto or New York. A few blocks east, she came to a small door in a windowed building flush against the sidewalk. The windows were hung with shabby curtains. The door caught her attention because it was so small. The word, Cybercafé, was handwritten in shaky white paint in the bottom right-hand corner of the window, closest to the door. Claire had seen no other Internet cafés since arriving, no booths for accessing e-mail in the airport, only slot machines, nothing in any of the casino hotels, no easy connections to the outer world. Maybe she'd missed them. Even Claire, not tall, had to duck as she passed through the lowered doorway. Her head throbbed like the beating of wings as she pushed on the glass of the door. She squeezed herself inside. There was no sign of anyone. Stuffing plumed from two armchairs. The dimness of this place seemed the murk of dereliction after the casinos' calculatingly artificial light. She was beginning to have trouble concentrating on external objects. The second Zomig hadn't worked. It was just after ten in the morning. How dark everything was.

A small, stooped man shambled out of the shadows. Claire asked to use one of the two computers and for something cold to drink — a juice, pineapple? She checked her mail. Nothing.

Nothing from Stefan, not that she'd expected him to write. Should she send a message to him? Apologizing, but for what, exactly? She pressed her fingertips to her clammy forehead and though she felt pain, it remained unreachable. In a search field, she entered three terms — migraine pain las vegas — and waited, bleary, sipping her pineapple juice, for a page of results to display itself.

Pro-Care Clinical Trials, **Las Vegas**: Have you suffered from the pain of migraine headaches for more than a year?

The Carter **Pain** Management Center, W. Charleston Blvd, Las Vegas.

Migraine Testimonials 0021 . . . we saw her . . . and she was in such pain. Her husband moved to Las Vegas.

Abstracts of the 14th Annual International Headache Symposium, April 14-16th, 2000, Alexis Park Hotel, **Las Vegas**: "evaluation of preference for naratriptan among migraine patients"; "a history of awakening with migraine pain"; "establishing a standard of speed for assessing the efficacy of serotonin 1B/1D agents (triptans) in migraine treatment"; etc.

Bull's eye. Pin in the right place. The dates fit. Her own haphazard methods had led to this. This was what must have brought Rachel to Las Vegas. And really what better place could there be to hold a conference on pain?

The Alexis Park Hotel was on Harmon, one block south of Flamingo Road, just east of the Strip, so that they must have passed within sight of it as they walked south along the Strip the night before. Yet there did not seem much point in going there now. Rachel could have come to the symposium to gather more research for her migraine article. Claire wondered what a headache symposium would consist of, exactly. Talks on headaches, panel discussions on headaches, booths on every remedy imaginable, a mingling of doctors and anthropologists and psychics and snake-oil salesmen? What sort of freebies would you get? Maybe Rachel simply wished to commune (commune!) with fellow sufferers, or maybe she was urgently seeking some further understanding of what made her own head ache. (Wasn't there a risk that attending a headache conference would make your pain worse?)

One of the papers listed among those delivered at the symposium, "speed vs. duration in current migraine pain treatments" was by a Dr. J. T. Reza affiliated with the University of Nevada at Las Vegas, a contact which seemed worth pursuing, since there was a chance, even if it was the middle of summer, that Dr. Reza would be in town. Back in her hotel room, Claire called the university, a few blocks to the east, where the switchboard directed her to the University Medical Center, a separate number. Then she was bounced back to the main campus where Dr. Reza had a second office and where he was more likely to be reached. She left a message on his voice mail, although, given that it was a Saturday, it seemed unlikely that she would hear back before Monday at the earliest. She could not find a listing for him at home.

She fell briefly into a deep sleep and woke abruptly at 2:16 p.m., remembering with a start that today was Star's birthday party. Allison had promised Star a party, the kind with games and loot bags that Star had desperately wanted, and was holding it two weeks after Star's actual birthday, since Allison and her family had been out of town on the day. It was past five in Toronto, which likely meant the party was over, or almost over. Allison's line rang repeatedly, and given the probable din in the house, Claire waited to be redirected to voice mail, but then the line clicked and, to her surprise, Stefan picked up.

So he'd gone to the party, presumably with the present (the little cup and saucer with Le Petit Prince on them) that she'd bought for Star in Amsterdam, without Claire even reminding him about it. She did not know whether he was doing this out of loyalty to her or in an attempt to show her up, or what he had said about her absence to Allison, or Allison to him.

"Stef, I should have called you earlier," she said. "I'm sorry. I'm sorry I'm not there. I'm glad you went. How's Star? How are the girls?" High-pitched laughter filled the air behind him.

"Oh, they're having a great time. Claire, come home."

"Stef, not yet."

"You're hurting me."

She felt helpless to respond to this. "Can I speak to Allison?"

Without another word, he set the receiver down. Moments later, Allison came on the line. "Claire, have you found anything?"

"I have a lead. A doctor out here. It looks like she was here for a conference."

"Listen, it's fantastic you're doing all this. We're grateful, we all are, but I think it's fine, you know, if you just come home. For Stefan – We'll be all right. Star will be all right. Maybe it's better this way. Better for Star. Maybe it's Rachel's way of really letting her go."

This took Claire aback. Since when had Allison decided that she was prepared to let Rachel slip away? Better for Star, but perhaps also better for Allison if Rachel was out of the picture. Easier to mother Star, as Allison had once thrown herself into mothering Dido, if there was no second, ambiguous mother hovering in the background.

Or perhaps Allison was pulling back as an act of self-protection, to guard herself, guard them all, against the ongoing risk of being hurt by Rachel. At this distance, it was hard to tell what was grievance and what a kind of weary acceptance — or what.

"Claire, I really don't think Rachel would kill herself."

"But you don't know." She had Rachel's pain diary packed in her travel bag. She couldn't get the anguished voice of Rachel's diary out of her head, or her own fear. She couldn't take anyone else's word for Rachel's state of mind. Somehow she had to find Rachel and see for herself.

There was a knock on her hotel-room door. Discombobulated, still half in Toronto, Claire rose to let Brad in. He sank onto the sofa, rubbing his hair, and told her he'd finally got hold of his friend Altha (who'd been out overnight but thought her daughter Susie would be in), and talked to Rita. The woman she'd seen was a dancer, not Rachel, but he remained convinced that he would find some trace of Rachel somewhere, if he looked hard enough. He was cheered when Claire told him about the conference and the possible proximity of Dr. Reza. She said nothing about speaking to Stefan or Allison. "I'm thinking of going for a swim," he said, as if, whatever his degree of concern, there was still room for a little relaxation.

"I'll stay here."

"Do you have a headache?" It was true, as Rachel had said, that there was no judgment in his tone. His question was an observation rather than a comment that implied she was somehow failing to look after herself.

"A bit. But I don't have a bathing suit."

He nodded. "I'll be back." She assumed that he'd left her while he went down to the pool and so curled herself once more on the bed, but a short time later, after another knock, Brad re-entered, letting himself in with the extra room key this time, and tossed a white plastic bag in front of her. Claire sat up and, from the bag, pulled a woman's bathing suit, a black, orange, and purple one-piece in a floral pattern, with fitted bra cups. Hideous. She did not know what to say.

"It was on sale. I know it's ugly but there wasn't a lot of choice. I found it in this chintzy little boutique downstairs. I hope it's the right size."

"You didn't need to buy me a bathing suit." No matter how hard she tried to thrust money at him, he wouldn't take any. There seemed to be no point in fighting his generosity.

And so, whether she wanted to or not, Claire changed into the suit (which sort of fit) and joined Brad, who'd brought his own black Speedo, in one of the Flamingo's five swimming pools tucked among the groves of palm trees. It was ninety-five degrees in the shade. At an outdoor bar, Brad bought himself a beer and Claire the virgin pina colada she requested, before abandoning his drink to dive into the blue water. He swam like an eel, doing laps of front crawl while Claire lowered herself into the water, the bra cups floating like independent body parts, the odour of chlorine swelling around her strong as bleach, making her eyes sting with tears.

That night, Brad said he could get them free tickets to a show featuring girls and a midget magician but Claire said she wasn't sure she felt up to it. He did convince her to go up the half-size forty-six-storey Eiffel Tower, although as soon as they stepped into the elevator to begin their ascent, she was certain she'd made a mistake. She did not know why she'd let him talk her into it. She had never been up the real Eiffel Tower. She did not particularly want to be reminded of her last trip to Paris. Her porousness to the world, or the world's own porousness, felt stronger than ever.

They had reached the elevator from inside the casino, across a metal bridge that spanned the casino floor. Outfitted young men and women leered at them, garbling Bonjour so that it came out sounding like Bun Shewer. She had come for the view of the Strip itself, which would be nothing like that over the city of Paris, but, up in the air, the impressive scale of the casinos was lost. The whirligigs of neon appeared flattened and far away. Claire was not by nature frightened of heights but something about the stomach-lurching ascent and the metal grill beneath her feet through which was exposed the street directly below made her more woozy than she already felt, and the cool breeze (it was several degrees colder this high up) did little to lessen her wooziness. (What if it were possible to be genetically altered so that she didn't get migraines? Would Stefan prefer her this way?)

When she closed her eyes, she saw herself standing on a bridge. No, she was looking at a woman balanced precariously on the stone railing of a bridge, waving her arms.

She dropped to her knees. "Claire," Brad was saying. "Maybe we should go back down."

Back in the casino, they got lost in an interior maze of mall-like streets that either led to dead ends or returned them to the card tables. Brad's sense of direction was not good. In fact, it was awful. In pain and some despair, Claire's was failing her. She couldn't connect the dots. There were no clocks. It had taken her this long to notice: not only were there no windows but no clocks anywhere. Lovers flung themselves at shrieking slot machines. At the tables dealers dealt not cards at all but the white paper slips of prescriptions. Stacks of chips were not chips but mountains of multicoloured pills.

"You're a maverick," Claire croaked to Dr. James T. Reza, who nodded wildly. Jamie Reza was how he'd introduced himself, yanking her hand so hard her brain shook. She was shocked, given that he was a doctor, by the deepness of his tan. Maybe the tan was fake. Right from his introduction, he struck her as cowboy-like: the T-shirt, jeans, trim waist, the pointy boots, the oversized gestures that swept towards her and away, as if made for a place with a far horizon.

He had surprised her by calling on the Sunday morning and agreeing to meet that afternoon. She had picked up his message at the ranch-style bungalow of Brad's friend Altha, a sinewy fortyish woman with a former cocaine habit and a truculent late-teenage daughter who slumped silently about the house. In the morning, Brad, who had spent the night there, picked up Claire at the Flamingo and brought her out to join them. She was lying on the couch in the air-conditioned living room, her head still aching, thinking of Rachel, of Stefan. She was convinced that he was going to leave her. She tried to block out the noise of the television that Susie had turned on before sloping out of the room, while Brad and Altha strategized about Rachel in the kitchen. At three, Brad dropped Claire off at the university.

Now the light in his office dissolved Jamie Reza into a dazzling blackness, from which he returned, swivelling in his chair, gesticulating, the chair squeaking beneath him. She wished he would pull shut the drapes, yet closing the curtains would mean shutting out the fifth-floor view, which was helping to anchor her: to the northwest, a slice of the Strip, a space needle, to the north, the mountains.

"Even if we did, if we do have ways of controlling pain, certain kinds of pain at least, say pain like yours, headache pain, migraine pain, just say, just say, why would anyone release it? Or market it? Presuming we're talking about a drug. Even if it wasn't. But let's say a drug. What value does it have if there's no way to make money off it? Okay? Even if people say they want it, even if they say they're looking for it, really? I'm saying even if such a thing is possible, you'd never hear about it. Headaches. Huge economic cost in lost days. Huge military problem, by the by. Great if they could be eliminated. I'm saying, even if in the best of all possible worlds, there's a cure, you're not going to see it. What you'll see — how fast you can get something into the system. Optimal length of time of pain relief. What is it? Four hours, twelve hours? New generations of nonopiate drugs."

Jamie Reza was cannier, Claire thought, than he let on. A lot of his display was a bluffer's, a showman's energy. She wondered if any of his research was military, given the part of the world they were in. What if he himself had developed a pill, a panacea, that eradicated pain like hers? What if Rachel (based on a hunch or some research she'd found) had suspected as much? What if she'd come in pursuit of him? How much would she herself give for a cure like that?

She showed him the photograph of Rachel, which had begun to feel so out-of-date, a relic, nearly antique. She asked if there was a way to get a list not only of conference attendees but the media. Who knew what address and contact information Rachel had given. She would pass on what information she could to Detective Bird, and if she had trouble ask him to request more.

There'd been quite a few attractive dark-haired women of approximately five-foot-six at the 14th International Headache Symposium, Dr. Reza said. Of various nationalities. He couldn't say he hadn't met Rachel, couldn't say he had.

Claire pressed her fingers to the point above her right eyebrow that ached, touched the three points across the top of her head. Even when she buried her hands in her lap, she found her cold fingertips, despite herself, moving back to the burning point on her forehead.

Dr. Reza leaned across his desk. "Believe me, I will never deny that a bad headache is a terrible thing."

The evening before, Claire had taken her third Zomig, along with an Anaprox. At dawn, after waking without relief, she'd gambled and taken the last Zomig because sometimes taking one at such an hour proved lucky. She'd had no caffeine since arriving in Las Vegas. No milk, no alcohol. Her pain would diminish a little but kept coming back.

She took the business card that Dr. Reza handed to her and rose to her feet. She could ask him for a prescription for Zomig, for Elavil, since she was now out of Zomig and the only Elavil she had were the pills from Rachel's expired bottle, which were two years out of date. Yet she was supposed to be home by the end of the next day, and she was feeling a little hopeless, currently, about any pill's ability to help her.

What if the medications she depended on stopped working? Would fear that the drugs were failing her make the pain worse? Was she, like Rachel, growing sensitive to smaller and smaller stimuli, the pain grooves in her nerves growing deeper and easier to fall into, every new pain a culmination of every previous one, or was she, along with everyone else, approaching some collective threshold?

She and Brad had arranged to meet at five, at a place called The Hookah Lounge. Claire had misunderstood. Not hooker, *hookah*, he'd mimed. Not on the Strip but in a strip mall. On the southwest corner of Flamingo and Maryland Parkway.

All roads seemed to be lined with nearly identical strip malls. The only grace was the expanse of sky above the flattened landscape. On Maryland, a school bus refitted for a summer camp was stopped, its hazard lights flashing, in the middle of six lanes of traffic behind a dented car. There were no ambulances, only silent police cruisers and, at the curb, a pack of giant idling sport-utility vehicles. Apparently the bus doors could not be opened. Parents huddled at the roadside, desperate to reach their children. Small trapped hands and faces were visible inside.

A doorknob, shiny and bright. Beyond the door, a fountain in a kind of covered courtyard. There were wrought-iron tables and trees in pots. A young woman pointed Claire towards another door, on her left. She counted four steps and entered a darkened room, a room full of hookahs. The hookahs were set on low stands, and different coloured floodlights had been built into the stands, illuminating the hookahs from below so that their glass bowls glowed pink blue yellow lime. They seemed to swell and gyrate as Claire approached. Their long pipes arced at their sides like the elegant necks of birds. Only one hookah was in use. Brad was seated behind it on a cushioned banquette that ran along the far wall. Velvet and embroidered pillows surrounded him. He lolled like a pasha, the only person in the room, lips to the hookah's long, caterpillarish neck as he inhaled. His hair, lit by the floodlamp, was green. He waved. She floated towards him. The air held none of the acridity of cigarette smoke, but was tinged with a curious sweetness. There were no windows here either. The plum-dark walls were hung with curtains, interspersed with shadowy paintings. The womblike room enveloped them. It was hard to believe they were still in Las Vegas. The illusion of the Strip gave way to a sense of being transported elsewhere. Happy hookah hour, Brad said. Or was it hookah happy hour? The pulsing music was loud, which made it difficult to hear him, especially since her brain felt partly disconnected from her body. Raising his eyebrows in query, Brad offered Claire a small plastic tip, her own, to fit over the end of the pipe's mouthpiece, then leaned close to whisper in her ear. "It's very mild. Maybe it'll even help you." She nodded. What, in her current state, did she have to lose by trying? When she inhaled, the water in the glass bowl bubbled. Her tongue was touched by the taste of orange. Her throat didn't burn. She didn't cough. The smoke was unexpectedly calming.

She managed to form the words, Did you find anything?

"Maybe," she thought Brad said. "I'm meeting this woman later who works at the spa at the MGM Grand. What did the doctor say?"

"He could have met her but doesn't know for sure."

There was an empty glass in front of him, a martini or a Cosmopolitan. "I still believe we'll find something."

"We haven't tried the desert." Whatever Allison decided, whatever Stefan said, Claire wouldn't give up.

Brad was frowning at the hookah. "Maybe I have this effect on women."

"What?" He made them disappear? He gave them migraines? He made their migraines worse?

"Why don't you let me give you a massage?"

"No." Claire shook her head. "But thanks."

He brought her back to her hotel room. Gingerly, she laid herself on the bed while Brad stood looking down at her. She smelled alcohol on his breath, the raw trace of sunscreen on his skin. "I can't bear to see you like this."

"I'll be fine, really."

"Massage may help you. I won't hurt you. At any point you can tell me to stop." People waited months to be seen by him. She was probably insane to turn him down.

"Maybe it's the place," she said. "Maybe it's something about Las Vegas that's making me sick."

"Maybe," he said, "but not necessarily."

From outside, lights bright as klieg lamps blasted in at them. Brad closed the curtains. He turned the thermostat up high, killing the air conditioning, and let the room grow warm. He asked if she minded lying on the floor, on the cushions from the sofa, which, while far from a perfect arrangement, would make it easier for him to reach both sides of her body than if she were on the bed. At what point had she agreed to this? But she no longer had the energy to argue with him. Only take off as much clothing as you feel comfortable removing. She thought of Ariel in Amsterdam. She should be at home but she no longer knew where home was. She could not call Stefan in this state because he would only get angry and blame her, convinced that what she was doing was making her own headaches worse. She frightened him. What she was doing frightened him. She was pulling apart the order of their lives. Brad retreated to the bathroom. Claire stripped to her underwear, wrapped herself in a sheet, and lay on the cushions.

He had no massage oil on him so they had to improvise with hand lotion. He rubbed his hands together to warm them but they were still cool when he first touched her back, moving over the terrain as if reading it. Then he began to press into the muscles of her lower back, muscles she hadn't even realized were tight. The sensations that he created were painful, almost unbearable at times, and perhaps masochistically she wanted this series of countervailing pains (on her scalp, behind her shoulders, at the back of her ribs) to match and distract from what she was already feeling. No, he was articulating something in her body, using her body. What was her body saying? The articulation became a kind of release. She trusted him. Kneeling, he pressed his arm from wrist to elbow down her back, throwing his weight behind it. He stood up, resting his own back, because his positions, leaning over her, were awkward. They barely talked. She did not think about Rachel, what Rachel was to him or to her. He, too, absented himself, was present only through his actions. She did not, now, want him to stop.

Long after Brad had left her on her own once more, the phone rang in the dark. Roused from sleep, Claire scrambled to pick up the receiver. It was 1:17 a.m. She was simultaneously aware of a slight bruised sensation beneath her skin, although her memory of the massage had receded to the blurring of hallucination. The pain behind her right eye continued to throb. "Claire." It was not Stefan but Brad, hoarsely, calling from Altha's. "She went to Mexico."

After leaving Claire, Brad told her, he'd gone to have a drink with Cleo, who was a four-foot-tall masseuse. Some people refused to believe that Cleo was strong enough to do the work but she was incredibly strong, she just had to stand on a box to reach her clients on the table. Those in the know knew to ask for her. Brad had been worked on by Cleo in the past. He thought it was likely he'd told Rachel about her.

In April, Cleo had seen a woman whom she recognized as Rachel from the photograph that Brad showed her, although in April, the woman's hair had been shorter and Cleo didn't remember the name. Journalist from New York, lived in the East Village, wrote about medical stuff and was in town for a conference – all this sounded about right, although Cleo thought the woman she'd seen was European, for some reason. The muscles of her shoulders and neck and mid-back were all striated and ropy, Cleo said, the fascia tight, too. Obviously some work had been done on her but she still wasn't releasing well. Did she say anything about headaches, Claire asked. Apparently, she got bad ones but didn't talk about them much. According to Cleo, she didn't talk that much at all. She was quite thin and complained about not sleeping well. She didn't seem obviously depressed but was perhaps a little subdued. What Cleo remembered most clearly was that the woman said she was on her way to Mexico, to Puerto Escondido in Oaxaca, which was somewhere Cleo had always wanted to go. The woman said she was driving down, driving with someone, whether a man or another woman, Cleo didn't know. She said she was on her way to a retreat, not somewhere religious but somewhere you could kind of shut yourself away from the world. It was outside the town in the hills. The woman said she was thinking of staying there for a while.

After drinks, Brad and Cleo had gone to the spa, where Cleo unlocked the doors. Inside, they searched through the appointment book until, on April 15, they came across the name Sylvia di Castro, and Cleo said, that's her. The only address given was a room number in the Flamingo Hotel. (What number, Claire asked, but Brad couldn't remember.) Cleo found the client form that Sylvia di Castro had filled in before receiving her services. The writing was definitely Rachel's.

"Claire, I think we should drive down to Puerto Escondido."

"Drive." Holding on to the phone, she sat up in bed to consider this more thoroughly.

"I've been talking to Altha. She says you can't take a rental car or a borrowed car across the border but she'll sell me this car that Susie isn't using any more. Sell it cheap. We can do the ownership exchange in the morning, and then the drive should take a couple of days."

"You don't think longer?"

"Well, about that."

"Do you know the name of the retreat?"

"All Cleo knows is that it's somewhere near Puerto Escondido. I don't think there can be that many. We'll find it when we get down there. And if we drive, maybe we'll find traces of her along the way."

"And she really said she was staying for a while?"

"Cleo seemed to think so." Though how long a while remained an open question.

"What about your job?" she asked.

"I figure I can put things on hold for about a week. Rearrange clients. People will wait. I'll have to make some calls and work like a maniac when I get back."

There was a certain mania to going, a leap into further disorder on both their parts. Who knew if she even had a job to get back to? She would only anger Stefan by going and she would be setting off without any Zomig – which would be a gamble, yet as long as they had something to go on, it seemed wrong to turn back. She had crossed some threshold: it was impossible to turn back.

How quickly the mirage of the city fell away. There were two more metastatic bumps of gambling towers, in Jean and Primm, before they were past and sandhills swallowed up all towns and the road began to climb. The car was a black '94 Chevy Cavalier, a colour that was probably not ideal for driving in such heat, but the vehicle seemed functional, which was the main thing. They had brought sandwiches, apples, bananas, bags of nuts, cartons of soy milk, and bottles and bottles of water, all stashed in the back seat.

Brad wanted to drive the California desert roads through the Mojàve and Joshua Tree National Park and cross the border at Mexicali. He said that he and Rachel, when they had discussed flying out to Las Vegas, had spoken of taking a side trip to Joshua Tree.

The throbbing in Claire's head had weakened but she still felt a little queasy. She was glad to be in a car, not in a bus or on a plane. Although a car was cell-like and involved entrapment (they were driving with the windows sealed and chemically cooled air blowing at them), a car was also porous. If the chemicals in the air conditioning began to bother her, she could roll down her window, stare unimpeded out at the desert, and let air that was hot and dusty, but blissfully untreated, blow in.

As they drove, she asked Brad how he'd come to massage and he said he'd discovered he had a talent for it, mostly through working on friends. When he first moved to New York, some of his closest friends were dancers who spent half their time in pain. He told her about massaging a friend through childbirth. Francie was a single mom who had asked him to help her through the birth – she wanted a man there and who better than a male friend who knew how to massage? Of course the doctor and nurses had all assumed he was the father and it had been too much trouble to disabuse them of the notion. He said he liked Francie well enough and had been happy to help, up to the point when she'd bit his hand during a particularly difficult contraction, but a nurse had slapped some ointment on him and they'd gone on and some hours later, there he was, bewildered, holding Francie's newborn daughter in his arms.

He said he wondered sometimes what he would do when he was older, because he wasn't sure he could see doing this forever. Did Claire know any old massage therapists? He didn't. You needed to be fit for it, you needed to train — at least for the kind of work he did. He could open his own clinic, but he wasn't sure he wanted to. He liked massage partly because it was portable, you could take it almost anywhere. He'd always thought he would travel more than he had. He still wanted to go abroad, to train — to Thailand, to Hawaii to learn *lomi lomi*, two strong men hefting your body back and forth between them. He wanted to experience it, anyway.

"Did you give Rachel massages even after you were involved with her?"

"Professionally? No, no, I wouldn't do that. I couldn't see her as a client. At home, of course. Not as often towards the end. It was kind of a sticking point. She wanted me to and I wanted her to see someone else, to find another professional relationship, not to depend — because in a way she was inexhaustible and I didn't want — after that guy, the one from the support group who could see in the dark — I looked him up, I asked him if he'd heard anything from her, I thought there was a chance she'd gone to him, but she hadn't."

At the Kelso Road, they turned off the interstate and pulled up outside a grey and desiccated structure, the only building between them and the horizon. Brad wanted a coffee. The weathered sign above the door promised gas, although there was none, none until Amboy and then only the possibility of it.

Two giant towing rigs were parked by the abandoned gas pumps, advertising their twenty-four-hour services, as if rescuing the gas-less was clearly the more profitable business. Inside, two men and a woman, none young, all wreathed in spires of cigarette smoke, sat at a battered table, a baby in a car seat resting at the feet of one of the men, who rocked it sharply with his foot while chanting, You're a mess, you're a mess, you're a mess.

Were there elevations ahead? Claire asked the woman. Elevations? Were there mountains, she persisted, or hills? There are knolls, the woman responded.

The desert held its own illusions. The scale of the landscape was so great — mountains lunar in aspect, their bases running with scree, the strange forest of Joshua trees, all shaggy arms and shock-headed protuberances, a forest you could see through — that no matter how fast they drove, they seemed to creep because everything around them was so slow to change.

They slid through ghostly Cima, a mere tumble of buildings, one truck and no evident sign of human life. Kelso appeared just as uninhabited.

They stopped outside an abandoned and now boarded-up railway station to pee. There were two turquoise Johnny-on-the-spots under some bedraggled trees to one side of a gravel parking area. Black cap on his head, Brad did a funny dance as he walked — shaking one leg at a time, rolling his shoulders, waving his arms, stretching, Claire presumed.

When she climbed out of the car, a hot wind buffeted her,

tugging at her hat, thrusting her sundress between her thighs. Cumulonimbus clouds crowded the southern horizon. The vast sky up above was blue and sere. Each time the wind spasmed to a stop, silence descended. She breathed in and out with a kind of wonder, amazed at how far she'd travelled, how far Toronto was from here.

They crossed the border towards the end of the afternoon. Claire offered to take the wheel but Brad said he was fine, he liked driving, distance driving especially, and he never got to do any in New York. Before crossing, they had to stop to buy Mexican auto insurance and more gas. An itching had begun in Claire's left eye, as if a speck of grit were lodged there, although when she peered into the mirror above her sun visor, nothing was apparent. Maybe the sun was bothering her eyes because she'd lost her hat; it had blown out the window when she'd rolled the glass all the way down one time, the hat bouncing like a tumbleweed across the road to be crushed by the car behind them.

They drove around a bit looking for a replacement sun hat and came up empty-handed, finding nothing but baseball caps and those ridiculous mile-wide sombreros sold in tourist shops, one of which Claire finally gave up and bought. With a knife borrowed from a gas station attendant, Brad hacked at the brim until he'd brought it down to a wearable size.

Once they entered Mexico, Claire grew aware of a certain slurring of the landscape, a somewhat familiar failure on her part to be able to fix on external details. The butchered sombrero scratched the back of her neck when she leaned against her headrest. She kept testing her internal perimeters to see what condition they were in.

They pulled into a motel just before dusk, since they'd been advised that it was unsafe to drive after dark. If they were awake at dawn, they could be on their way early in the morning. Before they'd set off from Las Vegas, Brad had taken the photograph of Rachel and made it into a poster, with the words MISSING PERSON printed across the top and his New York phone and cellphone numbers beneath. He had been handing out the poster whenever they stopped and taping it to utility poles, or, if given permission, inside gas stations, or, as now, in the lobby of the motel.

They unloaded their bags, along with two bottles of water and a carton of soy milk and a bag of nuts, and made their way into a room with unravelling carpets and twin beds, a room which, to Claire's nose, smelled rancid with the odours of all manner of human activity although she didn't have the heart to complain.

Lying on the bed closest to the bathroom, she searched through her knapsack and bag of toiletries, checking to see what medications she had left, just in case. Gravol for nausea, a couple of Anaprox and Tylenol 3s rattling in an orange plastic prescription bottle, the Imitrex packet and probably useless Elavil, which she'd stopped taking, anyway. Nothing as innocuous as a simple aspirin. Her migraine was definitely coming back on the other side, which was part of its pattern, but under her current circumstances worrying. She could try downing a cup of strong coffee, which might constrict her now-dilating blood vessels. If she was lucky, and intervened at exactly the right moment in the cycle, caffeine might abort the headache. Uneasily, she rubbed the left side of her forehead.

Brad came over and grasped the back of her neck.

"Ow. Yes. Left side. Ow."

He rubbed the nape of her neck for a few minutes then released her. "Try to relax, Claire."

She came back to the room after drinking a cup of coffee. They would go out for dinner but first Brad, too, wanted to lie down. She was aware of his breath from the next bed as it slowed, a little hoarse gust at each exhalation. She tried to lengthen her breaths, rounding through her belly and her ribs. Her hands and feet, despite the heat, were freezing. She tried to guide the warmth of her body towards her fingertips, to even the flow of blood along her agitated blood vessels. She was aware of Brad's body in the bed beside hers and tried to ignore it. To relax was to fall back, to let things fall, to trust, not to strive too hard or be distracted. She was not particularly good at it. Sometimes, true relaxation seemed to her a little like praying: she didn't as much imagine as sense a vast sky like the one over the California desert spreading above her, as she, or some interior version of her body (her spirit), fell back open-armed – released – beneath it.

In the morning, her headache had grown worse. At breakfast, Claire tried another cup of coffee but this time, the caffeine only made the pounding behind her left eye stronger. She hadn't called Stefan. She couldn't call Stefan. (Brad, who might have noticed her failure to do so, hadn't said anything about it.) Back in the room, she locked herself in the bathroom with her toilet bag. Even if she could hold on without drugs, she wasn't sure it would be wise; she wasn't at home but on the road with a man who might be familiar with her symptoms through his familiarity with her sister's, but who in any case she barely knew, and if things got unpleasant for her, they weren't going to be too pleasant for him, either. She took out the small cardboard Imitrex packet and unfolded its two enclosing panels. Inside were four foil-sealed spots for pills. Three were clearly empty, the foil over them broken; the fourth, slightly punctured, appeared to contain a pill until Claire pressed on the foil and it popped too easily. There was nothing inside.

She must have moaned or made some sound because Brad called her name through the door. (Rachel must likewise have thought there was one pill left, for why would she have kept the packet otherwise?) Unless Rachel was laughing at her.

Thankfully there was little navigating to do, beyond pointing themselves south, and when Brad had a question about their route, Claire was still able to rouse herself to consult the map. Mostly he left her alone, which was good. Now he was approaching the car carrying a blue plastic bag. Sliding back into the driver's seat, he showed her its contents: toilet paper and toothpaste, crackers and oranges and avocados. He snacked on the avocados as he drove, peeling back the skin and eating the flesh down to the pit. Then he chugged back some soy milk from one of his vacuum-sealed containers. The next time they stopped, he returned bearing a packet of rough, turquoise-coloured paper, which he unwrapped to reveal five damp, warm tortillas, fresh from a market tortilla machine. He said he'd held up five fingers and at first they thought he meant five kilos. At every stop, he showed around the poster of Rachel. He was outside the car, ges-ticulating as he tried to make himself understood in fractured Spanish, surrounded by a circle of small, dark men in shining white shirts. Back in the car, he offered Claire crackers, an avocado, a piece of chicken. She took the proffered piece of chicken.

They drove on. She turned to look at him, struggling to overcome, even momentarily, the frightful solipsism of her pain, her helpless absorption in it.

"Did Rachel ever talk much to you about Star?"

"Not a lot," he said. "It was a difficult subject. I mean, I knew about her, of course, but I never met her."

"Do you, have you ever wanted a child?"

"Not really. I've always felt I spend enough time as it is looking after people. Why, do you?"

"I'm trying to decide."

When her nausea grew, she took a Gravol, which did nothing to appease her headache but made her groggy. The whole world felt suspect, subject to forces beyond her control. Perhaps she, Claire, was indeed a weakling, so pervious that she felt everything, quaked at a scratch, winced at what others deemed a tic. Only she could drink hot liquids at temperatures that made her mother and Stefan recoil, scalded. She had pressed the soles of her feet to a radiator until they burned. It was impossible to know what others' pain was or what it meant that some could tolerate more, some less. Rachel had always resolved the problem of doubt. She was there like a mirror, her evident pain proof of the substance of Claire's. Claire had always assumed their pain was similar. And yet —

She had never personified her pain. She had only occasionally thought of it as an animal, as a dog, a big black dog. She had
never felt the need to bring God into the picture, although, yes,
sometimes the pain felt like punishment. She had never imagined someone sitting at the end of her bed asking, What would
you give up to be free of it? Of course she had asked herself what
would she give up and how she would change her life if only she
could figure out the thing that would make the headaches disappear. Inevitably there was bargaining, even pleading. What
would she give up now, at this moment?

She had to stop fighting. Fighting for this to end. Fighting
her anger, the bad twin of despair. She was near tears. With pain
comes desire. Part of pain is desire, the longing for somewhere,
another state, anything else. To be in that elongated palm tree,
up in that sky. She was the hills, the mountains. A policeman
(soldier? a man with a gun in his hand?) peered into the car and
waved them on. There must be some comfort, some source of
consolation somewhere, if only she knew where to look for it,
although thoughts of Rachel, who might have travelled this road
in a similar state, were no longer providing any. The daemonic
flash of the ocean. A toll booth. The hairy legs of a burro. Let
me be healed.

"What did you say?" Brad asked.

She was lying in another motel room, given over to the vertigi-
nous sensation that the road was still speeding beneath her.
When she opened her eyes, Brad was standing on his head.

A moment later, he was upright, looking down at her. "How bad is this?"

"About as bad as it gets. Only I'm frightened because I don't know how bad it's going to get."

"You don't think we need to find you a hospital, do you?"

"No, no hospital." Even if she'd wanted to, she couldn't get back to Toronto, because she had no way to get there. She had only the haziest idea where she was. They had passed through Mexican towns, skirted cities. It was impossible to imagine flying. She was pretty sure they were, now, nowhere near an airport (or a hospital). In any case, no one would let her on a plane in this state. If Stefan had been with her, he would not have been as calm as Brad. His anxiety — his helplessness in the face of her greater helplessness, his need to be useful — would have permeated the room and infiltrated her. He would perhaps have fought harder to get her to a hospital, get her out of here.

"Is there anything I can do?" Brad asked gently.

"Hit me on the head with a hammer."

"If you want, we can rest tomorrow, take a break."

She was losing all sense of what they were up to other than being in motion. She no longer knew if she was doing whatever she was doing for Rachel, or for herself, although she still had some sense that fear and loss and the fear of loss were propelling her. She was still looking for something. "Might as well be in the car. Let's keep going."

In the morning, she sent Brad out in search of a farmacia and suppositories, some kind of anti-nausea medication in the form of a suppository since her nausea kept growing and she wasn't certain she would be able to keep even a pill down. Neither of them knew the Spanish word for suppository which meant, unhappily, that there might be some sign language involved. He set off and returned apologetically without them.

In the car, the vinyl of the seat beat beneath her legs. Her hat clutched her head. The windshield enwrapped her. Such things weren't themselves any more as much as they were aspects of what she felt, the shape, the pattern of her pain. Perhaps the place of pain changed constantly. Perhaps all places were the place of pain.

She closed her eyes. The road carried her onward. She was falling. No, she was walking down a corridor off which rooms kept branching. In the rooms, people began to materialize.

She was on a mattress set upon a wooden floor, among rumpled yellow sheets and a fibrous green blanket, lying beside Kevin Giddings. They were alone in his shared apartment, on a Saturday afternoon. Kevin was small, nearly as small as Claire, but had a bass voice so sonorous he should have been in radio, a voice that seemed particularly striking given his small size. He wanted her to take off all her clothes, her unbuttoned blouse, her creased pink skirt, her bra, her underwear, for them to be naked together, which was normal, but then the process of seduction, their slow, delicious unwrapping of each other, which she loved, would be over, and she would be left with nothing but the momentousness of Kevin's desire, and equally, her awareness of his fear, his need not just to see and touch her body but to work his way inside her head and dissolve her secrets. She was unnerved, above all, by this sense of invasion. Even as she began to feel the urge to retreat, to extricate herself from him, she had a premonition, if she allowed herself to think about it (she did not really want to think about it), that he would be the one to leave her, however much she tried to shield herself from the knowledge.

She was living in a two-room apartment on Cowan Avenue when she met Tom Speck, for whom she would have done almost anything. The night he told her he was leaving his girlfriend because he wanted to be with her, she opened her door to him and led him up the stairs to her apartment; that night and other nights, she opened herself to him. She had never felt so giddy, so craven, so smitten, so eager to be with anyone, never felt so moved by someone's presence, in someone's presence, awed that his desire for her seemed to match hers for him. When he left her, simply walking through those rooms became devastating. She moved out of the apartment on Cowan and had never been able to walk down that block again.

A room with a wide, rectangular window. A teak desk with four drawers, two on each side. A man in a grey sports shirt was sitting at the desk with his back to her. What was he doing? He was painting. But he had stopped long ago. He had a good eye, a gift for composition and colour, he had taken almost all the photographs in their family albums, photos which were, in their framing and composition, far beyond most people's tipsy, blurry snapshots. When he gave himself over to the teaching of mathematics, he stopped painting. He was whistling softly, the hairs along his bare arms individually illuminated. She was very small. She wanted him to turn around and look at her without her having to call out to him but he had not noticed her. She could not see what he was painting.

They had found a couple of their father's oil paintings when they cleaned out the house, landscapes, Ontario landscapes. Allison had taken one, a grove of birch trees at the edge of a lake, which had been hanging above his desk, and Claire a farm scene found stacked against the back wall of his closet. It reminded her of day trips that she used to take alone while still in college, out into the countryside north of Toronto, to practise triangulation techniques. There was no need for her to do this, it was an old-fashioned way of mapping distance, still functional but hopelessly outdated. She liked its simplicity, and the heroism that had once been involved in mapping great distances this way, the length and breadth of France, Peru, Lapland. She would pull her borrowed car onto the shoulder of a quiet road whose gravel surface had been tamped down with tar. She set up two card tables along the side of the road and measured the distance between them. If you knew the distance between two points, you could figure out the distance to a third, far-off point. She drew lines on the paper affixed to each of the card tables, lines that if continued would intersect at the rusty roof of a barn set back from the road, beyond a copse of trees. Then she calculated all three angles. In a tree to her right, a flock of crows was gathering. Of course, knowing the distance (straight as an arrow) to the third point gave you no clue how to reach it. In the future, a flock of crows in a tree inevitably made her think of her father.

In her bedroom in the apartment on Booth Avenue, the phone rings. It is so late at night or early in the morning that, struggling from sleep, Claire is tempted not to answer, for as likely as not it's a wrong number, unless it's Stefan, as it's not all that long since they hung up on each other after talking for hours, until almost 2 a.m., for these are their very early days, their days of folly and ardour; what if it is Stefan calling to say he cannot sleep because he is thinking of her as she has lain awake at night thinking of him. She negotiates the room with ease even in the dark, knowing instinctively the placement of her dresser and small blue armchair, aware of indistinct sounds, quickening voices, from Allison and Lennie's apartment below hers, which is puzzling because she has no idea why they would be awake at this hour. Before she can pick up the phone from her desk, a pounding begins on the door below, the door that separates the two apartments. Allison is banging on the door, screaming her name. Now she is frightened. She thinks, Fire. A man with a knife. Someone has broken in and murdered Lennie. She runs down the stairs towards Allison even as the phone goes on ringing and ringing.

They are in a hotel room, she and Allison and Rachel. In Frankfurt. Lennie is there, too. At first he is the one shouting at Claire and Rachel. And then Allison, distraught and in tears. How could you do this, how could you run off and leave me at a time like this?

Why had she left Frankfurt and gone to Paris that day with Rachel? Because Rachel had asked her to. Because she'd felt obscurely flattered that Rachel had asked her, even if this meant leaving Allison behind. Always she had wanted Rachel's attention, ever since childhood, Rachel's more than Allison's, because Allison was always there. Her love for Allison was the love of the one close by, the one whose voice was heard daily rising through the floorboards when they lived one on top of the other in the house on Booth Avenue. Even in childhood, Rachel had seemed elusive, as if she might at any moment slip away. And yet Rachel had drawn close – years ago, it was Rachel who had lain in Allison's bed beside Claire, a guardian presence despite her own headaches. For all her self-absorption there were times when Rachel paid attention. It was Rachel who had leaned over Claire in her Frankfurt hotel room the morning of their arrival, who, before pulling out her blue injector, had brushed the hair from Claire's face, like a mother, their lost mother, and yet, on the surface, so unlike their real mother that perhaps she was all the more seductive because of this.

The day of their arrival, after Rachel had injected Claire, Rachel and Allison had gone together to the hospital. Claire had not wanted to go with them. She had refused to accompany them to make the formal identification and to begin the travel arrangements for the transport of their parents' bodies back to Toronto. She could not bear the thought of seeing her parents in this state. Instead she had gone back to bed and lay clutching a pillow to her chest, trying not to move. If on the night of the fourteenth or early in the morning of the fifteenth of May, she had done something, anything, different – not talked so long to Stefan, stayed awake instead settling into bed after setting down the phone, some microscopically alternative gesture – perhaps her parents would still be alive. They would not have stepped onto an escalator, that escalator, not picked out that defective luggage cart. (Let them have travelled on a different day, let them have had no desire to go to Germany at all.) If she and Allison had caught an earlier flight (they'd caught the first flight they could) and reached their mother in hospital (their father was pronounced dead at the scene but their mother died four hours later, never fully regaining consciousness, before they'd even left Toronto), perhaps they could have saved her (no, the doctors insisted, her internal injuries were too great). Surely there was something Claire could have done (she had no idea what) that would have saved them from this awful, ridiculous death.

After a while she rose and dressed and spoke briefly to Stefan by phone, although it was hard to know what to say. She called her Uncle Alan in Vancouver, as she had promised Rachel and Allison she would do. Carefully, she gathered her bag from the table by the window and left the room.

She rode an elevator downstairs. Outside she passed a fountain. The air was grey and misty, leaves the pale green of spring. She walked along a road. Out of the mist, an airplane sheared close overhead, landing gear outstretched. The ground quaked. Claire crouched low, hugging her knees, holding herself together, trying to keep the roar building inside her from tearing her apart. Her parents were not going to walk into her hotel room, however much she longed for them to do so. They weren't going to attend a conference or drive towards Strasbourg. Every journey led to death.

At 5:07 a.m., just after midnight Toronto time, there was a knock on her door. She wasn't sleeping. The three of them had only parted a few hours before, after staying up in Allison's room, crying, talking, Rachel pacing back and forth and calling out about lawyers and lawsuits, to hell with how helpful and aghast the airport officials were. Allison said she just wanted to get through the funeral. In the dark of her own room, Claire was sitting up in bed, eyes open to keep herself from imagining –

Rachel softly called out her name. When Claire opened the door, there was Rachel, in her white coat, a black handbag slung over her right shoulder. She came and perched on the very edge of Claire's bed, inspecting Claire closely, her right foot, in a red boot, tapping the floor. She seemed, not calm but calmer, if glazed with fatigue. No doubt she'd had no sleep either.

"You up for a little trip?"

"A trip where?"

"I need to get away from here for a bit, for a few hours."

"Into town?" *At this hour?*

"Maybe."

"What about Allison? And aren't there things we have to do today?"

"Allison has to be here when Lennie arrives. We won't be gone long."

Did she believe Rachel when she said that? Had she herself felt any desire to get away before Rachel introduced the idea, or was she simply taken up with convincing herself that Rachel wanted her company in particular, rather than that of the closest available escape partner. In any event, Allison could not have come. (When, as quietly as possible, Claire left a brief note propped against Allison's door, there was no stirring from within her room.)

There was a moment, after she and Rachel were already in a taxi, as soon as it became clear that they were not going into town but to the airport, when Claire begged to be returned to the hotel, but Rachel wouldn't hear of it. They were not going to the same terminal, she said. Claire had to get over her fear, starting now. The accident had happened on an escalator. There were escalators everywhere. She could not allow this to make her frightened of airports. It sounded as if Rachel were talking to herself as much as to Claire. She needed to stay in motion. At moments of crisis, she needed to be in motion, be elsewhere, this seemed clear. But she was not simply impulsive. She must have done some admittedly last-minute planning after the three of them had parted hours before, because when they approached the Air France ticket counter, she pulled out a piece of paper and asked in French if there were two seats available on the 7:30 a.m. flight to Charles de Gaulle, returning that evening on the 21:30. Even then Claire could have pulled back, or tried to argue Rachel out of this folly but she didn't. This was a chance not only to be with Rachel but, in the midst of grief, to be, for once, as reckless as Rachel was.

In Paris, they took a train from the airport into the city. A drum beat in Claire's head. Sometimes even allowing herself to feel something strongly meant she ended up with a migraine. If she let herself cry. At Châtelet, they followed the signs for the exit that led to the river and Notre Dame. Somehow she was going to have to tell Rachel that she had a headache coming on, even here, even now. They reached the top of the stairs, stepping into the blazing light. I have a headache, I have a headache.

Rachel led Claire over to a thick stone wall on the near side of a small square, unzipped her handbag and pulled out the pen-like injector. This time, she told Claire to inject herself. (Where? Here? Like this? But what choice did she have? She lifted her skirt and pressed the injector to her thigh.) When Claire asked, Rachel swore she was fine, although she kept touching the skin under her right eye, as if she might be on the verge of a migraine but didn't want to admit this, among other things.

Since her arrival in Frankfurt, Rachel had not mentioned Michael Straw, which struck Claire as odd. He had not accompanied her nor did it seem that he was coming to join her, as Lennie had flown to Allison's side. She would ask Rachel about him, just not yet.

She wondered why Rachel had wanted to come to Paris. They had visited as a family, the summer that Rachel was eleven and Claire on the verge of turning seven. It was Rachel, not Allison, who had mooned over creatures made of bread (a coiled snake, a frog, an alligator) glimpsed in the window of a Left Bank boulangerie. Their father had bought a bread alligator and they'd sat in a row on a bench in the Jardins du Luxembourg, all five of them, tearing at its limbs. But Rachel, like Claire, had definitely been back to Paris since then, at least once with Michael, Claire was certain.

They began to walk – over the Petit Pont, the Cathedral of Notre Dame to their right across a wide square dappled with the shadows of clouds and babbling drifts of tourists. Rachel seemed to have no real plan now that they'd actually arrived, other than to keep moving, as if in this way to distract herself from grief. Street names moored Claire. She tried, in spite of everything, to keep track of them.

As they crossed the Quai de Montebello, Rachel began to talk. She said they should have gone to Naples instead. There was a place she would have shown Claire, a chapel that she loved.

All these details returned to Claire now, as if she were once again walking the streets of Paris with Rachel. Rachel said she'd gone back to the chapel in Naples three times during her last visit to the city. Perhaps Claire would have understood why she loved the chapel of San Severo so much. Inside was the most extraordinary sculpture, a veiled Christ, the marble veil over the prone figure carved as thin as tissue, allowing the lineaments of the stricken body, the bones protruding through the flesh, to be visible through the veil, so lifelike that she'd wanted to run her hands over the stone. But that was not all. In the basement of the chapel, in an alcove at the bottom of a small, metal spiral staircase were two bodies, standing upright. The bodies were flayed, all their skin removed, leaving the blackened masses of veins and muscle exposed, out of which their eyeballs, blue irises surrounded by gleaming whites, stared. They dated from the eighteenth century, and were apparently fabricated anatomical models, although some mystery surrounded their origin and there was a chance that they were actual preserved bodies. In any case, what were they doing in a chapel, albeit in the basement? Some kind of bizarre *memento mori*? Testament to the frailties or the marvels of the flesh?

And there was another church, Gesu Nuovo, a baroque church now dedicated as a shrine to a twentieth-century doctor, who had been made a saint. Inside, whole side chapels and hallways were completely covered in small silver replicas of body parts — eyes, ears, legs, breasts — that people had fixed to the walls in a bid to be healed. Worshippers knelt in front of the doctor's statue. At the sight, Rachel had burst into tears.

They crossed the rue St. Jacques, turned again to the right, and found themselves walking east along a narrow street that it took Claire a moment to recognize as the rue St.-Séverin, the stone wall on their left that of L'Église St.-Séverin. On her last trip to Paris, she had approached the block from the opposite direction. She was on the verge of pointing out this geographic convergence — San Severo, St. Séverin — to Rachel, but Rachel had already hurried to the far side of the street, as if putting all her talk of Naples and suffering bodies behind her. She stopped outside an épicerie, dove her hand into a display of fresh almonds, furry and green, and, as Claire caught up to her, asked, "Ever eaten them fresh?"

Claire followed her into the store where two men, one at the cash register, the other sorting fruit, turned to look at Rachel, not ogling but alert to her beauty, which her misery muted but could not altogether hide. Rachel brought a little paper bag of almonds to the older man behind the counter, who asked her in French if she knew how to open their skins. In his country, Morocco, this was women's work not men's. He spoke these words with more wistfulness than dismay as he demonstrated. It was into Claire's palm rather than Rachel's that he tipped the first, peeled almond. She set it on her tongue and ate it, its taste nearly lemony, as if it were still connected to the tree. She wanted to tell the man that her parents had just been killed — no, she didn't want to confess it, she wanted simply to have the knowledge shared. She was glad to be here, which was not the same as being happy, but for the space of a few breaths, she did not wish to be anywhere else. She was thankful to Rachel for bringing her, to the man for his gift. And then thoughts of her parents, and guilt about leaving Allison, began to rise again, for all that Lennie should have arrived from

Toronto by now, so Allison wouldn't be on her own. She could find a public phone and call her, even if this was not among Rachel's plans – and yet she was overwhelmed by a kind of torpor as if to call would be to break the spell that Paris, and Rachel, had cast over her.

From the Rue St. Germain, they walked east along the Rue du Four and then along the Rue de Grenelle, Rachel pressing them onwards now, as if she had recovered or gained some sense of purpose. They walked still without speaking much, without discussing the idea of a destination. After lunch at a restaurant on the far side of Les Invalides, they made their way along the Avenue des Bourdonnais into the gardens surrounding the Eiffel Tower. Here Rachel announced that she wanted to climb the tower, an ambition that baffled Claire, since greenish rain clouds were gathering and they would have to take their place among the throngs of tourists already waiting in line.

But Rachel, who had never before, in Claire's presence, expressed any particular interest in views from great heights or visiting major tourist attractions, seemed adamant. "When it rains everyone will scatter."

"What if they don't?" Claire said. "We have so little time. Why waste it doing something like this?"

Without warning, Rachel took off, white coat waving in her wake, running across the wide square beneath the tower, towards the Pont d'Iéna. Midway across the bridge, Rachel hoisted herself onto its stone parapet and stood above the sidewalk and the river, flapping her arms.

"Rachel!" Breathless, Claire flung her arms across the stone as if to reach Rachel's ankles.

"We're orphans," Rachel cried, right at the edge, teetering. "Rachel, come down!"

A sightseeing boat was making a lugubrious three-point turn below. A couple of people on board glanced up.

Rachel turned and looked at Claire. She pushed strands of hair out of her face as she climbed down from the parapet. What had she been doing? Before Claire had a chance to consider whether Rachel had really been intending to jump, or to ask Rachel what she thought she was up to, Rachel shoved her hands in the pockets of her coat, and said in an almost shockingly offhand manner, "You know, don't you, that Dad was engaged before he met Mum?"

"Before — you mean a while before or he was engaged when he met her?"

"About a year before. But she died. She killed herself. Janna Berkowicz. She was a pharmacy student. They were engaged and then she got pregnant, not the other way around, as I understand it. Then she found out she had lupus, which is not a good thing to have if you're pregnant. Anyway, apparently he offered to help her get an abortion, being a medical student and all, which would be the best thing for her health, but she refused. He told her he would stick by her no matter what happened. But I suppose she decided she couldn't bear to be sick or have an abortion, that she couldn't bear for him to put up with her under either of these circumstances, or whatever, something proved unbearable, because she jumped off the Bloor Street Viaduct."

Claire was standing on a bridge, its stonework solid and frail beneath her. "When did you find this out?"

"Mum told me. The last time I was up in Toronto. We were driving to the liquor store. I was asking about Dad's decision to quit medical school and all of a sudden she came out with this. She said she thought it was time we knew."

"We?"

"I told Allison. I thought Allison said she was going to talk to you. Or Mum was. I know Allison talked to Dad about it."

"But all these years they never said anything. And no one said anything to me."

"Mum said he didn't want it to intrude on our sense of family. He didn't want us to have to think about it. He wanted it to stay in the past. Which you could argue is never really possible but that's what he wanted."

She'd flung herself, like numerous suicides before and after her, from a bridge whose great arches spanned a ravine, a half-hidden river, and the wide lanes of the Don Valley Parkway. Claire had never heard of anyone who'd survived the plunge. She had driven countless times across the Bloor Street Viaduct, from east to west, from west to east, knowing nothing of this crucial episode in her father's life.

"Did Mum know this when she married him?"

"I don't know. I didn't ask her that." Now, of course, it was too late to ask. Unless Allison had thought to, they would never know the answer to this question.

She was taken aback by the fact that no one in the family had told her. (Did it matter now whether the failure was deliberate or careless? What else was being hidden from her?) This revelation would be forever tied to the agony of her parents' death. Jana Berkowicz falling, her mother and father falling, although her parents had made no decision to end anything. They had exercised no choice. No sooner was her father killed than he was transformed again – his whole past, the life that he'd lived with them, recast in the light of this knowledge. Between her parents lay this spectre of loss, of illness that led to madness if suicide was indeed a form of madness. Beneath her mother's guilt over her migraines and her father's helplessness in the face of them lay this. Why had he never spoken of it? He'd wanted to spare them, but spare them what exactly? The hidden will still be revealed. What isn't spoken simply finds another language. Perhaps their headaches gave voice to his grief, among other hidden things. Pain will out.

The horror, the senselessness of her parents' death convulsed Claire once more. The waste of it, the outrage.

She did not know why Rachel had suddenly decided to tell her about Janna Berkowicz after climbing down from the stone parapet of the Pont d'Iéna. Had Rachel been thinking of her even before she scrambled onto the bridge? Afterwards, they never discussed her bridge-climbing incident or spoke much to each other about that day in Paris. Claire had always thought, had wanted to believe that Rachel was, at that moment, simply playing with her, acting out a dare, giving in to a wild spasm of lament, but this was perhaps to ignore the way Rachel had looked, after Claire's shout, before descending from the parapet. (And what of her strange desire to climb the Eiffel Tower?) Yet if she had come to Paris intending to kill herself, why bring Claire, unless she had wanted Claire there in order to save her, to pull her back from whatever she was contemplating. Or perhaps something had happened in Paris that had pushed her to the brink (something Claire had done or failed to do?). Was there some crucial trigger that Claire had failed to see?

Did Rachel need her again now? Was she calling to her, giving her another chance, or was she, wherever she was, not thinking of Claire at all at all at all?

They were on a stretch of winding, hummocky road, each jolt of the car ricocheting through Claire. Brad slowed as they came up behind a struggling truck that spewed black clouds of diesel smoke, the fumes reaching them, entering her, even with the car vents sealed and the windows closed.

The road was shoulderless, a single lane in either direction.

"I can't go on like this." She vomited into a plastic bag.

"Hold on, I'm going to pass."

Brad veered the car in behind another truck. More clouds of noxious diesel smoke. Jungle verdure closed around them, the sides of the road crawling with vines. Beyond this truck was yet another, straining on a hill, so now they were sandwiched between two of them. For miles. Neurology is destiny, Rachel had once cried. As if to say that living like this was their fate. There would be no escape. Claire vomited again. She was in a dark place. She was the dark place, the thin white line of the self dissolving —

She undid her seat belt and unlocked her car door. Opening the door, she leaned all her weight against it.

"Claire!"

Brad swerved them into the ditch at the side of the road, tilting them at an angle as Claire tumbled out into bushes that were cool and green and studded with thorns.

When she awoke, the pain was on the right side again but fainter and then, perhaps half an hour later, it moved across her forehead to the left side. It zigzagged back and forth like a weary traveller as it receded.

They were in a sparsely furnished room. Beside her on the bed, Brad lay asleep in his clothes. A fan rotated slowly on the ceiling. She was uncertain how much time had elapsed — hours, days — since she'd lost track.

Claire rose, a little wobbly, her muscles sore as after strenuous physical exercise. She was in her bra and underwear, and bruised, at least down the right side of her body, from where she'd fallen out of the car. No, not fallen, she'd practically thrown herself out of the car. She could have — But she hadn't. She was all right. Mostly. She'd borne what had seemed at first unbearable and reached the far side — for now, anyway. Elation filled her, which might be a chemical high, but that hardly mattered. She felt exhausted but cleansed. The world flowed back towards her and she took it in, took herself in with a new kind of clarity, which wasn't precision but a different, more expansive awareness.

The overhead fan creaked and swayed a little as it turned. A crack ran down the wall beyond the double bed, from the ceiling almost to the floor. There was nothing to indicate where they were, geographically speaking. Their window overlooked a courtyard in which there was a small, drained swimming pool, with a crack, even more severe than the one in their room, cutting through one of its blue, paint-chipped walls. According to Claire's watch, it was a little before 6 a.m. A man in flip-flops was watering the flowerbeds with an air of sober concentration. She debated calling out to him and decided not to. In the bathroom, on the back of the door, she found a sign listing prices, in Spanish and English, at the Hotel Santa Monica, but the sign did not say where the Hotel Santa Monica was.

Brad had not yet awoken, and she figured she should let him sleep, after all his driving and what she'd put him through. She was still trying to determine how long it had been since they'd arrived in this place — how long she'd spent in that bed. One day or two? There had definitely been stretches when she'd thought the pain would never retreat and she'd be stuck in that state forever.

She was aware that Brad had carried her into the room, lifting her in his arms up a flight of stairs. But then she'd not been in much condition to walk. He had undressed her and laid her on the bed and pulled a sheet over top of her. He had been gentle but had kept his distance, even when they were both lying on the bed, and had hardly spoken to her, except to ask if there was anything she needed. He had come and gone a few times. There was respect in his withdrawal, a sympathetic acknowledgement that she just had to get through whatever it was she was going through. His acceptance made the experience oddly intimate, though not shared. In the midst of the worst of it, she did not have to pretend or strive to feel anything other than what she was feeling.

In a plastic bag, beside their overnight bags, which Brad must have brought upstairs, Claire found an orange and the remains of the package of almonds they'd bought, long ago, in Las Vegas. She ate some nuts and the orange, which took the edge off her hunger — a normal appetite, now, no nausea or panicky sense of famishment.

When she sat back on the bed, Brad opened his eyes. "Hey," he said, and stretched out his arms. There was stubble on his chin, and his hair was matted and flattened, his left cheek creased and pink where it had been pressed to his pillow. "How are you feeling?"

"Much, much better, thank you." She smiled and slid down the mattress until she was lying, facing him. He reached out and touched her temples with his fingertips. His gaze glanced over the bruises on her arm.

"I'm sorry about my, you know, leap out of the car."

"A little scary there for a moment," he said, "but understandable, I guess."

He rolled to one side, flexing his left wrist back and forth, feeling the joint with the fingers of his other hand as if his wrist were sore.

"Did you hurt yourself?"

"Not really. Just a bit of an awkward lift getting you out of the car."

She drew his arm close and pressed her lips to his skin, to the place that he had been touching. The last thing she wanted was injure the massage therapist. He shook out his wrist as if it were indeed fine.

Laying her hand against his right cheek, the exposed, pale one, she was washed with tenderness, with a gratitude so deep that it became something else. He wrapped his arms around her, as if the tenderness and gratitude were mutual.

His fingers made their way up the ridge of her spine, following the line of her vertebrae, not with a masseur's pressure but simply making contact. She slid her hand beneath his shirt, inside the back of his jeans and pressed it to the warm triangle of skin at the base of his spine, drawing his calm heat into her. In her arms, his body was sturdier than she would have expected. Touch was layered over the residue of pain. It moored them in the present, allowed them to shut out Rachel and concentrate on each other for a little while.

And while it was tempting, in the midst of her surprise and temporary serenity, to believe that something in Brad's presence was her cure, the cure that her journey had been leading her towards all along, it seemed unwise, even dangerous to think this.

Lying on his back, Brad took hold of her hand and caressed the webbed skin between her thumb and forefinger. He did not appear self-conscious, or surprised to find himself doing this. His gesture seemed to punctuate his thoughts. "Once I burned out and stopped massaging altogether. I just couldn't deal with it. I was doing all this therapeutic work and there were so many hardcore cases. Dancers desperate to get back to performing, stroke victims, journalists, musicians with overuse injuries terrified they'd never play their instruments again. A friend got me a job as a gaffer. I'd always wanted to work in film. I know that may sound like an insane way to take a break. The hours were gruelling but I just couldn't take making a movie as seriously as most people did. I liked it, but the whole time friends kept saying to me, you have a talent, you can't waste it. Only I had to figure out a way to make things feel different. I kept telling myself, pain is a mystery not the enemy. I can help people but I can't always heal them. Healing's mysterious, too. Less pain is definitely good but you need a certain amount around to listen to. Of course, I admire people who figure out ways of dealing with massive amounts of it."

"So you gave up the therapeutic work."

"No, oh no, I still do quite a lot, on the days I'm not at Pure, and I'm not saying the people I see at Pure don't need help —"

She was giving up on the idea of a cure. She would find an accommodation with her pain, make a place for it. The possibility, no, the necessity of doing so was something he, too, understood. If she concentrated only on pain's constraints, she would lose sight of what it had given her. She would lose sight of part of herself. Free of her headaches, there would perhaps be less of her. They kissed, Claire winding the fingers of her left hand with Brad's right, aware of the pressure of their joined palms.

They went out for breakfast at a restaurant, little more than a taqueria, down the street from the hotel, their bodies brushing against each other as they walked, coming this close and no closer. They were in a little town called Rio Grande, about two hours north of Puerto Escondido, and had arrived on the Wednesday afternoon. It was now Friday. So near then, if Rachel were indeed somewhere in the vicinity.

Back at the hotel, they were greeted by the owner, Felipe, a middle-aged man whose taut belly pressed against the confines of his navy T-shirt. "Hola, girl with headache," he called out, as if a headache were a mark of distinction. "How are you feeling?"

"Very well," Claire said.

He hoped they were not too worried by the crack in the wall of their room. It was from the earthquake of a year ago, as was the crack in the pool and the spidery lines in the hotel's exterior stucco, which he pointed out to them. His own house had fallen down – while his children were at school, thanks God. The hotel had not. He did not seem frightened that it was going to.

Claire asked Felipe if he knew of any sort of retreat near Puerto Escondido. A retreat? There was a very small place, where a man, a magician, lived and where local people went, on the road to Puerto Escondido. He treated headaches by pulling on people's hair. His wife went for treatment to this man, Felipe said, but he did not because – he tugged at the air – he did not have enough hair to pull on. People visited but did not stay there.

They gathered their bags and prepared to head onwards. It was difficult stepping back into the car, given all that Claire had gone through inside it, but the car's interior felt altered by the shift in intimacy between Brad and herself, their new ease in each other's presence.

It was possible, surrounded by the ridge of mountains in the distance to the left and grassland sweeping towards the ocean on their right, to prolong the sensation that they were cut off from the rest of the world, for Claire to put off worrying about Stefan for a little longer. Potholes were marked with piles of stones. A hawk roosted near the top of a tree. Cattle grazed among stumps, a line of trees left standing between the fields and a strip of sandy beach. A continent lay between her and Stefan. From this distance, he seemed small and far away. And yet she owed him answers, about having a child, about what they were, what she was doing.

When an unmarked pothole loomed, Brad swerved to avoid it. He glanced across and touched Claire's leg – no more than that. What she took from him, what he seemed to take from her, was something potentially seductive but, above all, steadying.

A straightaway carried them into Puerto Escondido, and then the road began to curve around the harbour, the hidden port, part of the town rising up the hill to the left and the other part continuing down a slope towards the ocean on the right. Water glittered at them through a scattering of low buildings and palm trees. They had made no plans as to where to stay but since this was a tourist town and it was not high season they assumed they would find somewhere without difficulty. They took the first turn past the harbour, just beyond a little ravine in which scrubby trees half-hid a river or creek, and turned right, down a small road. A hotel appeared, on their left, just up from the beach, pink-walled and gated and more picturesque than the Hotel Santa Monica. Having arrived here, and liking what they saw, they had neither the inclination nor energy to look anywhere else.

There were rooms available. A fountain warbled in the colonnaded courtyard. There were fewer Americans at this time of year, said the woman who was checking them in at the Maria del Flor, just Europeans, and mostly Italians. "Double or twin?"

"Double," Brad replied without pause, his sunglasses pushed back into the hanks of his blond hair.

"We're looking for a retreat," Claire said to the woman. "We don't have a name but we heard there was a place near here. Maybe not right in town but outside. I'm not sure what sort of place exactly but somewhere people go to get away from the world."

"Temazcalli?" the woman asked.

"I don't know." Claire looked at Brad.

"It is in the hills. There is a special kind of massage they do there. A traditional Indian way. There is steam. There is fasting, I believe, if you wish. You can go to stay. If you stay, it must be at least a week. Some people stay longer. They go to meditate, detoxify."

"Can you spell the name?" Claire asked. She was trying to write it down. "Do you have the phone number?"

"There is also the nunnery," said the woman. "Do you know about the nunnery? Sometimes people go there. They do —" She pointed to her eyes "how is this called? Healing through the eye?"

Claire had no idea. "Iridology," Brad said.

"But the nunnery is far," the woman said, flicking one hand as she spoke. "Past Puerto Angel."

Up in their room, Claire called the number that the woman had given her. A man answered in Spanish. Habla inglés, she managed, and gathered from his response, in rapid Spanish, that he didn't. Perhaps he understood English even if he didn't speak it.

"Is this Temazcalli? I'm looking for a woman named Rachel Barber. Is she staying there?"

When his reply proved once again incomprehensible, she passed the receiver to Brad, whose grasp of Spanish, while rudimentary, was better than hers. "Alguian habla inglés? I'm looking for una mujer, Rachel Barber, de New York, canadiense – is she there?"

"Or Sylvia di Castro," Claire interjected.

Brad made a kind of grimace as he listened, then he covered the receiver with his palm. "I'm sorry, I can't really make it out. He keeps saying, I think he keeps saying something about silence, but I'm not catching it. I know I'm not getting a yes or no answer."

"We could call back. We could ask the woman downstairs for help."

"Gracias." Brad hung up the phone.

"Do you know if Rachel speaks Spanish?" Claire asked.

"Maybe she picked some up in New York. Maybe she's learned more down here." Brad rubbed his hand over his mouth. "Maybe we should just figure out where this place is and go. If she's there and gets word that someone's looking for her, maybe she'll bolt."

"What's your hunch – do you think she's there?"

"On a hunch, I'll say yes."

For all that Rachel was potentially so close, Claire was feeling a measure of hesitation. She did not know what they would do or say to Rachel, when and if they found her. What Rachel would do at the sight of them — the two of them together. Or what she was going to do if Rachel wasn't there. She had to return to Toronto. Whatever happened, she was preparing herself to return to Toronto, to Stefan, even though she was no longer convinced that she would be able to slip back, like the missing piece of a puzzle, into her life as it had been. And yet she did not regret what she'd done, or what she'd gone through: the journey, the immeasurable ways in which she'd been touched. She would go back, although she did not know what awaited her. Mystery. Disorder. Not necessarily bad things. She did not know what Stefan would want from her.

When she and Brad went downstairs, the woman at the desk had been replaced by a small sign in Spanish and English. Someone would return at five o'clock. It was, now, a little before three. No one seemed to be about. Even the bakery up the street was closed until the next morning. They debated whether to head into the centre of town, to try to find someone who could point them towards Temazcalli, or wait and, as seemed most likely, set off in the morning.

"Before we do anything," Claire said, "I really have to eat or else." So far the brightness inside her head was holding.

They made their way down to the beach and walked until they came upon a strip of restaurants, set back from a long, straight stretch of sand where the surf was high. After a late lunch, they kept walking until a fierce downpour sent them scurrying inside and up a set of stairs to a second-floor bar. They shook out their hair and clothes and patted their faces dry with paper napkins. Protected from the elements by a palm-thatched roof, they seated themselves on stools open to the air, with a view, through a curtain of rain, of the ocean.

"Will you tell me," Claire asked, sipping from a can of pineapple juice and looking not at Brad but at the sea, "how you came to get involved with Rachel?"

"She was a client," Brad said, "and we'd done a piece of work together, but she wasn't coming in as regularly, so it wasn't like — of course, it's odd we hadn't run into each other before, given how close we live, but we hadn't. Anyway, one day I was in Commodities, the health food store on First, when she came in. We started talking. She asked me if I wanted to go for a coffee. Maybe she felt something right from the start, from when she first met me. I do think she's drawn to people who've had some intense experience of pain themselves. I don't know how conscious she is of it. I don't know if it makes her symptoms worse or shapes them in any way. It's not something I ever found easy to talk about with her. She'd get very defensive. We went to this café and she told me she had a feeling that I'd experienced some deep pain and wondered if I'd tell her about it. I was shocked. That she'd seen this about me. And one way and another, things went from there."

"What happened to you?" She had sensed the depth of his empathy and responded to it, but had assumed his familiarity with pain grew out of his talent, out of his professional life. Unlike Rachel, she had not asked him about it, until now — but then the circumstances under which she'd met Brad were entirely different.

"I had a bad case of rheumatoid arthritis." He rubbed his wrist. "This was a long time ago, back when I was in college. It took a long time to diagnose. No one seemed to recognize the trouble was in my joints and because I wrestled, at first everyone thought it was a sports injury. So it was pretty hard for a while, because no one knew what the problem was, and it would go away and then come back. I'd ache and not make it out of bed for days. I had to drop out and move back home. My mother would pray over me. Eventually, this was in St. Paul, before I moved to New York, I met this woman, who did a lot of work on my muscles, on the tissue around the joints. A massage therapist. She was amazing. When they finally made the diagnosis, the doctor who was treating me wanted to put me on this incredible drug cocktail but I wouldn't do it. I was doing all this research on my own. I took all these vitamins. I worked out as much as I could. At a certain point, my symptoms started to recede. It's hard to know exactly why, because some people aren't so lucky, but they did."

"And never came back?"

"Not in the same way. I have to look after myself. I can't take anything for granted. Everything changed because of it."

He was bearing lightly on an experience that could not have been light at all. Those days and days in bed. His mother praying over him. "I thought for a while I was going to end up as some kind of invalid." He shrugged, his fingers smoothing over his bottle of beer, the joints of his knuckles shifting easily to Claire's eye, and she was moved by the sight, by his skin, by the thought that he carried this invisible history within him, not weakness, a legacy of mysterious healing; empathy was called up out of her, too.

"I'm sorry," she said.

"Sorry? What's there to be sorry about?"

For an instant, she entertained the thought of a life with him. Whatever happened with Rachel, they would keep going, to Hawaii, to Thailand. But something stopped her. It seemed like another form of escape.

When the rain let up (it had been nothing more than a late-afternoon shower), they stood, adjusting their still-damp clothes. At the top of the stairs leading down to the street, Brad leaned in close. "I'm sorry about what happened to your parents. For days and days, I've been meaning to say that."

Claire nodded: grief rustled in her chest and subsided.

At the hotel, the woman was back at her post behind the counter. Claire asked if she would call Temazcalli for them and explained that they were looking for her sister, whom they had reason to believe was there. She wrote two names on a piece of paper, Rachel Barber and Sylvia di Castro, and handed the paper to the woman.

Hola, hola. The woman's voice rolled on in Spanish, now animated, now accommodating, then quiet, her head cocked as she listened to the voice on the other end of the line.

"Okay." Without hanging up, she set the receiver down on the wood of the counter. "Rachel Barber, the Canadian, she is there. For nearly three months she is there. But there is a difficulty if you wish to see and speak to her because she is in the most extreme retreat. She does not speak to anyone."

"Doesn't speak to anyone," Claire said.

"There are a few people who do this. They have small separate houses for them."

"But is she well, she's not sick?"

The woman picked up the receiver once more and spoke into it before resting it against her shoulder. "She is well. She walks in the hills. She meditates. If you wish, you can pass by in the morning."

They sat side by side on the bed, their backs to the carved wooden headboard.

"She's there," Claire said, hugging her knees to her chest. Her relief, her joy were matched by a degree of incredulity — she did not quite dare to believe that they had found her. Or that Rachel, who, for all her single-mindedness, had never struck Claire as a silent person, had removed herself so far from the world that she would not speak. Repeatedly, Rachel had referred to her need to give up something: this time, she seemed to be renouncing almost all human contact. (And was it working, was her renunciation bringing her the solace she sought?)

"So what do we do?" Brad asked. He lay down and stared at the stuccoed ceiling. His face looked pale and angular. She could not now think of touching him.

"I guess we'll go there in the morning."

"And then?"

"I don't know exactly. We'll have to see when we get there. We'll ask them to let her know we're there —"

"What if she doesn't want to see us?"

Which was possible, although Claire didn't much want to consider this. "We have to see for certain she's all right. And make sure it's really her. We can't just take someone else's word for it over the phone. I mean, I can't. I would feel — And we need to know, we need to have some idea when she's coming back."

"Only maybe — maybe, Claire, maybe it would be better not to disturb her. Okay, we have to confirm it's her, but if she needs to be alone — if she's chosen, if she's put herself in seclusion and whatever she's doing is making her feel better, and then we come along and burst in and wreck that — I'm not sure I want to live with the responsibility."

Claire's eyes filled with tears. "But we can't be here, be so close, and not go."

They fell silent, inwardly wrestling. A shutter banged and at the sound, a dog began to bark. Light from the setting sun fell across the far wall.

That night, warily, they got ready for bed. In the dark, after some hours of near sleeplessness, Brad pressed his body to Claire's, his breath ragged in her ear. "We'll go," he said.

In the morning, they ate breakfast at the bakery just up the street. Back at the Maria del Flor, they debated whether to leave their bags or check out. Since they did not know altogether what lay ahead and it would be easy enough to return, they took their bags, along with a page of directions, with them.

Claire navigated. At the top of the hill, where their small road met the highway, she instructed Brad to turn right, which led them out of town. They were to continue down the highway, still a narrow single lane in either direction, for perhaps two kilometres, past a couple of turnoffs on the right, both of which ran down a short, sharp slope to the beach. A haze of mist marked the line of surf. They were looking for a turning on the left, away from the ocean. There would be only a small wooden sign. It was easy to miss. They missed it, although Claire, half-blinded by the sun rising over the hills, shouted out as they passed. Brad pulled up, and since there was no other traffic in sight, reversed speedily until they were opposite what seemed to be little more than a dirt track. The woman at the hotel had said the retreat was not far up the lane, at most half a kilometre.

Brad nosed the car off the road, into a grassy dip. He switched off the engine but kept his hands on the wheel. "You go," he said.

"On my own."

"She doesn't need to see both of us."

Nervous and a little discomfited, Claire waited a moment. "All right." She opened her door and stepped out, and, after glancing in either direction, jogged across the road.

Almost immediately, the dirt track began to climb. Pebbles and grit slid between her feet and the soles of her sandals. She was anxious and dry-throated, and had forgotten to bring any water. To turn away from Rachel now, to leave without knowing how she was, still felt to her like a kind of abandonment, for all that there was a streak of selfishness to the desire to see Rachel and the place where Rachel was, if Rachel did not want to be seen.

On her right, an opening in the undergrowth led to a ram-shackle yard, an old brown sedan pulled up in front of the low rectangle of a house, chickens squawking and pecking at the bare ground that surrounded it. The hillside to her left was covered in small, scrubby trees. A little farther on, on her left, a containment wall began, running down the slope towards her for about fifty metres and turning to run for another fifty metres into the trees. The wall was plastered and painted white. Above it, and level with her, appeared the roofs of some small buildings, one roof of red clay tile, the others of palm thatch. A gurgle of water met Claire's ears: not a creek but perhaps an outdoor shower or a tap. She thought she heard the slap of footsteps hurrying up the hill on the other side of the wall, the velocity of another presence, and at the sound her heart quickened, but there were no voices.

Up ahead, where the hillside flattened out, rose a larger two-storey building, also stuccoed, its roof tiled, a balcony running along the second floor, under the overhang of the roof. A white rope hammock was strung up at the far end. A cluster of dark palm trees partly shaded the exterior. Near the house, Claire glimpsed some flowering shrubs, hibiscus and bougainvillea. A series of flagstone steps likely continued down the slope. All was still, cloaked in heat, bleached by the dazzling light. No one appeared. The very quiet of the place filled her with unease and a strange longing: she was curious about what sort of sanctuary lay within the walls.

Farther along the crest of the hill, a group of smaller buildings was scattered, each a short distance from the other. Perhaps it was in one of these that Rachel was living. Claire wondered if there were others at the retreat who had taken a similar vow of silence, and what kind of company Rachel kept or if she spent most, or all, of her time alone. She did not know what to make of Rachel's choice. Was there something sacrificial, penitential to her solitude, and if it was solitude that had proved so healing, would she then need solitude forever? If solitude failed, what else was left to her?

A gravel driveway opened on her left, following the line of the perimeter wall. Midway along the wall, within an arched entranceway, a wrought-iron gate was set, a seemingly ordinary doorbell attached to the wall beside it. A flutter of movement caught Claire's eye. In the distance, beyond the end of the drive-way, among the low slopes that continued to rise in slow and undulating folds towards the distant mountains, a woman was walking. Clad all in white (white trousers, white shirt), masked behind sunglasses and a wide-brimmed straw hat, she was making her way down a hillside, along a path that branched and wound among low shrubs and clumps of gorse. Her gait, as she approached, grew ever more familiar — that quick, firm stride. Bright flash of her shirt. The sound of stones skittering beneath her heels was carried across the distance between them. It *was* Rachel.

Claire pulled herself back, against the perimeter wall before it turned, pressing one hand to the folds of her blue dress, the other hand to her own straw hat. She did not think that Rachel, who continued her approach, had seen her.

Rachel did not seem to be in pain. There was a fluidity to her movements. She did not look anguished (no finger rubbing the skin beneath her right eye). There was a certain calm about her. Had she found what she was looking for? She was nearing the gate now, intent on her own progress, the intermittent breeze chasing loose strands of dark hair across her face and along her cheekbones, the crease between her eyebrows just visible in the gap between her sunglasses and hat.

Claire's voice burned in her throat. She longed to call out, step into sight, ask Rachel what her secret was. Pulling out a set of keys, Rachel stopped by the gate and glanced about her, in the direction from which she had come, in Claire's direction, the ghost of a smile on her lips, as if perhaps she sensed another presence.

Beyond her relief and bittersweet astonishment, Claire was aware of something else, a deeper sensation, as of something letting go. She had done what she needed to do, done all that she could do for Rachel. She could not follow her any farther.

Key to the wrought-iron lock, Rachel paused. It was still possible for Claire to call out, or make herself visible even if she said nothing. Once again, a remarkable quiet descended, enveloping the two of them, broken only by the humming of insects. Rachel stepped through the entranceway. The gate creaked on its hinges as it closed. Her receding footfalls began to fade.

Only then did Claire turn. A lizard rustled in the dry grass at her feet. A truck horn blared from the highway below. She set off, slowly at first but then with greater speed, down the hillside, towards the hurly-burly of the world.

ACKNOWLEDGEMENTS

I'm indebted, for neurological insight, to Oliver Sacks' *Migraine, Revised and Expanded*. Among the many texts on pain consulted during the writing of this novel, the elegant articulations of David Morris's *The Culture of Pain* stand out. The support of the Canada Council and the Ontario Arts Council is gratefully acknowledged, as is that of the MacDowell Colony, The Santa Maddalena Retreat for Writers, and Yaddo for time and space to write portions of the manuscript. Thanks to Patsy Aldana and the spirit of Matt Cohen, to those who shared their stories, and to those who read the work-in-progress and offered invaluable advice, including Shyam Selvadurai, my agent Denise Bukowski, editors Ellen Seligman and Jennifer Lambert, and above all, André Alexis, who gave so much and so unstintingly.

Miriam Berkley

Catherine Bush is the author of three acclaimed novels: *Minus Time*, a finalist for the SmithBooks/Books in Canada First Novel Award and the City of Toronto Book Award; the national bestselling *The Rules of Engagement*, which was shortlisted for the City of Toronto Book Award, was named one of the best books of the year in the *Globe and Mail* and the *Los Angeles Times*, and was a *New York Times* Notable Book; and *Claire's Head*, a finalist for the Trillium Book Award and a *Globe and Mail* Notable Book of the Year.

Catherine Bush lives in Toronto.